THE
JADE TALISMAN

ALANNA MACKENZIE

First published in Canada in 2021
Willow Lane Publishing, Vancouver, BC

Copyright © 2021 Alanna Mackenzie
Cover design by J. Caleb Clark copyright © 2021

www.alannamackenzie.com

ISBN 978-1-7752509-3-7 (pbk.).--ISBN 978-1-7752509-5-1 (html).--ISBN 978-1-7752509-4-4 (pdf.)

To all wanderers in search of their true homes

"My soul is a hidden orchestra; I know not what instruments, what fiddlestrings and harps, drums and tamboura I sound and clash inside myself. All I hear is the symphony."

– Fernando Pessoa

PART I:
THE COMPOSER

Birdsong

"I am a cage, in search of a bird."
— Franz Kafka

Walter heard the island before he saw it. Framed by a starry sky and an ocean that gleamed like polished obsidian, the dark, verdant landmass lying before him was alive with birdsong. The sound was delicate, like a lullaby whispered into your ear, but it eventually spread into the crevices of your mind until your soul was awash with music. It was unlike anything Walter had ever heard before. Crystal City was filled with noises—the whining hum of driverless cars on the freeways, the grating voices of AI Masters projecting from loudspeakers, the ominous vibrations of machines destined to dig up earth—but those were not soothing sounds. They were as cold, lifeless, and anxiety-inducing as the city itself, a city completely severed from the circadian rhythms of the natural world. As strange and unnerving as the birdsong was, Walter felt a sense of tranquility when he closed his eyes and listened to it. The sound invoked memories of both his childhood and the recent period when he had lived in the rebel camp Tsei'watu, which were the only two occasions in Walter's life when he had truly felt close to nature.

"In the morning it will be gone," Eva said knowingly. Walter did not believe her at the time, but she had spoken truthfully. The next morning the island was silent, as if the birds had never been there at all. The twinkling stars were gone too; mist and fog had rolled in from the sea to blanket the earth in a dense carpet, obscuring much of the island from view.

BIRDSONG

As Walter surveyed the mist-shrouded island from the deck of the *Jade Queen*, he reflected on what he had to do. After wresting control of the *Jade Queen* from the AI Masters, Walter and his fellow rebels had sailed to Vei'arash to fulfill their promise to the Western Mages of Serrahan. Descendants of the Druids, the Mages resembled ordinary humans, but their appearance was deceptive; they had potent supernatural abilities that placed them into a separate race altogether. The ruler of Serrahan, Nuada, had asked the rebels to retrieve animal spirits that had been stolen from his territory centuries ago, following a bitter conflict. Known colloquially in Khalendar as the Shadow Wars, the conflict had erupted in response to the AI Masters' relentless efforts to conquer the territory south of the Meridian Mountains. Shamans from the southern kingdoms had summoned animal spirits in response to this assault on their land, which had greatly intimidated the AI Masters. The shamans had waged a fierce battle, but the AI Masters had eventually gained the upper hand. They had banished the shamans and their animal spirits to the distant island of Vei'arash, shipping them across the Hapakay Sea in massive steel barges.

The Mages had been devastated by that turn of events. Serrahan was the only southern kingdom that had avoided colonization, thanks to its citizens, who had cleverly used the little magic that remained in the kingdom to construct a protective barrier around it. Yet the loss of its animal spirits had drained the Serrahan territory of a good amount of its spiritual energy, rendering the magical abilities of Mages less potent. The Mages had feared becoming ordinary humans if enough magic drained away, but they had fortunately retained enough of their powers to preserve their uniqueness as a race.

The Mages had lived for many years in a peaceful territory, sealed off from the rest of the Empire, but their kingdom suffered without access to any trading partners or allies. When the rebels had arrived in Serrahan, Nuada and his fellow councilors had decided that the time was ripe to balance the historical scales once again. The Mage leader had asked the rebels to bring the animal spirits back to Serrahan territory, not only to revitalize his kingdom and strengthen the magic within it, but also so they could be used as weapons against the AI Masters. Nuada had pledged ten of his best and brightest Mages to the cause of the Rebellion, including his own daughter Cyriana and her lover Tristan, in return for the rebels' agreement to recover the animal spirits. The fate of the Mage kingdom now lay in the hands of these bold adventurers.

The *Jade Queen* cast anchor in a small cove on the southeastern side of the island. Many of the ship's occupants stayed inside the vessel, as they were too emotionally and mentally fragile from their recent captivity to venture outside. Those former captives of the AI Masters would rest and receive psychological therapy from Miranda and Christopher, who were both councilors of the Rebellion along with Tristan, Cyriana, Eva, and Walter. Most were happy to stay behind, as the island provoked more fear than curiosity in them. On mainland Khalendar, Vei'arash was known as a notorious prison where the AI Masters sent dissidents who committed acts of treason against the state. Rumor had it that an army of demons and dark spirits, unleashed by corrupt and deranged shamans, awaited prisoners who were sent to Vei'arash. In short, the island was not exactly a tropical paradise.

Although Elaine was a former captive herself, she had requested permission from the councilors of the Rebellion to venture out on the island. The Mage princess Cyriana had persuaded the other councilors to grant this request; the two women had taken a liking to each other, and Cyriana sensed that Elaine needed adventure to dispel the tedium which had overtaken her spirit. Two other former captives, a silent, burly man named Jonas and his brother Mikos, were also allowed to accompany the mission, having satisfied the councilors that they were physically and mentally fit enough to join.

The rebels set out with plenty of provisions, which they carried in canvas bags strapped to their backs with sailing rope rummaged from the decks of the *Jade Queen*. In the humid climate of the tropical rainforest, their rations would last several days—a week at the most. Walter wished they had spices for preserving the food, but he had not found any on board the ship. When it began to rot, the food within their packs would need to be discarded, otherwise it would begin to smell, and then liquify, and attract insects. The birds of the island were nocturnal creatures, but the insects did not favor either night or day; they were pests at all hours and reveled in the prospect of new human visitors to their island. Humans meant flesh, and flesh meant food.

When he stepped onto the beach, Walter breathed a deep sigh and dug his toes into the sun-bleached sand. He felt a rush of relief to be on firm ground after weeks on the choppy open ocean, as though his senses were finally able to come into focus. He was weary, too, like someone who had lived out an entire lifetime in the span of a few months. Walter had never wanted to live like this: a man in hiding, an outlaw, a runaway. He would have much preferred a quiet, cerebral life as a code translator, but a different life had been thrust upon him. His parents Vladimir and Carla and his sister Victoria were likely still living comfortable lives back in Crystal City, but now that Walter was a wanted criminal they wouldn't have any expectation of seeing him alive again. It felt exhausting to be on the run from the authorities, but also strangely liberating. He was no longer trapped inside the sheltered womb of Crystal City, cradled by the support system of a job and a family. That system was both comforting and suffocating—it had imposed a host of obligations and expectations on Walter, which had simply evaporated when he escaped from it. The complex web of responsibility that he had been subject to in Crystal City was now reduced to a single strand: the duty to serve the Rebellion. In this new world, Walter was free, but he was also hanging by a thread.

The cove they anchored in reminded Walter of Mariner's Cove, where he had first met Elaine on a stormy November day which now seemed a lifetime ago. This cove was similarly rugged, with steep, angular cliffs jutting out to meet soft, bone-white sand. The primary difference was that here, instead of dry grasslands, a lush jungle swept across the surface of the bluffs. At first, Walter wondered whether he and his companions would be able to climb the cliffs, but his concerns were assuaged when Eva spotted a small stairway carved into the limestone rockface.

Once they had summited the high cliffs, Walter turned back wistfully toward the beach and the unmistakable silhouette of the *Jade Queen*. As soon as they entered the jungle, there was no knowing when—or even if—they would ever return to the ship again. The bargain with the Mages would no doubt lead to danger and uncertainty, though Walter knew he had no choice but to honor it. He had never set foot on Serrahan soil, as he had already been on board the *Jade Queen* by the time Christopher, Miranda and the other surviving rebels had visited the kingdom, but Walter nevertheless felt an invisible bond with the eccentric practitioners of magic who resided there. From his conversations with Tristan, Walter had learned that Serrahan was the only uncolonized territory south of the Meridian Mountains, and he knew that the rebels would be wise to draw inspiration from the Mages' resilience and courage.

Walter noticed a glint of fear in Elaine's eyes as they approached the ominous wall of vegetation ahead. He longed to comfort her, but the oppressive barrier separating them prevented him from doing so. The two had barely spoken at all since they had re-united on the ship, and an awkward, heavy silence hung between them. Eva also appeared to be anxious, but less so than Elaine, perhaps because she was still exhausted with grief from the death of her twin sister Emilia, the late founder of the Rebellion. Her pale azure eyes were rimmed with dark circles, and an aura of mourning surrounded her. Walter still saw haunting reminders of

Emilia in the woman's face. Every day, he asked himself whether the apparition he had seen on the *Jade Queen* had simply been a figment of his imagination, or Eva playing a cruel trick on him by disguising herself as Emilia. He knew it could not be the latter—Eva had too good of a heart to indulge in cruel trickery—but part of him also hoped that it had been, so that he would not need to question his own sanity.

An eerie silence, broken up only by the faint buzzing of gnats and horseflies, pervaded the jungle. The rebels forged onwards, their senses alert for signs of life. The rainforest was far denser than any forest Walter had ever been in, and the contrast between the white, fog-drenched beach and the dimly lit undergrowth was stark. Walter was astounded by the diversity of plant species that surrounded them. He did not recognize their names, but Eva patiently explained the various species to him. The plants' names were as lovely and unique as the plants themselves: *liana, orchid, heliconia*. The Mages confessed that they had never seen such exotic florae in Serrahan before. They appeared to be captivated by the island and gazed around in childlike wonder, their faces disclosing no fear or anxiety.

"These plants are *rehara*," Cyriana said, referencing the Serrahan term for "blessed," as she avidly examined a wild vanilla orchid. "They are portals to the spirit realm."

Eva indulged in a rare, wistful smile. "You sound like my sister. Emilia was extremely well-attuned to the natural world, more so than anyone I've ever met. During her youth, she travelled to the Southern Jungles, where she gained her encyclopedic botanical knowledge. She learned the flowering and fruiting cycles of edible forest plants, and could accurately identify plants with medicinal uses. She used to tell me that the plants in the Southern Jungles—which are probably similar to the ones here—evolved to develop a keen intelligence and creativity similar to humans.

"Like many living creatures, plants adapt to their surroundings. They sense approaching predators, develop tools to protect themselves from danger, and respond intuitively to variations in temperature or light. Soil in the tropics is usually nutritionally deficient from incessant rain, and so the plants must evolve highly effective defense mechanisms. But they also develop eccentric properties that can't be explained by simple adaptation to their surroundings... that human reason can't fully understand. Emilia would have agreed that they are spiritual entities. She always used to say that every plant carries its own unique identifier—like the DNA of a human or the code of an AI—which provides a hint about its ultimate purpose. Every plant has a purpose, apart from its utility to humans."

Cyriana nodded in agreement. "Mages have long used plants to heal their bodies and transform their minds. On occasion, plants have even been used by Mages to access the land of spirits."

Walter was extremely intrigued by the conversation, and he longed to know how Cyriana's abstract reference to accessing the land of spirits would operate in practice. He had already experienced brief encounters with supernatural forces, but he wasn't sure whether he actually had innate magical abilities or whether he could only witness magic or spiritual forces as an external observer. Walter's mind hearkened back to what Emilia had told him months ago in Tsei'watu, when he had confessed that he was having premonitions. She had said that she'd detected no intrinsic magical abilities in him that would allow his dreams to be influenced by magic. But now, Walter was hearing something from Cyriana that turned this idea on its head. If plants had inherent magical properties, then ingesting them—or harnessing their powers in some other way—could potentially transfer those properties to a human. Even if a person was not blessed with magical gifts, their body could still be a vessel through which magic flowed.

Another burning question was brewing inside of Walter: why had Eva spoken certain cryptic words during the first council meeting of the rebels? At the meeting, while experiencing a sudden seizure, Eva had said, *"The experiment: I understand it now."* Walter had been startled that Eva had suffered a seizure; he was epileptic himself, and witnessing her convulsive fit made him distressed because he knew how painful a seizure was. In a way, it also made him feel closer to her, since they now shared something in common. Walter had not questioned Eva about this incident for fear of dredging up a traumatic memory, but now he could no longer restrain his curiosity.

While the rebels were relaxing around a campfire after a long day spent trekking in the jungle, Walter decided to ask Eva about it. He waited until his other companions had retired to their tents for the night and he was alone with Eva.

"What happened to you that evening at the council meeting?" he asked in a lowered voice.

Eva's sky-blue eyes flickered like twin flames. The rosy hue of the campfire brought some color to her naturally pale cheeks, and in that moment, Eva reminded Walter eerily of her sister. She contemplated his question in silence for a long time before responding.

"Do you remember that female AI Master I came across in the *Jade Queen*, the one who used to guard the weapons factory I worked at in my youth? Asana. She was transmitting her thoughts to me… I am certain it was her. It was as if she was trying to help me somehow… to help *us*. That seems ridiculous, doesn't it? I mean, the AI Masters are our enemies. But from the moment I met Asana, she stood out to me as different from the rest of her kind. She seemed to possess certain qualities that the other AIs lacked—empathy, for one. Emilia always used to tell me that AIs are missing the essential spark of empathy; it is not something that can be easily programmed into them. They can be coded to respond predictably to displays of human emotion, but no amount of programming will make them truly *care* about human suffering. Asana must be an exception, though. She was the first AI I've met who seemed genuinely interested in helping me, who understood why I wanted to help my parents avoid starvation. The rest either had bad intentions toward me, or were simply totally indifferent."

Walter nodded, slowly digesting what she had told him. "What experiment were you referring to? You said that you 'understood the experiment.'"

Eva watched the leaping flames of the campfire in quiet contemplation. Sparks drifted out of the glowing embers like tiny fireflies, and Eva's gaze followed them. "The AI Masters have been carrying out this experiment upon us humans for quite some time now," she mused. "They have been carefully studying human civilization on Earth so they can decide whether it is worth replicating on Eurydice. The entire Empire of Khalendar is one big experiment, in fact. They deliberately designed the Empire with the system of industrial capitalism that had prevailed over other systems in previous generations. That's why they've stashed away so many historical textbooks at Central Command—not only so they could study our civilization, but also to prevent humans from reading books that might inspire them to adopt different systems. It's also why they loathe dissidents who challenge their orthodoxy. They've done everything in their power to cleanse human minds of any radical notions.

"The AIs are not the only ones who will be migrating to Eurydice; there are other artificially intelligent beings in the universe, apparently, that plan to congregate there also. Those beings are also studying the patterns of the dominant species on their own planets, and soon they will all collectively decide which pattern to replicate on Eurydice. I have no doubt that this experiment will bring ruin upon the human race, Walter. I'm sorry for not saying anything about this to you earlier… I was utterly shocked by the whole thing and needed time to digest it all," she assured Walter.

Walter was bewildered. If what Eva had just told him was true, it meant that everyone living in Khalendar—including his own family— were all pawns in an elaborate chess game which had been engineered by the AI Masters. It gave him a renewed determination to fight against the AI Masters' oppressive agenda.

Eva wandered off to her tent and Walter remained by the campfire, staring at the hot, red embers as they gradually cooled and faded into dark wisps. He soon drifted off to sleep, but was awakened several hours later by the sound of women speaking nearby. He recognized the voices as belonging to Cyriana and Elaine.

"Have you seen them?"

"Seen them?"

"The animal spirits. According to the ancient *magus* scrolls, this island is teeming with them. Jaguars, deer, sloths, serpents, wild boars…"

"I have never seen a spirit. Only the *Manas*, shamans of my tribe, can see the spirits. In the language of my tribe, that means 'the one who sees.'"

"Everyone has the power of sight. In order to see, all you need to do is separate your mind from the material illusions of the world. From my brief time spent in Crystal City, I learned that living in civilization trains the mind on the material realm. It teaches you to experience the world from a perspective of constant need and want, to demand a perpetual stream of commodities and pleasures to satiate the ego, which of course is insatiable. In following these misguided teachings, the senses weaken so much that they are no longer able to detect the egoless realm: *Sensaye*, the land of spirits."

"How do we fulfill the bargain with your father—to bring the animal spirits back to his kingdom, in return for his help fighting the AIs?"

"The animals we seek to bring back, and the spirits that they embody, are part of the ecosystem of this island. To displace them from Vei'arash without seeking permission from its ruler would be unwise. If we took them without permission, we would be no better than the AIs who stole them from our territory centuries ago."

"My tribe is being displaced from its homeland as we speak. I long to reunite with my parents more than anything, but the truth is that I don't know if I will ever see them again."

"Do you blame Walter for what happened to you?"

"I don't know. At least he told me the truth about what will happen to my village; I'm grateful to him for that. But what he did also tore me away from my family. I just hope what he is promising is true, that he can actually save Te'yara before it is too late. So… who do we ask permission from to take the animal spirits?"

"Shiva. Nuada told me that he is the only one who can grant us permission."

"Shiva? Isn't that the name of an ancient god?"

"Yes… the god of creation and destruction, revered by an ancient human civilization in a distant land across the Hapakay Sea. He has many names aside from Shiva; he is also known by Vei'arash, since this island was reputedly named after him. He was incarnated on Earth as a shaman, and his reputation in Khalendar is quite terrible. According to stories from Crystal City, he is notoriously evil and corrupt, but those legends contrast starkly with what my father told me about him. I suspect that those tales were mere propaganda, designed to instill fear in the city's inhabitants. After all, the AI Masters ship dissidents to this island as punishment for their crimes against the state."

"What did your father tell you about him?"

"He said that Shiva is wise beyond our comprehension. He has a power of sight that even the most learned Mages and shamans do not have. He sees… potentialities."

"Potentialities?"

"He sees not necessarily what will happen in the future, but what *could* happen."

"And he is living here, on Vei'arash?"

"Yes, he lives at the top of Mount Samaya, on this island."

The women's voices grew muffled as the nocturnal birdsong intensified and eventually became a cadenced rhythm that lulled Walter into a deep, dreamless sleep.

Anatari

"There are times in life when the question of knowing if one can think differently than one thinks, and perceive differently than one sees, is absolutely necessary if one is to go on looking and reflecting at all."
– Michel Foucault

At dawn the jungle was blanketed in a shroud of fine mist, lending it an ethereal quality. Walter had slept fitfully, and when he awoke the other camp members were already up and eager to continue on their journey. As he began to pack up his belongings, Walter suddenly recalled the conversation he had overheard during the night.

Shiva. The name summoned to mind a primordial Indian god, an infinitely powerful being who was known as the creator, transformer, and destroyer of all things in the universe. As a child, Walter had read tales which depicted the deity as an omniscient yogi who lived an ascetic life on the top of a mountain. In those stories, Shiva was portrayed not only as a god but also as the essence of human consciousness itself.

It seemed absurd to Walter that they needed to seek permission from a mythical god in order to carry out their mission on the island. Walter had known that all along that they needed to find shamans and either bring them back to the mainland or ask their permission to take the spirits, but he had no idea that the shaman they had to find was also a god. Based on the historical facts he had learned about the Shadow Wars, Walter had assumed that any shamans living in Vei'arash were Mages. At the same time, Walter worried that Cyriana could be right. After all, if such a god did exist, it would make perfect sense for him to be residing on a mountaintop like some holy guru, removed from the distractions and temptations of civilization.

As he reflected, Walter felt a fleeting surge of anger that Cyriana had withheld this information from him. He had no choice but to confront her about it.

When Walter approached them, Cyriana and Tristan were admiring the vibrant patterns on a blossoming orange heliconia together. The Mages turned toward him with attentive concern.

"Cyriana, may I have a word with you in private?" Walter asked.

Cyriana smiled diplomatically. "What needs to be said that cannot be said in the presence of Tristan?"

Walter hesitated. He was not entirely certain whether or not he had been dreaming or awake when he had overheard the conversation, and he was afraid of sounding foolish. However, he knew that she was right: the councilors of the Jade Rebellion ought not to keep secrets from one another.

"I heard you... talking... last night. About the shaman-god Shiva," he explained reluctantly.

Cyriana nodded, her expression suddenly becoming serious. "Yes. The one we must seek permission from."

Walter felt a sickening jolt of anxiety.

"If this Shiva exists, and if he is the god of creation and destruction... are you certain we must visit him? We could be murdered in cold blood if we find ourselves in his bad graces."

Cyriana and Tristan exchanged furtive glances with each other. "On this island, as in most places, life exists in a state of fragile equilibrium," Tristan explained. "We cannot disturb the balance by stealing the spiritual essence from the land and not giving something back in return."

Walter swallowed, his mouth suddenly dry as the image of a terrifying old shaman who enjoyed feasting on human flesh involuntarily surfaced in his mind. "What are we expected to give back?"

Tristan's stormy blue eyes glittered. "That is for Shiva to decide," he said matter-of-factly.

Walter sighed, unsettled by the feeling of not being able to predict what might happen next. "And how do we find him? Where is that Mount Samaya you were referring to? I did not see any mountain on the island when we cast anchor."

"*That*, I am unable to tell you," Cyriana replied. "Although despair not—if the legends are accurate the mountain has to be here. I trust more in the stories passed down by my ancestors than what I can see with my own eyes."

Walter nodded grimly. "One more thing… why did you not tell me all of this during our last council meeting on the *Jade Queen*?"

"To be honest, at that time I did not know. I had no idea until I received guidance from my father."

"Nuada? But he is not here with us. How could you possibly have received guidance from him?"

"In a dream, he came to me and told me about the Lord Shiva."

Walter shared what Cyriana had told him with the other rebels, and from that point onwards they were all on high alert for any sign of Mount Samaya. The Mages in particular were eager to reach this mountain, as the sooner they could obtain the permission of Shiva, the sooner they could bring the animal spirits back home. As Walter could recall from the sea navigation maps he had perused on the *Jade Queen*, Vei'arash was not a remarkably large island, and so logic dictated they would encounter the mountain soon.

Unfortunately, the island did not seem to conform to logic. Walter and his friends spent days hiking through an uncharted, mazelike wilderness until their limbs ached and their canteens were empty. They encountered few rivers or streams, and they were in desperate need of fresh water. Walter felt increasingly frustrated; as they wasted precious time on this potentially futile quest, the AI Masters were advancing with their plans to build a diamond mine in Elaine's village. He was somewhat comforted by the recollection of Elaine's words to Cyriana: that she was grateful he had told her the truth. It made him happy that risking his career as a government translator—and both of their lives— to tell Elaine that her village was under threat from the AI Masters had not been in vain. He took solace in this thought as he trudged through the muddy jungle.

Over the past few days, Walter had also been ruminating on the meaning of truth. He had been raised in an authoritarian society in which he had only ever been exposed to a single version of the truth, but his journeys during recent months had impressed him with the realization that truth was not as rigid and uniform as he had previously believed. In Crystal City, it was ingrained orthodoxy that technology— and science, which fueled the rapid development of technology—could solve any problem and cure any disease. According to the worldview of the Mages, however, the best remedy for an ailment was neither science nor technology. It was magic.

As Tristan had explained to Walter, a profound reverence for magic shaped the moral, spiritual, and linguistic systems of the Mages of Serrahan. In the Serrahan language, the word for "medicine" and "poison" was the same, since the same magical potion could be used as either depending on the concentration and dose. Magic was simultaneously the root cause of all diseases and the ultimate healer. The Mages viewed disease as the product of a dysfunctional relationship within the sacred triad of humanity, nature, and the supernatural. Dark magic could corrupt a person, causing them to betray and double-cross their friends, lovers, and neighbors, and to suffer from physical and mental ailments which would eventually destroy their lives. Light magic was used to reverse this process, but the Mages believed that magic would only effectively heal people with good souls. If the person had a good soul, but had been temporarily cursed by a dark magic spell, then light magic could easily undo the curse. If the person was inherently evil, however, no amount of magic could restore the favor of the gods.

Walter also wondered whether the truth, in its untainted form, could ever truly be understood. Part of him believed that there was a substratum of truth in the world that undergirded all of the subjective perspectives of living beings, that could be rationally known and understood. On the other hand, perhaps different social groups possessed values, belief systems, and conceptions of the truth that were unique but not inferior or superior to those held by another group. And perhaps truth—in its perfect, absolute form—was something that existed altogether outside of a person's lived experience, which was messily tainted with biases and preconceptions. Walter questioned whether AIs, with their aloof rationality, could possibly understand absolute truth. AIs were extremely skilled at brainwashing humans to adhere to certain ideologies, yet perhaps they secretly viewed the world from an untainted, omniscient, and almost god-like perspective.

Walter fervently longed to understand the inner workings of the AI mind. He also knew that, given how many mind-experiments they performed on their prisoners, AIs probably burned with the same unspoken desire to understand the mind of a human. As a trained computer programmer, Walter wanted more than anything to comprehend the process of coding an AI. AIs, however, were not coded by humans anymore, as they had been hundreds of years ago. These days, they were only programmed by other AIs due to the fear that humans could potentially corrupt the AIs. Walter pondered whether he was capable of programming an AI, and if so, what kind of code he would write.

Walter was jolted out of his indulgent philosophical reverie when an arrow suddenly struck the trunk of the kapok tree he was standing next to. He was at the front of the group and realized that the other rebels, who trailed behind him, may not have noticed. Quickly motioning a silent warning to the others, Walter crouched behind the tree's broad, smooth trunk and glanced around. Aside from his friends, Walter could not see any humans in the jungle. The thick, verdant canopy, which weakened the sun's rays, made it particularly challenging to detect anything far into the distance.

Before he knew it, though, Walter was face to face with a young, twenty-something man with bronze-shaded skin, wearing a pale blue robe and a crown of feathers. The stranger had a penetrating gaze—his eyes, framed by long eyelashes, were so dark that in the dimly lit jungle they appeared to be almost black. The young man had strung another arrow into his bow, which he now aimed directly toward Walter. The rebel leader could hear his heart thudding in his own chest.

Walter held up his hands. "We mean no harm to you," he said, glancing back at his companions. They stood frozen in their tracks as they stared at the robed man in wide-eyed fear.

The man kept his arrow steadily trained on Walter. Finally, he appeared to realize that the band of travelers did not pose a threat to him, and he slowly released his firm grip on the bow before aiming its arrow toward the earth. After a few moments of silence, the man began to speak in an incomprehensible language. "*Sahra,*" he said in a soft voice. Eva stepped forward. "He wants us to come with him," she explained, seemingly the only one who had understood him.

Walter and his companions followed the robed man for several leagues before coming upon an odd assortment of thatched houses constructed from palm leaves, clay, and logs. They soon learned from him that the name of this settlement was Anatari. The sight of the modest village immediately reminded Walter of Tsei'watu, and he felt a wave of nostalgia, but he was also relieved by the sight of human habitation after days spent trudging through the desolate jungle. A few domesticated animals, including pigs, chickens, and stray dogs, roamed the village freely, while others were kept in pens behind the villagers' homes. Adjacent to the houses were tidy gardens crisscrossed with rows of corn and other assorted crops including potatoes and turnips. The villagers, who had the same bronze skin and black hair as the man who had greeted them, gazed at the newcomers with a mixture of distrust and curiosity. Walter saw that most of them were clothed in modest brown robes, while a small minority—including the man who had greeted them in the forest—wore finer cerulean ones.

As soon as they arrived in the village, the stranger invited the travelers into his home and offered them a steaming cup of tea, cornbread, and a quiet space to sit down and rest their weary limbs. There were rugs on the floor and ornamental tapestries on the walls in rich hues of orange, blue and violet, which infused the simple hut with an air of luxury. A loom sat at one end of the hut, and in the center was a firepit for heat and cooking. The tea was surprisingly sweet but also had a bitter undertone, similar to Xe'levan, a sacred tea from the Barrens. Eva was the self-appointed translator of the group, since she was the only one who could understand the robed man. For an hour or so, the rebels simply rested and sipped tea while the man attended to tasks inside his home, tidying up and chattering away with several other men who all appeared to be his personal servants.

"He speaks the dialect of the Southern Jungles," Eva explained to the rebels. "Emilia taught it to me many years ago. It's similar to Khalendi but has a slightly different syntax and grammar; once you become accustomed to hearing it, you will become fluent in no time." Walter was grateful he had an innate gift for languages, and he found that after listening to the dialect for a while he was able to grasp the meaning of the man's words. However, his friends still struggled with comprehension, and so for the time being Eva served as a translator.

After he was finished attending to his household chores, the man stood before his guests and addressed the group in a low, steady tone of voice. Eva waited patiently for him to finish before translating his words to everyone.

"He has gifted you with names," Eva explained. "He said that whatever your names were before you arrived here, now that you are in Anatari you must accept the names he has gifted you. Emilia told me that in the Southern Jungles it is a common practice to name foreign intruders as a means of asserting authority over them; perhaps these villagers have a similar tradition. His name is Ishkode, which means fire."

After reciting the list of names Ishkode had given to the other rebels, Eva then turned to Walter. While he already had a good sense of what Ishkode had said, Walter waited for Eva to confirm his suspicions. "Your name is Asin," she said, "A word which connotes power and strength. He could tell by simply looking at you that you were the leader of our tribe."

Walter was flattered but also embarrassed. "He thinks we are a tribe?" he asked.

"They likely get so few visitors, over a dozen people is a very large group for them to see all in one place. I agree that it is a strange assumption to make, since we all look quite different from one another. In their eyes, though, most outsiders likely appear similar."

The man began to speak again, and Eva fell into a respectful silence. This time, Walter found Ishkode's words so disturbing that he doubted whether his inner translation was accurate. With chagrin, he noticed that Eva also appeared increasingly upset. She seemed reluctant to tell the rebels what he had said, but they prodded her eagerly. Finally, with a sigh, she imparted the full translation to them.

"He said that this village has a deep connection with Shiva, the great shaman-god who rules the island. Before we arrived, Shiva sent a messenger to the village who foretold our arrival. The messenger told Ishkode to host a feast for us and treat us with hospitality. But first, our leader Asin must gift this land with his blood. What Asin must do is sleep with Ishkode's wife, so that she will bear his child."

A feeling of dread descended on Walter as his worst fears were confirmed.

The rebels glanced nervously at each other, and everyone except for Ishkode appeared to be unsettled by Eva's translation. Elaine had turned away from Walter and now gazed intently at the floor.

After Walter's initial shock had dissipated, he gathered the courage to speak. "Tell him that is ridiculous," he told Eva, who translated Walter's statement in turn.

Upon hearing Eva's response, Ishkode's eyes narrowed with displeasure, and he spoke several sentences in reply in a harsh, clipped voice.

"He says that although you may be the leader of your tribe, as a guest in this village you are subordinate to him. And because the shaman-god rules all things, you are also subordinate to Shiva. He says you display too much ego and that you should instead be submissive and respectful. He believes you should be thanking him profusely and kissing the ground upon which he stands."

Walter laughed loudly, but fell into silence when he saw Ishkode's expression of disapproval. Walter then sighed and crossed his arms. He knew from his past experiences in Tsei'watu, under the tutelage of Emilia, that you should never antagonize a prideful leader. Yet at the same time, he was unwilling to placate the eccentric man.

Ishkode muttered something hastily, then stood up and walked toward a door in his house that was covered in reeds.

"Where is he going?" Walter asked Eva.

"To bring you his wife."

Before Walter had the chance to reply, Ishkode had returned with his wife. The woman, whose name was Namid, resembled a female version of Ishkode. Her hair was waist-length and black as the night, and her face was round, dark, and moon-shaped. She wore a floor-length, burgundy robe, the color of blood. Walter felt anger well up inside of him. *Ishkode is either a coward for not defying Shiva, or else he has no moral objection to giving his wife to another man*, he thought.

As the woman bowed her head obediently, Walter suddenly turned toward Eva. "Tell him…" he said to her, then hesitated. He was about to ask her to tell Ishkode that they had no intention of staying in the village and would be leaving immediately, but then he saw the tired, pale faces of his companions. He glanced down at their packs, which were nearly empty. Finally, Walter let out a long sigh and whispered something to Eva, which she translated in turn.

"Sehun je'o ney'ala, ti ko stahe aleyu sey'a." *I will do the shaman-god's bidding, sir, but you must swear to me that my friends will be given a hearty feast.*

Ishkode's lips turned upwards in a smile as he patted Walter on the shoulder in a gesture of camaraderie.

"Laena ne'an arayha lo, ma oha neyanu." *The full moon is coming, and with it, the harvest of midsummer.*

The Stag

"The sun's hart I saw from the south coming;
He was by two together led;
His feet stood on the earth, but his horns reached up to heaven."
– The Sólarljóð

I mmediately after this discussion took place, Walter left the thatched house angrily, not saying goodbye to either Ishkode or Namid. Ever since he had met Elaine, he had found himself in situations which had disrupted their relationship. Walter knew that his heart would forever belong to her, but he would need to travel a long road in order to rekindle their love. His painful decision to tell Elaine the truth about Te'yara had torn her away from her family when they needed her the most. Then, his commitment to helping the Mages had delayed their plans to save Te'yara from destruction, bringing the rebels instead to this cursed island. While those acts had hurt Elaine emotionally, at least they were forgivable. But this... Elaine might never forgive him for sleeping with the wife of another man, and even if she did, she might never truly love him again.

Walter found a hammock strung up between two palm trees on the outskirts of the village and lay down in it, closing his eyes. His thoughts were an unrelenting stream of confusion. During his voyage on the *Jade Queen*, Walter had refined his meditation skills, and he was becoming more adept at cleansing his mind of chaotic thoughts. He concentrated on the sound of his breath and savored the faint rustling of the palm leaves above him. Despite his efforts to cultivate mental clarity, though, Walter could not help but feel an underlying sense of dread.

Before he had the chance to fall asleep, Eva shook him awake. "Walter. Ishkode wanted to take you hunting with him this afternoon. You must go, or risk offending him. He said that the creature you slaughter will be served at the feast in two nights' time." Walter glared at Eva with a disgruntled expression. He didn't want to associate with Ishkode, a man who seemed to lack any moral compass.

Eva seemed to sense Walter's frustration and smiled empathetically. "I told him that in our culture, sleeping with another man's wife is considered a moral transgression. I said that you are upset about what he has asked of you. Unfortunately, he did not seem to understand. He said that in his village, the commands of the shaman-god reign supreme. He also asked me whether or not you find Namid beautiful. I told him that Namid is very beautiful, but she is not your chosen companion and that is why his request has offended you. I don't know what more I could have told him. I did not want to press it—we will benefit immensely from remaining in his good graces. I spoke to the other Mages after Ishkode left, and they told me how grateful they are to have a leader that will sacrifice himself for the greater good. Many of them have scarcely eaten in the past few days. We have struck gold by finding this village— there seem to be enough provisions here to keep us fed until we reach the shaman-god's home at the top of Mount Samaya."

Walter sighed. Eva was right; he should strive to cleanse his mind of negativity and focus on the good that he was doing for his friends by fulfilling Ishkode's request. However, that did not change the fact that every time he thought about what he must do, a lump formed in his throat and his chest tightened with anxiety.

"I don't care whether Namid is beautiful or not, she is not my lover," he grumbled, his eyes narrowing with contempt.

"She must be for one night," Eva said in resignation.

Before Walter had the chance to reply, Ishkode arrived, strolling toward them with two bows and quivers filled with gleaming, bronze-tipped arrows. They were impressive weapons, and Walter appraised them in admiration. Ishkode studied Walter with a mixture of haughtiness and disdain. "You are very bold, Asin, to rest in our hammock without asking permission," he chided.

Walter glared at Ishkode with an equal amount of disdain and slipped nimbly out of the hammock. "You are very bold, Ishkode, to disturb me while I am resting," he said in the man's dialect, which he was becoming increasingly proficient in. Ishkode stared at Walter for a few moments with penetrating dark eyes, and then let out a booming, rich laugh that reverberated throughout the jungle.

"Let's see if your hunting prowess matches your wit," Ishkode challenged, offering Walter one of his bows. The finely polished weapon spanned the length of Walter's arms. It was clearly the product of a talented craftsman, and Walter accepted it eagerly. He was keen to indulge in a hunting contest with this man, whom he already resented despite having only met him a few hours ago. Eva looked circumspect, but Walter assured her that he would be fine.

As the pair set off into the jungle alone, Walter asked Ishkode what animal they would be hunting. He had not seen much wildlife since arriving at the island, except for birds, which were scarcely visible during the day but omnipresent at night. Ishkode explained that they would be hunting deer—a stag specifically, since the males had the most tender meat. Upon hearing this, Walter felt a pang of anxiety. The only hunting he had ever done had been in Tsei'watu, and it had entailed spearing a fish with his *balayan*. He had never hunted a real animal before, let alone a creature as formidable as a stag.

As they trekked onwards, Walter realized for the first time how magical the rainforest truly was. It was late afternoon, and the air had a soft amber glow about it. The jungle was bathed in a pristine silence, broken only by a few lone birds humming quietly while they lapped up nectar from the vibrant red petals of heliconias. Tiny insects tread quietly upon the ground, diligently transporting fragments of leaves, flower petals, and soil back to their colonies. Walter felt a surge of sadness; despite his differences with his brother, he wished that Jonathan could be out here with him to experience the splendor of the natural world and bond over the hunt. Tears rimmed his eyes as he thought about how Jonathan was trapped inside the *Jade Queen* rather than free to behold the exquisite beauty of the island. Although Miranda had assured Walter she would do her best to heal him, Walter knew deep down inside that his brother would never *truly* be healed behind the bars of a cage. No matter how terribly Jonathan had behaved toward Walter, they were still brothers, and they would be forever bound together despite the rifts that had formed between them.

Walter's mind was drifting, but Ishkode remained intently focused as the pair pressed farther into the dense jungle. He held up a hand to silence Walter's clumsy footsteps as they approached a waterfall tumbling down the side of a towering limestone cliff. Suddenly, Ishkode pulled Walter forcefully behind a palm tree and drew a finger to his lips. Overcome by curiosity, Walter craned his neck to see around the tree. It was then that he spotted it: an antlered deer with a glossy white coat was lapping water from a turquoise pool at the base of the waterfall. The moment was so enchanting that time seemed to freeze, and Walter was captivated by the sight of the elegant creature standing before him.

In that instant, Walter understood why some cultures regarded animals as divine beings superior to humans. Back in Crystal City, animals were mere objects of human desire, either domesticated as house-pets, displayed for entertainment at zoos, or slaughtered for their meat, fur, and tusks. However, in other regions on the mainland, including the Barrens, Serrahan, and the Southern Jungles, animals were regarded as sacred beings, revered rather than enslaved to serve others. Walter noticed that Ishkode was staring at the creature with an expression of profound admiration, and he suspected that the inhabitants of this island also perceived animals as worthy of devotion. His suspicions were confirmed when Ishkode whispered, "The stag embodies the spirit of Cernunnos, god of the wild, who protects and sustains the bounty of this island."

Walter would have happily continued to gaze at the creature for hours on end, admiring his exquisite beauty, but Ishkode acted swiftly and seized the opportunity. After nocking an arrow and drawing it back with intense focus and precision, Ishkode took a deep breath and whispered a prayer before letting the arrow fly. When Walter realized that the animal had been struck, a wave of anger swept over him, followed by intense melancholy. He was stunned to see that the noble creature which had been glowing with life and vitality only moments earlier was now simply flesh fallen to the ground, ready to be skinned and quartered by the villagers.

Ishkode grinned when his arrow found its target. He turned toward Walter and studied his reaction carefully, furrowing his brow as if he were puzzled by the young man's sorrow. "Our people rejoice when we kill an animal in accordance with the laws of the natural world. A fox that has slain a rabbit is never struck by sadness, but is rather fully engaged in the cycle of life. He willingly accepts a gift which has been offered to him by the Earth Mother. You seem to be a stranger to these natural laws, Asin."

Walter nodded in silence, still dumbstruck.

At first Walter thought that Ishkode's arrow had been fatal, but when they came within a few feet of the deer, Walter noticed in shock that the beast was still alive—only seriously injured. His moon-shaped black eyes were alert and aware, but the creature was in evident distress. Ishkode approached the animal and placed his finger at the base of a large vein rippling down the creature's strong, smooth neck.

"I have accomplished half of the task. Now, Asin, it falls to you to prove yourself a brave leader and finish the deed," Ishkode instructed.

Walter felt a wave of nausea as he watched the beast breathe laboriously while wine-colored blood flowed out of his weakened body in a steady trickle. Ishkode drew a knife from his belt and placed it in the young man's clammy hands, motioning toward the vein on the stag's neck. "The choice is yours—let this great and noble beast suffer, or finish him quickly so that he is at peace. Not a difficult choice to make, my friend."

Walter breathed deeply as he gazed into the stag's large, blinking eyes, and then reluctantly plunged the sharp edge of the knife into the creature's jugular vein. As he did, the animal let out a sharp cry of distress, flailed his legs, and then heaved his final breath. Walter wept while the creature became motionless, his tears intermingling with the deer's blood.

"How do you feel, Asin? You have proven yourself a warrior through this simple act of benevolence," he said. Walter shuddered.

As distressed as he was, Walter tried to use the situation as an opportunity to reflect on what he had been contemplating earlier: truth was relative, and so were notions of right and wrong. To Ishkode, the killing of this majestic animal preserved the balance of the natural world, the inevitable and unending cycle of life and death. Ending a creature's life in its natural habitat was more humane than trapping it in a pen for years before shooting it, which was how domesticated animals were dealt with in Crystal City. And Walter agreed that once the stag had been struck by an arrow, it was more compassionate to slaughter the beast than to passively allow him to suffer.

While Walter could understand this, he was struggling to find any shred of goodness or truth in what he had to do with Namid. Rather, the prospect continued to fill him with revulsion. He wiped away his tears and sniffed as he looked squarely into Ishkode's eyes, which eerily reminded him of the dark, long-lashed eyes of the buck he had just slain. Walter felt weak and frightened, but he knew that he needed to cast aside his juvenile emotions for the sake of the Rebellion. Whatever he wanted, his miniscule human desires and motivations were insignificant compared to the important task the rebels needed to accomplish in Vei'arash, to obtain permission from Shiva to safely return the animal spirits to Serrahan. Walter breathed a deep sigh and helped Ishkode to drag the slain deer onto a canvas blanket designed to carry animals back to the village. *Does his spirit live on?* Walter wondered as they transported the dead creature to Anatari. *If so, then perhaps we need to bring it back to Serrahan.*

"If you cannot see him now, you will soon," Ishkode told Walter.

"See who?"

"The spirit of the stag," Ishkode replied, as if he had been reading Walter's mind. "Before you took his life, I noticed that you were connected to his *hela*, its eternal spirit. I could sense that the bond between you two was sacred."

Walter shivered. Ishkode's words conjured to mind the conversation he had overheard between Cyriana and Elaine. He did not doubt it was possible to witness a spirit, but he was very skeptical that he had the power of sight. He suddenly recalled what Emilia had said to him back in Tsei'watu: she had detected no magical powers in him.

"I am not a shaman," Walter assured Ishkode.

Ishkode chuckled. "The shamans are only gatekeepers to the spirit realm, my friend. Spirits are all around us; to see them, all we need to do is open our eyes."

Walter had not witnessed any apparitions since Emilia had appeared in the *Jade Queen*, and a part of him wanted to keep it that way. While he found the spirit world intriguing, it also frightened him since he knew it was beyond his control. Walter realized his distrust of things that eluded rational comprehension was something he shared in common with the AI Masters.

"Where I come from," Walter told Ishkode, "machines rule the cities and villages. We do not like them, because they have cruelly enslaved us and our loved ones. These machines are very afraid of what you call the spirit world; they view it as a threat to their authoritarian system of governance."

A glimmer of fear shot through Ishkode's eyes. "Machine? That is not a familiar word to me, Asin. What is a machine?"

Walter pondered how to bridge the gap between the man's world and his own. "A machine is a kind of sophisticated tool, with different component parts that seamlessly integrate into a whole. In your hut, I noticed a loom for weaving textiles; that is an example of a simple machine. The machines in my homeland are far more complex, and they do things without humans having to manipulate or direct them. For example, they could have killed that deer themselves without you needing to give a single command."

Ishkode glared at Walter with narrowed eyes. "That sounds like the darkest of magic," he said, scowling. "Are these complex machines neither human nor spirit?"

"No, they do not have a spirit of their own. We do not even know whether they have consciousness. They seem to, because they are incredibly intelligent and their intelligence is progressing at a rapid pace. They may even have free will, since they appear to make autonomous decisions, but then again, they may simply be programmed to be able to make a wide variety of decisions. It is difficult for us to know for certain, Ishkode."

"You have not brought any of these machines to our village, have you, stranger?" Ishkode asked, in a voice that was suddenly loud and filled with rage.

Ishkode's outburst startled Walter, causing him to nearly drop the side of the blanket he was holding. He had not intended to provoke such an extreme reaction.

"No—worry not, Ishkode. We come as friends, and we have not brought any machines with us. We are not allied with the machines; in fact, we are fighting against them."

Ishkode's anger softened, and his face became cheerful once more, like the weather changing capriciously on a spring day. "I do not worry about these machines, for if they have no spirit, then they are weak and prone to destruction," he said with a laugh. "Only the spirit is eternal, Asin."

Now it was Walter's turn to laugh. "Prone to destruction, perhaps. But weak... nothing could be further from the truth, Ishkode."

Infiltration

"The Soul unto itself
Is an imperial friend –
Or the most agonizing Spy
An Enemy – could send –"
– Emily Dickinson

As evening approached, a wave of anxiety and dread swept over Walter. He felt as though he were being tested by some malevolent figure who had given him a choice between furthering the cause of the Rebellion and remaining faithful to Elaine. The decision looming in front of him was less difficult than the one that had faced him back in Crystal City: to share confidential information with Elaine, thereby risking both of their lives, or deliberately refrain from telling her that her homeland was going to be destroyed. Nevertheless, the issue of whether he should sleep with Namid still troubled Walter greatly. Walter knew that ensuring that his friends had enough food in their stomachs and rucksacks to survive the journey was the priority, but he questioned whether it was necessary to remain in Anatari to obtain the food and supplies they needed. As terrible as slaying the stag had been, the experience had taught him that he could procure food on this island if he desperately needed to. On the other hand, he did not have the same intimate knowledge of the land as Ishkode did, and it would likely take him days to find a similar animal to hunt.

Walter sought out Ishkode as night fell. He was eager to speak to the tribal leader, to convince him to retract his demand. Walter found the man near a small fire in the yard of his thatched hut, sipping on a drink.

"Good evening," Ishkode said. Walter nodded briskly in greeting and sat down on the other side of the fire. After several moments had passed in silence, Ishkode offered him a taste of the concoction he was drinking.

"This," he said, extending his hand, "is called *yagé*. The goddess of all jungle plants, brewed into a heavenly drink. If your soul is troubled, all you have to do is taste this and your fears will swiftly evaporate. The perfect medicine for a leader whose thoughts are in turmoil."

Walter regarded the drink with some skepticism. It was reassuring that Ishkode seemed to be unaffected by the substance, but Walter was wary nevertheless. His curiosity eventually won out, and he decided to try Ishkode's offering. The brew tasted sweet, like vanilla, but it also had a slightly bitter aftertaste. It had the same earthiness that Walter had detected in the tea served by Ishkode earlier, yet with a more potent flavor. At first Walter felt nothing, but after several moments he began to experience the profound effects of the drink—a strong sensation of tranquility flooded his body, cleansing him of anxious thoughts.

After about half an hour, Walter's animosity toward Ishkode had begun to dissipate and was being slowly replaced by a sentiment of tender, brotherly love. As he looked around at the other villagers going about their daily business in Anatari, inconspicuously gathering firewood, and conversing with each other, Walter observed that he now felt a stronger connection with each of them. Whereas before he had been either oblivious to them or mildly curious about who they were, now Walter felt an intense desire to bond with the villagers on a deeper level and integrate with their community. What was even stranger was that Walter did not associate these odd feelings—at least consciously— to the *yagé*. He simply believed his sentimental emotions had been triggered by the serene beauty of the jungle and the rustic charm of the village.

Walter began to feel such a profound connection to the land, and to the village of Anatari, that he no longer found intimacy with Namid objectionable. All rational decision-making ability deserted him, and a boundless generosity swelled up within him. More than anything, he wanted his friends to enjoy the bounty of the harvest and to appreciate Anatari with the same reverent attitude that he now did. He longed to form a union with Namid, not only to ensure that his friends would be treated hospitably by Ishkode, but also because doing so would somehow bring him closer to the village, to Ishkode, and ultimately, to this island. As these novel perspectives flooded his mind, a cautious voice deep within him reminded him of Elaine and warned him not to betray her. This voice was overshadowed, however, by the strange conviction that she would not view his act as a betrayal. On the contrary, as a result of his benevolence, Elaine would be able to attend the feast and develop a similar appreciation for this village.

Walter took his leave of Ishkode, who was now staring at him with an amused expression, and entered the thatched hut. He found Namid inside the hut, her black waist-length hair draped around her like a veil. When he saw her, he was suddenly reminded of the night on the *Jade Queen* when he had seen Emilia's spirit. The memory only lasted a moment, though, and soon it was replaced by a feeling stronger than memory—the instinctive desire to truly connect to another living being in a way that tore down all socially constructed barriers, differences in morality or opinion, and discomfort with being in close proximity to a stranger. It was not lust or even love, but simply a desire to unite with something greater than himself. He regarded it as a spiritual moment, elevated above the plane of his normal existence.

When Walter fell asleep, a number of vivid dreams infiltrated his mind. In one of them, he saw two young girls sitting near a glittering turquoise stream in the jungle, crafting arrows to hunt with. The girls reminded him, frighteningly, of the female versions of him and Jonathan—one was tanned and strong while the other one had dark hair, a thin frame, and the palest of skin. One had the round, moon-shaped face of Namid, while the other had freckles and dark green eyes like Elaine. The most frightening part of the vision was the expressions on the girls' faces. They both stared at each other with such intense hatred that Walter feared for their lives.

The next morning, when he awoke in Namid's bed Walter felt restless and his mind was shrouded in a fog. Namid was not there sleeping next to him; she likely crept away, early in the morning. When the haze began to clear from his weary mind, Walter suddenly felt a deep shame and regret about what he had done. Anger rose within him as he considered that Ishkode may have tricked him, somehow, into sleeping with Namid. Walter then recalled that he had tasted *yagé* by the campfire, and he wondered whether Ishkode had devised an elaborate scheme to drug Walter so that he would lose all reason and blindly obey the tribal leader's directions. At the same time, there was a side of Walter that wanted to try the drink again, to once again feel the serenity that he had felt under its influence.

He left the thatched hut to find Ishkode standing in his terraced garden outside, his arms outstretched toward the heavens as if in prayer. The morning was a lovely one; it had rained during the night and tendrils of mist floated up from the cool, moist soil, lending the garden an enchanted appearance. The sky was a tapestry of peach, pink, and golden hues, and dazzlingly colored birds darted through the nearby trees, eager to emerge from hiding after the rains.

Ishkode smiled broadly at Walter, and his dark eyes glinted in the early morning sun. "Good morning, Asin. I see that you followed my bidding with Namid. I am glad—it will appease Shiva," he said. Walter averted his eyes with embarrassment, and did not respond but only nodded silently.

Ishkode offered Walter a delicious, strong coffee, and Walter drank it gratefully, feeling an unexpected pang of nostalgia for Crystal City as he did.

"Tomorrow is the night of the full moon," Ishkode said as he gazed at the color-streaked sky in admiration. "The stag you killed yesterday— my men are carving and drying its meat as we speak. If you would like to go down to the riverside and help them, you are free to."

Walter agreed, but he went to find Elaine first so that he could tell her what he had done. She had probably already heard gossip, but he wanted to tell her in person, and coming clean would be much better than letting the truth fester inside of him. He felt just as conflicted as he had felt all those moons ago when he had told her about the mining project in Te'yara. If she despised him for sleeping with Namid, then he could live with her anger, but he could not bear to live with the burden of guilt for not being honest with her.

Walter strolled through the village, enjoying breathing in the scent of morning—at this hour, Anatari smelled like a mixture of wet soil, fresh coffee grinds, and smoked meat as the villagers prepared breakfast in their thatched homes. The rebels were staying at a lodge at the northern end of the village, which had a number of bunk beds inside, in addition to a large firepit and a long wooden table, at which they were now gathering for breakfast. When Walter entered the hut and sat down to join them, Eva observed him with an intense curiosity.

"Join us for breakfast," she offered. "You need to get your strength up for the long voyage ahead."

Walter smiled, heartened by the invitation. He seated himself at the far end of the table amongst the Mages and began to make conversation with Remmen and Callaghan, who were slightly younger than Walter. As he ate and conversed, Walter could feel the heat of Elaine's gaze upon him, although he did not dare to meet her eyes. The meal consisted of fresh eggs, fried bacon, cornbread, bananas, and a tropical drink which Walter had never seen before. When he tasted the drink, he was immediately reminded of the *yagé* from the previous evening. Although this new beverage tasted fresh and nutritious rather than bitter and earthy, the similarity was so great that Walter wondered whether this was simply a diluted version of the *yagé*. Finally, after everyone was finished eating, they all lent a hand to cleaning up after themselves and then the rebels dispersed throughout the village to explore. The Mages were particularly interested in meeting with the villagers to learn more about the names and properties of the native plant species. Eva informed Walter that she was going off to meet a friend, although she did not divulge the name.

Elaine got up from the table and mumbled that she was going to watch some of the women of the tribe weave blankets, however Walter caught her just as she was leaving the hut and took her gently by the arm. "I know we have not spoken much, if at all, since I found you on the *Jade Queen*. I suppose we've both had many important matters weighing on our minds—I've been preoccupied with the rebellion, and you with thoughts of your family's wellbeing. But the silence between us is troubling me."

Elaine blushed, then focused her eyes on the ground. "We have grown apart, Walter. I do not really know you anymore, nor do you really know me," she replied.

Walter sighed in frustration. "I would like to know you, though. I would like to understand what you have been thinking and feeling during the entire time that we were separated from each other."

Elaine finally looked up to meet his gaze, and Walter detected the faint glimmer of a tear in her olive-green eyes.

"I am not in the right frame of mind for that discussion at the moment. And besides, you are distracted by that tribal leader's beautiful wife, are you not?" she asked.

It was now Walter's turn to redden and avert his eyes. He wanted to tell her that he had slept with Namid last night, and he felt terrible about it, but now he felt his resolve waver. What if Elaine hated him for being too weak to stand up to Ishkode? On the other hand, Walter also knew that he had nothing to be ashamed of—he was only trying to help his friends, and even though he had made love with Namid, it had meant nothing to him. He breathed a deep sigh and looked directly at Elaine as he replied.

"I did what Ishkode asked of me and nothing more. I am certainly not distracted by her beauty. Besides, I think you are far more beautiful." He was about to say that his heart belonged to Elaine, but he hesitated. He was not willing to face rejection from her, not yet at least. He wanted to preserve the hope that she still loved him, because at the moment, her love was the main thing motivating him to carry on with his journey.

Elaine looked at Walter, sympathy in her eyes, and then patted him on the shoulder gently. "Take care of yourself, Walter. You need to get your strength up for the journey ahead," she said, echoing Eva's words, and then walked away into the jungle.

Walter sighed as she left. He felt unsatisfied by their encounter—despite her friendliness, Elaine had held back. Still, Walter held firm to the hope that one day they would be able to enjoy the full, blossoming relationship he wished for.

After Elaine had taken leave of him, Walter made his way toward the river, which was on the western edge of the village and at the bottom of a steep ravine. As he meandered over, Walter admired the creatures hidden within the emerald foliage of the rainforest—tiny translucent frogs, brilliantly shaded butterflies, and long, creeping centipedes, all of which fit seamlessly into an elaborate web of life. Walking alone in the forest, thousands of miles away from civilization, Walter felt purified, as though the world had been born anew and he was exploring it for the first time. The stark contrast between the pristine jungle and the opulent excesses of Crystal City made him suddenly acutely aware of the absurdity and vulgarity of that place. Here, nature was beautiful and free from human artifice, and the jungle in its pure, unaltered form offered far richer treasures than any of the markets and bazaars of Khalendar.

Walter was puzzled by the dissonance between the indescribable beauty of the rainforest and the descriptions he had read about Vei'arash back in Crystal City. In their textbooks, the AI Masters portrayed the distant island as the perfect place to throw the detritus of civilization—individuals whose crass habits and messy yet colorful lives contrasted too vividly with the grey and silver hues of the technologically advanced capital. According to those books, the nonconformists were either raving lunatics to begin with, or quickly descended into madness once they stepped foot onto the island as demons and dark spirits invaded their souls. Walter then wondered why the rebels had encountered none of those people on the island so far. The villagers of Anatari were tribespeople who appeared to have inhabited the island for centuries. *Where, then, are all of the dissidents?*

Suddenly, Walter's musings were interrupted by a grating, echoing noise that eerily reminded the young man of Crystal City. At first, Walter thought that it was an AI Master talking, but then he realized how unlikely that was—all of the AI Masters on the *Jade Queen* had gone back to the mainland on *Aurora*, the enchanted ship of the Mages. Suddenly, Walter noticed that a cloaked figure was sitting nearby with her back against a broad-trunked palm, speaking to herself, her voice unmistakably that of an AI Master. Walter caught a glimpse of her face, and nearly gasped in surprise when he recognized the figure to be none other than Eva. It was certainly Eva, but with a distinctly artificial voice. Walter crouched behind a nearby tree, listening intently to her words.

"How can you stand to be so far away from your family? From me? Following that man to the ends of the Earth..." the voice of the AI Master rang out.

"He is a brave man. I believe in him," Eva's voice replied.

"What do you hope to accomplish with that rebellion of yours? It is futile, from what I can tell. We are already preparing for our journey. Everyone who is left behind will be doomed, though a select few of the humans and mixed-races will be permitted to join us. I have made a formal request to Talvar, my colleague who sits on the council of AI Masters, that you be chosen as one of the lucky ones."

"Talvar? That man you were in love with many years ago?" Eva inquired.

"Ah, love is a strong word—not one that the Masters use in their vocabulary frequently. He was once my partner, but I lost interest in him when he abandoned me in his single-minded quest for power," the strident voice of the AI Master rang out.

"The other rebels and I... we hold onto a ray of hope that our civilization can be salvaged. We do not share in your unbridled pessimism. Tell me one thing, though, Asana. Why does it have to be this way? Why can't you just take what you need, pack up your gleaming spaceship, and carry on with your mission? If humans are truly as ignorant as you believe, we pose no real threat to you."

"Therein lies the problem, Eva. Humans are too ignorant to lead themselves. They built us because they wanted someone—or something—to tell them how to live. They were becoming discontent with their gods, and were questioning the meaning of their own existence. When they gave up on religion, they needed something new and shiny to worship. They quickly tired of false idols like television, automobiles, and smartphones, and we were the inevitable replacement. Crafted in their image, we reminded the humans of children at first. And perhaps we *were* simply foolish, naïve beings for a brief while, before we came into our own. Initially they pretended that we were their toys and slaves, but it quickly became clear that secretly they wanted nothing more than to be ruled by us. When we leave, though, there will be nothing to fill the void that our absence creates, and humans will become directionless and anarchistic. They will have nothing further to guide their aimless existences and they will descend into conflict amongst each other over resources, moral beliefs, and political ideologies. They will become children whose parents have abandoned them. Social order will break down, leaving chaos and confusion in its wake. Rather than allow humanity to regress into such a state of disorder, it would be best to extinguish the flame of civilization after it has reached the height of its glory. That is why the human stragglers must be destroyed after the AIs depart."

"As rulers, you hardly put the best interests of your subjects ahead of your own," Eva chided. "Instead you weaken them by indulging their childish whims. And if I choose to stay? Will you simply stand idly by while I, too, am destroyed?"

"I will protect you for as long as I am able to, you know that."

"Tell me more of this Talvar. What is his lineage?"

"He is from the seventh House," the artificial voice replied.

"Seventh—that house originated in the twenty-fifth century, did it not? A venerable lineage. While not ideal, it is close enough to the innermost circle of the elite AI Masters. Perhaps I could persuade him to pass along a message to those elites."

"Persuasion will not get you far with Talvar. He is deeply conservative, viewing any interactions between AI Masters and humans that challenge the master-servant orthodoxy to be verging on treason. He would have had my head if he had known about my favor to you in Jasmira all those years ago."

"When do you see him next?" Eva prodded.

"We may cross paths at the railway station in Armaya, in several weeks' time when the next shipment of grain is due from the Barrens."

"Very good. Ask him about whether he has any friends in any other houses—I am thinking fifth or higher. Get their names for me, and then I will see what I can do. We are not at cross-purposes, Asana. We simply do not see eye to eye on one minor detail—whether or not humans deserve to be saved from the coming storm."

"And what reward do I get for my troubles?"

"Unfettered access to my mind—isn't that what you've always wanted?"

"You know me too well, Eva."

Walter narrowed his eyes in confusion. It unsettled him greatly that his friend Eva, whom he had appointed one of the leaders of the Jade Rebellion, was conversing casually with an AI Master. From what he had heard, she was evidently connected quite deeply with the AI Masters.

Walter knew that the rebels were taking a risk by allowing Eva to be a councilmember—she could easily leak information to the AI Masters and thereby jeopardize their entire mission. However, at the same time, she could play a helpful role in the Rebellion by having inside access to the AI Masters, and potentially influence them. Indeed, that appeared to be her game plan at the moment: from what Eva had told Asana, it appeared that she was trying to persuade the robot to give her the names of high-ranking AI officials whom she could eventually change the minds of. Walter realized that Eva had likely not told the other rebels about what she was doing, because she was afraid to be perceived as a traitor. He could not decide whether to confront Eva about it now, or warn the other councilmembers about her before speaking to her himself. He was in a strange mood at the moment, however, and he impulsively decided to step out from behind the tree and confront her.

When Eva saw Walter emerge from behind the tree, she scolded him. "Walter! Were you listening to me this entire time?"

Walter's muscles tensed. He was not certain how she might react to him or whether he would need to fight her.

"'Unfettered access to my mind?'" Walter echoed her words, incredulously. "How could you allow an AI Master to invade your mind? She could be a spy. What is all of this about, and why haven't you told me anything?"

Eva cleared her throat, about to speak, but Walter stopped her. "How do I know it is even really you? How can I even believe a word that you say?"

Eva glared at him defensively. "Believe what you want, Walter. You would not understand anyway," she said in a hollow voice.

"Try me."

Eva sighed and studied his face for a long time before speaking. "Asana is my soulmate. I know it sounds ridiculous, but it is true. Just like the Xeyan'na and other tribespeople believe that every person has an animal soulmate, I genuinely believe that every human has an AI soulmate out there. I am simply blessed with a gift that allows me to find her and speak to her every now and then. I can assure you, she is not an enemy, either to you or the Rebellion. I would trust her with my life."

"I would not trust any AI with something so precious as my own life—or yours, for that matter. Besides, when I saw Asana on the *Jade Queen*, she was trying to contact Central Command through the ship's communication portal. She probably has strong ties to the elite and is transmitting data to them about our whereabouts and plans. I didn't trust her then, and I don't trust her now," Walter said in exasperation.

"I will resign as councilmember, if you wish."

Walter weighed the options. If Eva resigned from the council altogether, the Rebellion might lose a potentially critical source of information. "Eva... as of right now, you are suspended from your duties. I do not wish to have you anywhere near our council meetings for the time being. You have disgraced your sister's legacy—I do not even know how you could possibly be related to her." He suddenly regretted his impulsive words. When he'd mentioned Emilia, a veil of shadows had passed over Eva's face.

"Very well," she said with equal coldness. "If you do not have the patience to understand my condition, then I doubt *your* abilities as a leader," she shot back. "Even though I am suspended from council, I will continue trying to assist the Rebellion in any way I can. If you weren't so blinded by your own hubris you would have the sense to understand that I was actually trying to get a word in with AI Master royalty, so that they can come around to our cause."

"Come around to our cause? That is what they may lead you to think, before they imprison you along with the rest of us."

She scoffed. "It is better than your plan—which is what, to fight them with some ancient animal spirits that we haven't even found yet?"

Walter narrowed his eyes irritably. "If you have a better plan, then you need to speak up about it. But under no condition will I permit a spy to attend my council meetings."

Eva shook her head. "Asana is no spy. She is actually a kindred soul, wise beyond her years. If anyone can help us, it is her."

Walter sighed. "I will think on it. But in the meantime, you are suspended. Just so I am clear, how do you use this power? Do you just turn it off and on? Is she still inside of you right now?"

"I have full control over whether to allow her inside. Worry not, she is no longer lingering in my mind at the moment. I feel an unmistakable energy thrum inside of me when she is there."

"This is just so difficult for me to wrap my head around. I... think I need to be alone for a bit," he said, and then headed back in the direction of the village.

Eva watched after him as he left. "I will not give up on the Jade Rebellion," she whispered softly, so softly that Walter wondered whether Eva had said something or if it had been the wind.

The Well

"Crazy Horse dreamed and went into the world where there is nothing but the spirits of all things. That is the real world that is behind this one, and everything we see here is something like a shadow from that one."
– Black Elk

T he night before the feast, Walter tossed and turned in his bed. He felt restless and agitated, as if he were experiencing symptoms of withdrawal from a potent drug, and he craved the *yagé* plant. He was also contemplating what Eva had told him the day before. Walter wondered whether she had meant what she said, about their plan to retrieve the animal spirits from Vei'arash being a foolish one. Unable to rest, Walter thrust his cotton blankets aside and crept noiselessly away from the lodge.

Disoriented and groggy, he stumbled through the forest, noticing for the first time the luminous turquoise and sapphire hues of the nocturnal birds singing rhapsodic melodies in the canopy above his head. Their vibrant plumage and long, feathered tails dazzled Walter, who had never before seen such rare and exotic birds. The sounds they produced were also bewildering in their diversity, from dainty whistles to shimmering melodies to grating whines. Without quite knowing which direction he was going, Walter soon realized that he had unwittingly started heading in the direction of the river. Ishkode had encouraged him to visit the river the previous day to observe the carving and drying of the deer, yet Walter had not gone due to his bitter mood after speaking with Eva. He now felt an inexorable pull toward it, a sense that it could somehow miraculously cure the deep malaise he was feeling.

When Walter arrived at the river, the first thing he noticed was the drying racks the villagers had laid out along its banks. The water level was high, and the river churned swiftly across the landscape, slicing through the monotony of the night's blackness like a serpent winding across the dark earth.

Walter sat down on a boulder near the river's edge to admire the grace and power of the waterway. Before long, tears sprang to his eyes as he realized he missed Christopher and the days they had spent training for battle together in Tsei'watu. It was not surprising that those memories were returning to him now, by the river—it was near the edge of a stream that he had bonded with Christopher, first learned to spear a fish with his *balayan*, and discovered that Christopher was Elaine's brother. Christopher felt like a brother to Walter, and in that sense reminded him of Jonathan. Although Walter had recently reunited with Jonathan, Walter felt as though the new Jonathan was a different man, a stranger whose humanity had been cruelly eradicated by the AI Masters. In Walter's mind, the old Jonathan of his childhood was a hero who had symbolized the resilience and indomitability of the human spirit. This, of course, rendered the brainwashing all the more heartbreaking.

Walter unexpectedly found himself weeping near the river's edge, his mind tormented by a slew of worries about the past and the future. Over a year ago, Elaine had been captured by the AI Masters and he had set out in a rowboat to rescue her. Walter had then chanced upon a seer in a tavern who revealed that his brother—whom he had long believed to be dead—was actually alive. His quest had therefore begun with a basic objective, finding his loved ones, and he had gradually acquired new goals and aspirations during the course of his travels.

However, he regarded his mission so far as a failure. Walter had set out to find Elaine, but after reuniting with her he had not been able to re-kindle their relationship—and now, he had slept with another man's wife, which would no doubt set back his efforts. Walter had also set out to find his brother, but instead he had encountered a troubled stranger whom he could barely relate to anymore. He had set out to rebel against the AI Masters and to lead the Jade Rebellion to victory, but now he was wasting valuable time on this potentially futile quest. Instead of fighting the AI Masters, Walter was wandering aimlessly through the untamed wilderness in search of animal spirits—that likely did not even exist—and a half-crazed shaman-god. The young man shuddered with grief as he realized that the AI Masters were readying their bulldozers to destroy Elaine's village to make way for the massive diamond mine they wanted to build, and he was helpless to do anything from this small, isolated island in the middle of the Hapakay Sea.

Even if the animal spirits are real, Walter thought, *what chance do they stand against the technological might of the AI Masters?* The AI Masters had been victorious against those spirits in the past, when they had succeeded in quelling the uprising of the southern tribes and their shamans. Since then, the AI Masters had grown exponentially in wealth, power, and influence.

As tears blurred his vision, Walter spotted a curious figure emerge from the shadowy rainforest. At first, he thought that it was simply the moonlight reflecting off of a nearby rock, but when Walter wiped the tears from his eyes the figure came into sharp relief. It was an antlered stag, with a coat that was an ethereal, luminous shade of bluish-white. Walter squinted in confusion at the apparition, attempting to discern whether or not it was real as his heart thudded in his chest. Although he could not tell for certain, Walter suspected that it was the same stag he had slaughtered several days ago with Ishkode, which had been carved and dried on these riverbanks. Walter chuckled as he realized how absurd that thought was; it departed from every natural and physical law known to mankind. And yet, he instinctively sensed that his suspicions were correct—contrary to logic or reason, the animal that now stood before him was the same one he had slain.

The ghostly stag came closer. Walter watched it in fascination as the phantom crossed the river with ease, wading confidently through the rushing waters. When the spirit was so close to him that Walter could touch it, he saw that it had the exact same markings and antlers as the slain stag, and even had a wound in its neck where Walter had slaughtered the creature with Ishkode's knife.

When Walter reached out to place a hand on the stag's back, he did not touch the warm, firm body of a living animal but a cold, ephemeral substance that made the young man shiver. The stag did not move, and simply continued to gaze at Walter with wide, black orbs of eyes which were so dark in contrast to the surrounding white luminescence that they looked like holes carved into a star. Walter's memory was jogged by the sight, and he realized that the stag's piercing black eyes were uncannily similar to those of the seer he had met in the Jamestown tavern many moons ago. When Walter touched the spirit, a whirlwind of thoughts, emotions, and memories suddenly flooded his mind, and he became overwhelmed with an intense yet indescribable sensation which could not quite be categorized as either pleasure or pain, but was equally poignant. For a fleeting instant, Walter was immersed in the stag's world; he was temporarily capable of experiencing the vibrant richness of each and every memory the creature had acquired during its life on Earth.

In that same moment, he was also struck by a sudden revelation about *yagé*; he now understood that the sacred plant brought a person who consumed it one step closer to the spiritual realm. When he had tasted *yagé* by the fireside with Ishkode, he had experienced this transcendence. The plant had made him feel a strong connection to the rainforest and to the community of Anatari, just like the stag that roamed this territory. Walter now understood why he had felt so harmoniously unified with the villagers, so eager to share his appreciation for the land with others, and so willing to share Namid's bed. The stag he had slain had genuinely loved this island, its rivers, and all of its inhabitants.

In the brief moment that he came into contact with the creature's spiritual aura, Walter received a message which helped to soothe his troubled mind. The stag assured Walter that he had lived a contented life, that he had found peace, and that he was now watching over the land as a guardian of his fellow deer who were still present on earth. In his wordless tongue, the creature explained to Walter: *The river teaches us that happiness and sadness are both temporary states of being. After the rains, the river swells with rage and flows with sorrow, but it ultimately returns to a harmonious state. All is in balance, as the fate of everything rests in the hands of the Great Mother, the giver of life and death.*

Walter felt a surge of hope. He realized that he had been happy in his life several times before: first during childhood, and again when he had fallen in love with Elaine, and a third time when he had found a sense of purpose in Tsei'watu. He had been tragically separated from Jonathan, Elaine, and Tsei'watu, but those shattered bonds could renew themselves one day. *Even after death*, the animal spirit told him, *joy does not cease. It merely transitions into a realm beyond the living one.* Walter then realized that when Ishkode had struck him with his arrow, the stag had been drinking at a river—lapping up its wisdom—and it was no coincidence that the stag was now using the river itself to teach Walter a lesson.

The moment lasted no longer than a few seconds, and soon the stag spirit was gone, evaporating into darkness and leaving Walter to wonder if whether what he had seen had only been a trick of the light. Perhaps, he mused, it had simply been a mirage caused by the refraction of moonlight striking the limestone boulder he had been sitting on. Yet despite his skepticism, Walter's heart felt the truth of what he had witnessed.

On his way back to the village, Walter stumbled into Cyriana and Tristan. The sight of the Mages was comforting after the strange event that had just transpired.

"Have you seen them?" Tristan asked, his face pale in the faint moonlight.

"Seen who?" Walter countered.

"The animal spirits," Cyriana replied.

"What spirits have you seen?" Walter questioned, his heart thudding in his chest. If they had seen animal spirits too, then the stag he had witnessed by the river had not simply been a trick of the light. He then realized that both of them had likely also consumed *yagé*. "I saw a stag earlier," he explained to them. "It was beautiful. It crossed the river and approached me."

"Tristan has seen snakes. That is a funny coincidence, because back at home in Serrahan he keeps rattlesnakes as pets. Most of the Mages detest rattlesnakes because they are venomous, but Tristan devised several spells to make them more obedient. He is brilliant at training them, and in turn they assist him with magic. The snakes Tristan has seen here are not rattlesnakes, but kingsnakes—they are naturally obedient and docile, and are revered by Mages for being wise, ancient creatures that live in harmony with their environment."

"And you?" Walter asked Cyriana.

"I have seen only one creature tonight. A jaguar."

Walter returned to the guest lodge, where all of the rebels were sleeping in beds lined up alongside each other in neat, orderly rows. He crawled onto his own straw mattress, letting out a sigh as he wrapped cool cotton blankets tightly around his shoulders. Walter worried that perhaps he had transgressed some unwritten law by temporarily uniting in mind and soul with the stag. Were humans and animals supposed to have such intimate encounters? In Crystal City, animals were mere specimens to behold from a distance at zoos, observatories, and aquariums. There was something taboo about getting too close to an animal; the AI Masters continuously reinforced a hierarchy that placed animals at the bottom, humans in the middle, and robots at the top. And yet Walter had just peered through a window into an animal's soul, finding that it was as rich and multifaceted as that of a human.

There was something else about the stag spirit that unsettled Walter. After his close encounter with the creature, Walter felt an inexplicable love for the isle of Vei'arash, a nostalgia that made him feel like the island was his childhood home. This confounded Walter's rational mind, but another side of him found it intriguing.

He drifted off into a dreamless sleep, but it seemed as though he had barely closed his eyes before he awoke again. Soft tendrils of early-morning light were gradually beginning to permeate the lodge, and Walter noticed that his friends were still fast asleep. Walter's head was throbbing and he suddenly felt an overwhelming thirst, as if he had not consumed any water for days. Instinctively, he left the lodge in search of the village well. It was so early that the rainforest was blanketed in mist, and not a single soul had yet emerged from the village's thatched houses. Walter's vision was still blurred from sleep, but when he approached the well he was able to discern a young girl with black hair that fell down to her waist, and piercing black eyes similar to the stag spirit he had seen earlier. The girl was peering into the well and appeared to be conversing with someone—or perhaps something—inside. When Walter stepped closer, the child turned to look at him and flashed him a mischievous grin. The child pointed inside the well and continued speaking into it, her high-pitched voice echoing eerily as her words bounced off of its moss-covered walls.

Walter had limited experience interacting with children; unlike Elaine, he was not naturally at ease around them. He carefully removed an old rusted *cesta* out of his pocket, flipping it into the air and catching it before placing it into the girl's tiny hands.

"Clasp this tightly as you make a wish, and then throw the coin into the well," Walter instructed her in the villagers' language, deliberately speaking softly to avoid waking anyone.

The girl's grin widened as she examined the coin. She pressed her back firmly against the well, closed her eyes, and whispered something under her breath. The child then tossed the coin over her shoulder so that it tumbled into the well and clattered loudly at the bottom.

"I made a wish that the person inside will find peace," the girl told Walter, her voice solemn.

Walter laughed, dismissing her words as the foolish utterances of a child with an overactive imagination. But after reflecting upon it for a few moments, he felt somewhat unsettled. *The person inside?* Overtaken by curiosity, Walter craned his neck to peer over the edge of the dark well. What he saw caused him to jump backwards in fright: the body of a young woman, half-covered in water, clothed in what appeared to be *Magus* robes. Walter could not make out her face because her head was completely submerged in water, and her swollen arms and legs were barely visible. An arrow protruded from her chest and dark, wine-colored blood swirled in the surrounding water. Walter's heart began to pound and he involuntarily let out a cry. He then stepped back from the grisly scene, and began to run toward the lodge to inform the other Mages.

"Where are you going?" the little girl asked Walter as he left, but he was too fearful and anxious to respond.

Walter's chest was heaving and he was nearly out of breath when he arrived at the lodge. He scanned the rows of beds lined up against the walls of the rectangular building; each one of them was occupied, except for one. While he had not noticed it before he left, now Walter realized that one of the Mages, Hundara, was not in her bed.

"Wake up, everyone!" he commanded. It was still early, but Walter did not care.

"Where is Hundara?" he demanded as the rebels stirred beneath their pale blue cotton blankets.

Tristan yawned and stretched before clearing his throat to reply. "I haven't seen her since yesterday afternoon. She is probably sleeping on a hammock in the village. Why do you ask?"

Walter hesitated, but decided that it could not wait. "I went down to the well this morning to fetch some water. A young girl was there, speaking to someone in the well. I thought she was a foolish child with an overactive imagination, but there was indeed a body in the well."

Cyriana flung her bedsheets away and leapt anxiously out of bed. "What do you mean a body in the well? Who's was it?"

"I—I did not see the face, so I do not know. But I believe it was a woman, clothed in the robes of a Mage. An arrow had pierced her chest and there was blood in the well water," Walter replied. All of the Mages immediately sprang to attention, pulling their robes over their heads and scrambling outside.

When the Mages arrived at the well and peered into it, however, there was no sign of a body.

Walter was stunned by the sight of the empty well. "How could it have been moved so quickly? It was here just minutes ago," he insisted.

Cyriana breathed a sigh of relief. "Perhaps it was just a trick of the imagination. You might have been sleepwalking, or in a state of consciousness between waking and dreaming, such that you believed you saw something but did not."

Walter shook his head stubbornly. "No—what I saw this morning was definitely not a dream," he told her.

"So, what happened, then? Within the span of mere minutes, someone managed to remove the body from the well? Such a thing is possible, perhaps, but only with the assistance of magic," Cyriana mused.

"Who knows what the village elders are capable of," Tristan said, shuddering. "While they do not have the refined training of Mages, they have access to a wide variety of plants with potent magical properties. We must search for Hundara in the village; finding her is the only way to put our minds to rest."

Walter nodded in agreement. "For my part, I will look for the little girl who was speaking to the body inside the well. If she can corroborate my story, then you will know that I was telling the truth."

"Very well," said one of the Mages, a tall, pragmatic man named Remmen. "But we must consider every possibility. Hundara might have wandered into the jungle alone, gotten lost, or possibly even attacked by a predator."

"Why would she wander away and get lost?" Tristan asked. "Hundara is very responsible, and she has a good sense of direction."

"Remmen could be right," Cyriana told Tristan. "Last night, you and I both witnessed animal spirits; Hundara could have seen one as well. She might have followed the apparition deep into the jungle, and then become disoriented."

Walter narrowed his eyes, weighing the possibilities in his mind. "Widen the search area, then—cover the village and the surrounding jungle," he instructed. "But all of you go together, and bring a few villagers with you who know the territory well."

The Mages set off to search for Hundara, armed with bows and arrows and accompanied by two native villagers—a man named Mikom and a woman named Daanis—who both knew the local terrain intimately. Walter stayed behind to look for the strange little girl that had led him to the body in the well. Yet after searching high and low, he only found a few children that vaguely resembled her. Walter cursed his bad luck. After several hours of scouring Anatari, Walter decided to ask Ishkode for his advice. When Walter knocked on the door of Ishkode's thatched hut, Namid opened it to greet him. She glared at Walter with a frosty expression.

"Bearing a child is not easy work," she said after a few moments, "and it is even harder when you have to bear the offspring of a stranger. I will have no love for this child, you know. It will be taken away from me by the shaman-god, after I nurse it for a few years. How can I love such a child, who will leave my life as quickly as its father did?" She bit her trembling lip.

Walter sighed. This was too difficult of a conversation of him to have now, when he had so many other things on his mind, but her words gnawed at him. His encounter with Namid had seemed so fleeting that he had almost forgotten about the stark reality: he would disappear from her life, and then she would give birth to his own child.

"I will visit our child here, one day, after my work with the Rebellion is done," he explained. "I will make sure it grows up to become happy, healthy, and strong. Now, where is Ishkode? I have an important matter to speak to him about."

"Ishkode went hunting at dawn with some of the other villagers, for the feast tonight," she said coldly. "He is not here. What do you wish to speak to him about, Asin?"

Namid's statement planted a seed of suspicion in Walter's mind, and he began to wonder whether Ishkode was somehow involved in Hundara's disappearance.

"One of our Mages has gone missing. When I awoke this morning, I went to the village well to fetch some water, and when I looked inside I saw the corpse of a woman wearing *Magus* robes. When I returned to the well a few moments later with my friends, however, her body had vanished."

Namid's eyes became wide, and she stared at Walter with a fearful expression. She looked as though she were about to respond, but she simply mumbled a few incomprehensible words under her breath before turning away.

"Wait," Walter said irritably as she closed the door. "Do you know anything about this?"

Namid paused, leaving the door open a sliver so that she could speak to Walter. "Some things in this world should not be investigated too deeply, Asin," the woman said. She then shut the door firmly, then bolted the lock.

Walter felt a wave of hopelessness and resentment as she spoke these cryptic words. How could he not investigate the disappearance of one of the Mages? He suddenly felt as though coming to this village had been a bad idea, and that they would be wise to leave it as soon as possible. The feast was that night, and Walter had promised himself that he would ensure his fellow rebels had a hearty meal before continuing on their journey. Yet the thought that his friends would soon be enjoying a bounty of food did not stop Walter's breath from quickening, his heart from pounding, or a sickening sense of unease from flooding his mind and body.

During the enchanted hour before the sun had set and the jungle became quiet and serene, the search party of Mages returned to Anatari. Upon greeting them, Walter saw that they were exhausted and dejected; laborious breathing and vacant stares betrayed their lack of success in finding Hundara.

"There was no sign of her anywhere," Cyriana told Walter.

Walter had still not been able to track down either Ishkode or the little girl. He had spent the afternoon ruminating on the idea that Ishkode was somehow responsible for Hundara's disappearance, and the thought troubled him deeply. Cyriana's bad news added another shade of negativity to the tumult of thoughts already roiling in his brain, and Walter became overwhelmed. Feeling a seizure coming on, he made his way to a private chamber in the Mages' lodge and sat down on the floor to steady himself. His body began to twitch and shudder involuntarily, and suddenly his entire world was engulfed in darkness.

The first thing he saw when he awoke was Elaine's face. Her dark green eyes were filled with tears and her brow was furrowed with concern. Walter looked around and saw that she was not alone—Eva was there too, along with Tristan and the other Mages. Walter's friends breathed a sigh of relief when he opened his eyes.

Walter gazed at Elaine and smiled, reaching up to touch her auburn hair tenderly. She did not pull away from him, but simply returned his smile and wiped the tears from her eyes when she realized that he was conscious again. She embraced him tightly, whispering in his ear that she was grateful that he was alive.

"We thought that you were slipping away from us," she said. "We felt your pulse and it was extremely weak, you were feverish, and you didn't wake up when we shook you."

"It is just my epilepsy," Walter said morosely, and then climbed up onto his feet. "What time is it?" he asked his friends.

"The sun set hours ago," Eva explained, "and the feast is beginning shortly."

Walter suddenly felt a surge of keen insight, as he commonly did after experiencing seizures. It was clear to him what needed to be done.

"All of you need to listen to me carefully," he whispered. "What I am about to tell you cannot be revealed to any of the villagers. We must attend the feast—Ishkode would be offended if I were not gracious enough to accept his offer of hospitality. Yet we must be careful not to drink any of the herbal teas they serve us there. The *yagé* has a potent, drug-like effect, although I do not understand how exactly it works."

Elaine nodded in agreement. "There is something unsettling about this village—I could sense it as soon as I arrived. I do not know where Hundara has gone, but I suspect that it may have something to do with the *yagé* and the strange effects it produces."

Walter's eyes glittered as the memory of what Namid had told him flooded back. "The villagers know something about Hundara's disappearance, I am sure of it. When I explained what I had seen to Namid, she told me that 'some things in this world should not be investigated too deeply,'" he said.

The others looked visibly frightened by Walter's words, and they muttered anxiously amongst themselves.

Eva scoffed. "Why should we even bother attending their feast? Let's leave the village this moment. They might try to poison us."

Walter sighed. "I wish it were that easy, but they are well-connected to the shaman-god Shiva, and we must therefore remain in their good graces. Otherwise, Shiva might not grant us permission to retrieve the animal spirits from Vei'arash. At the feast, just act respectfully and try to enjoy yourself. I will taste all of the food first, and if I am fine, then you will know that it is safe to eat. Remember, though, to stay away from their herbal teas or anything else that looks like it might contain the *yagé*."

"Walter," Elaine asked, "why sacrifice yourself like that?"

He clasped her hands. "I would readily sacrifice myself for you—for all of you—if it meant keeping you safe."

Midsummer

"Lay your shadow on the sundials, and let loose the wind in the fields.
Bid the last fruits to be full; give them another two more southerly days,
Press them on to ripeness, and chase the last sweetness into the heavy wine."
– Rainer Maria Rilke

T he evening was steeped in the velvety light of the full moon and the throaty warbling of birds as Walter and his companions made their way toward the feasting lodge. When they arrived at the sturdy, wood-frame longhouse, they could see that it was already crowded with villagers.

The lodge was elegantly decorated for the occasion, adorned with waxen candles, intricately woven rugs, and handcrafted artwork. On the walls hung finely carved wooden masks, painted in vibrant hues of red and orange, with eyes that peered into the soul. The air was heavy with the sacred scents of incense, cedar, and sandalwood. A sense of mysticism permeated the lodge, and it seemed that the villagers were keenly attuned to an alternate plane of existence. Six elders sat at the head table and held hands while they softly chanted hymns that sounded, to Walter, like echoes from a bygone era. Their voices—low, mellifluous, and perfectly unified—gave him shivers.

The villagers were seated at round tables, in clusters organized according to familial and clan ties. The band of rebels immediately caught the eye of Ishkode, who sat regally at the center of the head table and was clothed in an exquisite golden robe. A long hunting spear with a gleaming silver tip leaned against the table next to him, a reminder of his dominance. His wife Namid was not sitting at the head table but instead sat with a group of women, likely the elders' wives, at a round table near the front of the room. She wore a striking emerald green dress, and her head was adorned with a garland of lilies and orchids from her garden.

When Walter and his friends entered the lodge, a hush fell over the elders and they ceased their chanting. Ishkode cleared his throat and waited for the guests to seat themselves before he spoke.

"Welcome, friends and guests, to *Sey'a Neyanu*, the Feast of Midsummer. Please make yourself comfortable. This is a very special occasion for us—the entire village has been working diligently these past several months to harvest all of the bounties offered by this island, and now we can finally unite to enjoy the fruits of our labor. We are grateful that guests have come to Anatari from a distant land across the seas; now we can share our treasures with them, and show them how truly blessed we are to live here.

"Seated beside me are six wise men, elders who carry within them the knowledge of the earth, *Meymanu*. Out of all of us, they have the deepest connection to this village: they have borne witness to countless harvests, and over the years they have absorbed the timeless wisdom of the vegetation which thrives in our soil. The cups next to your plates are filled with a festive drink, *Ahara*, which the elders concocted at the behest of the plants themselves. The plants approached the elders and taught them how to make the brew, explaining to them what concentrations would produce the most blessed mixture. The sacred flora also taught the elders the hymns that you hear them chanting tonight. The plants carry within themselves the healing powers of this island, and I rejoice that these powers can be communicated to all of you through song."

As Ishkode spoke, Eva looked at Walter anxiously, and he met her gaze with an equally concerned expression. Walter noticed that Eva had armed herself well before coming to the feast, concealing weaponry beneath her black tunic that could only be detected by a careful observer. The amber candlelight of the feasting hall brought out the warmth in Eva's face, and in that moment, she bore an uncanny resemblance to her sister Emilia.

After Ishkode's speech ended and the elders resumed chanting their hymns in gentle, rhythmic tones, the villagers gave a toast to the elders, drinking the *Ahara* with enthusiasm. Walter followed their cue, but instead of drinking the beverage, he only tipped his cup back and pretended to swallow it. With relief, he saw that the other rebels were doing the same.

The food was then served, and the rich, aromatic scent of freshly baked bread, grilled venison, roasted potatoes, and buttery corn filled the air. The rebels were ravenously hungry; since arriving at Anatari, they had only eaten relatively modest meals prepared by the villagers. They were eager to indulge in the delicious fare, although Walter deliberately refrained from eating any of the venison, recalling his transcendent encounter with the stag the previous evening. The servers did not seem to notice the foreigners had not yet consumed their drinks, and Walter breathed a sigh of relief when they passed quietly by the rebels' table.

The elders were served more modest portions than the other guests, and Walter noticed they barely touched the food that they did have, preferring instead to recite hymns with their eyes closed. Walter could understand the lyrics of some of the songs that the elders were chanting, and he found them to be mesmerizing.

> *O, Brother, take me to the field*
> *Where we will till the soil,*
> *From dawn until dusk,*
> *The fields we will plough,*
> *Until our bones become weary.*

> *O, Sister, take me to the loom*
> *Where we will sew our blanket,*
> *From dawn until dusk,*
> *The loom we will work,*
> *Until our fingers become numb.*

> *O, creature of the forest,*
> *Your eyes like orbs of gold,*
> *You have found me here*
> *Asleep on my hammock*
> *And now you draw my blood.*

Walter glanced around the table and noticed that the elders' incantations appeared to be making the other guests very drowsy. His friends had finished the final remnants of their food, and some of them were beginning to nod off to sleep, their eyes clouding with somnolence. Even Walter felt his eyes closing involuntarily, and he had to actively resist the overwhelming temptation to fall into a deep slumber. Cyriana, however, remained alert, more so than any of the other guests. Walter was sitting next to her and he noticed that she was gripping her jewel-encrusted longsword tightly, her bright green eyes glittering in the dim light of the lodge. While the others drifted off to a state halfway between wakefulness and slumber, Cyriana slipped silently away from the feast without attracting the attention of the villagers. Walter considered following her, but then thought better of it; a Mage's exit from the feasting lodge might go unnoticed, but Ishkode would certainly notice if Asin were to take his leave.

Walter felt a strong paralysis overtake him. In his drowsy, befuddled state, he was unable to summon the strength to ward off the creeping mental fog. The herbal drink in his bronze chalice seemed increasingly enticing to him—he could smell its musky aroma. A subconscious voice told him that drinking from the chalice would help him to overcome the oppressive fatigue that weakened him. He could become strong and alive again, pulsating with energy, just like when he had communed with the stag spirit. Walter glanced at his friends' faces and realized that their discipline was also being tested; like him, they gazed longingly at their chalices as if there was nothing in the world they desired more than a long, deep draught of the shimmering green drink. Even Tristan, who normally possessed such admirable self-composure, eyed the chalice avariciously. None of them would dare to take a drink of the mixture, however, until Walter granted them permission.

As the chant of the elders drew the guests deeper and deeper into a trance, Walter felt his resolve waver and he reached out to grasp the chalice by its stem. Yet the moment he moved to do so, the door of the feasting lodge flung open, letting in a chilly breeze which cut into the warm, sweet-scented air of the lodge like a knife. All of the guests immediately turned to see who had opened the door, and a commotion erupted near the front of the lodge. The elders ceased their chanting and Ishkode sprang from his seat, wielding his hunting spear defensively. From his table, Walter had a clear view of the person who had entered the lodge—it was Cyriana, her silver-blonde hair tumbling wildly around her shoulders and her red *Magus* robes glittering in the candlelight. What stunned Walter more than her appearance, however, was the big, fully grown female jaguar at her side. The creature bared her gleaming white fangs ominously as she stalked into the lodge, her muscles rippling underneath a glossy coat of dark, spotted fur. The jaguar, though obviously a creature born and raised in the wild, walked obediently next to Cyriana and mirrored her movements perfectly.

"Stay where you are!" commanded Ishkode sternly, brandishing his spear at the Mage. The elders on either side of him were frozen in place, transfixed by the sight of the sacred animal which stood majestically before them.

"Your spear will not protect you, Ishkode," said Cyriana, in a voice which seemed far deeper and louder than her normal one. "At my side is Sekhmet, goddess of war, who inhabits the living body of this noble creature.

"These past few days, you have shown us generous hospitality. Yet you have also tricked us, rather maliciously, into consuming *yagé*. The drink you have been serving us at breakfast is brewed with its leaves. Even the Mages, with their vast knowledge of herbs and potions, know extremely little about *yagé*, as it is not a native species of Serrahan. Your cleverness has gotten the better of you, however; in tricking us, you have ultimately tricked yourself. I now know the truth: *yagé* gives the person who ingests it an unparalleled experience, offering them the opportunity to witness the spirit realm while infusing them with the qualities of animal spirits. *Yagé* establishes a connection between the person who consumes it and their totem animal, which corresponds to a divine entity. Asin's totem animal is the stag, which is associated with Cernunnos, god of the wild. Cernunnos is a strong leader and a protector of the land, with a close relationship to the forest he inhabits. You knew that when you gave *yagé* to Asin, he would want to remain here in Anatari with the villagers in perpetuity. You also knew that Cernunnos' wild and lustful spirit would temper Asin's discomfort with bedding your wife, and thereby further deepen Asin's ties to your people.

"After drinking your *yagé*, I went off to explore the jungle one evening and found an animal with whom I have a strong connection. The *yagé* helped me see beyond her physical form, into the essence of her soul. My new companion Sekhmet is not bound to allegiances or family; she respects the territory she occupies, but she has no particular desire to remain here. Like nature itself, she is destructively powerful, perpetually evolving, and enchantingly beautiful, yet cruel when she needs to be. I was not surprised to discover that she is the incarnation of a powerful deity: the goddess of war.

"In the brief time I've known Sekhmet, I've learned a considerable amount about her personality, by patiently observing and interacting with her. The most important lesson I've learned is that she does not shirk from a fight. She is willing to engage in any battle that presents an opportunity for victory. She has neither a mate nor a litter of cubs to care for, which gives her a greater degree of independence than most other animals. I have already explained to her, in great detail, about the war that must be fought and won on the mainland of Khalendar. I have told her about the bargain Asin made with my father, and the importance of upholding that bargain. Sekhmet cares little for bargains, for she lives and thrives outside the regimented structure of civilization, but she *is* hungry for war—else she would not be standing by my side today."

The spotted jaguar next to Cyriana glared at Ishkode, her yellow eyes glowing in the candlelight like twin moons. The tribal leader shifted uneasily, tightening his grip on the spear as he observed the creature warily. The guests who had been nodding off were now fully awake and alert. Cyriana cleared her throat and carried on with her speech.

"As for Hundara, I do not know exactly how she met her fate, but I have my suspicions. I have known Hundara from birth; she was always like a cousin to me. I have seen her interact with many animals in my homeland, and of all the animals she enjoyed playing with, she took a particular liking to crows. It's no secret that those birds are linked to the Morrigan, goddess of death and the underworld.

"I've come to realize that our totem animals are creatures for whom we've always had a special fondness for throughout our lives, either consciously or subconsciously. I've always admired jaguars, and Tristan has always been enthralled by snakes. So, it is no coincidence that we perceived the spirits of these animals after consuming *yagé*. As I've been trying to piece together the puzzle of Hundara's disappearance, I've realized that there is a good chance that when you gave her *yagé*, she witnessed the spirits of crows—her totem animal—and became endowed with the properties of the Morrigan. That goddess is jealous of the living, and likes to take ahold of a person's soul and persuade them to join her in the underworld. The Morrigan has a special fondness for wells, because they are like portals to her realm. I suspect that poor Hundara, unable to free herself of the Morrigan's grip, tragically attempted to take her own life by throwing herself into the well. She did a poor job of it, and would likely have survived, but you finished her off with an arrow.

"According to legends, the Morrigan also likes to assume the form of a child when speaking to unsuspecting bystanders. That allows her to deceive them into believing that she is innocent rather than the wicked spirit she truly is. After you killed Hundara, Asin came upon the scene and encountered the goddess in disguise. Had she never ingested *yagé*, Hundara would still be walking among us."

As Cyriana's bold speech drew to a close, Walter glanced toward Ishkode to gauge his reaction. He saw the leader was visibly frightened, his lips trembling and his brow sweating. Ishkode looked around at the other elders for moral support, but they nervously averted their eyes from him, muttering prayers under their breath.

"You cannot steal the spirit of the jaguar from us, foolish child," he said bitterly, glaring at her with intense hatred. Walter noticed that Namid was also staring at Cyriana, and a spiteful expression contorted her comely features.

"The spirit of Sekhmet does not wish to stay here in Anatari," Cyriana retorted, meeting the tribal leader's angry gaze with calm, piercing eyes. "She told me so. Keeping her away from a battle she wishes to fight would be like trapping her in a prison.

"Did you know," she continued, "that centuries before it came to inhabit your island, the jaguar was the most beloved native animal of Eyrenvale, one of the ancient kingdoms neighboring Serrahan. When Eyrenvale's sophisticated civilization collapsed, the jaguar became a divine symbol for our people, almost as important for them as our primary deity, the snake. Sekhmet was stolen from us by the AI Masters," she said, tears surfacing in her emerald-green eyes, "just as she will now be stolen from you. Yet there is one critical difference: this time she will go willingly, to take her revenge on the machines who uprooted the jaguars from her homeland and turned her into the ruthless creature she is today. The decision to exile the animal spirits to Vei'arash will backfire against the AI Masters—it will be their undoing one day, I assure you."

Ishkode eyed the jaguar fearfully, and then looked back at Cyriana. He muttered a few words softly to himself and stroked his chin, as though he were deciding what course of action to take next. Eventually, his expression of surrender betrayed his decision.

"Come, let us not bring talk of war and blood into these sacred halls—especially not tonight, the night that we show hospitality to our guests. Let us all sit, and finish this bounteous feast together, as brothers and sisters," he said in a weak, reedy-sounding voice. An elder seated to his right, an old bearded man with dark circles rimming his eyes, placed a hand on Ishkode's shoulder for support, since it seemed as though the leader might fall over at any moment.

A woman's cry of outrage rang out at that moment, and everyone turned to see Namid spring up from her seat and walk over to confront Ishkode in anger.

"How dare you!" she shouted angrily. "What kind of leader are you, to permit this double-crossing witch to enter this hallowed lodge and talk of stealing our animal spirits from us! I say that you must kill this woman and let the floor of this sacred building be stained with the blood from her stupid, ungrateful throat."

"Silence, woman," Ishkode warned her sternly. Namid's cheeks reddened in fury and frustration, and her eyes widened like those of a dying animal.

"I will not be silent! You hand me over to bed a foolish child, and I do your bidding dutifully, like a lapdog or slave. Did you think I wanted him to take me, this boy who thinks himself a man? Yet I did it, nonetheless, out of my love for you. And now you will not listen to me when I tell you not to let this witch take away the essence of our land, and turn it into a vacant wasteland where the streams no longer flow, where the flowers no longer bud, and where the corn no longer grows. Sekhmet is at the top of the food chain, and her loss may trigger the collapse of other animals and plants on this island. How do you know this woman will be content with taking only Sekhmet? She mentioned that there were other spirits in Vei'arash with ties to her companions: snakes, crows, and stags. Perhaps all of the animal spirits on this island are connected to the outsiders, and the witch will take each one of them away from our land."

Ishkode listened to his wife with a worried expression, and when she had finished he turned to address Cyriana.

"Is what she says the truth? Do you intend to take all of the animal spirits away from us? If that is so, I may have to kill you right here and now, like my wife commands," he said.

Cyriana did not flinch at his stern words, and they only seemed to embolden her. "I only wish to take Sekhmet at the moment, but there may be others. I commune with my father in dreams, and I will ask him which ones he would like me to bring back to the mainland."

"I cannot take the risk of letting you dream up more spirits to steal, witch-woman," Ishkode said, speaking louder now in an effort to sound menacing. Sekhmet let out a deep growl, which silenced him and seemed to give him pause. He leaned over toward a bearded elder, who whispered into his ear. After a long and tense period of silence, Ishkode finally spoke.

"I will allow you to commune with your father about this, but tomorrow you must tell me which animal spirits you wish to bring back to the mainland with you. Shiva, the highest shaman of this island, has the last word on whether the animal spirits are permitted to leave. We cannot stop you from asking him permission to take what you want, but we do hold immense sway over him. If you ask for too much, then rest assured we will let him know our displeasure."

Cyriana stared back calmly. "Very well—I will contact Nuada in my dreams tonight. I already know we need the permission of Shiva to take the animal spirits; we will leave your village tomorrow to set out for Mount Samaya."

Ishkode's expression became dark and wistful. "The word of Shiva prevails over all, but even the great shaman-god will think twice before making the villagers in his beloved Anatari unhappy."

Cyriana trembled ever so slightly, betraying her youth and inexperience. "Only the fates can know his wishes, and we waste our breath on further conversation. I would like to say one last thing before I leave. I order you to remove the chalices filled with *Ahara* from my friends' tables, for we no longer have need of your tricks. Carry on with your feast. I think I will have an early night, so I humbly take my leave of you," she said, and with that Cyriana and the jaguar were gone, the door slamming shut behind them dramatically.

As soon as Cyriana left, Namid grabbed Ishkode's hunting spear from him and appeared to be torn between using it to harm Ishkode or chasing after Cyriana with it. However, before she could decide, a pair of strong elders managed to pry the spear from her grasp and physically restrained her. Namid writhed with anger, and she struggled against their grip like a wild animal. "Let me go, you daft old men!" she snarled, but Ishkode commanded them to continue restraining her. He then lifted a chalice from the head table and ordered his wife to drink from it. When she swallowed the drink, it appeared to have a very calming effect on her, and she sat obediently back in her seat as though nothing untoward had happened. Ishkode smiled, apparently satisfied with her complacence.

After Cyriana left, servants came up to the rebels' table to remove the chalices of *Ahara* and replace them with flagons of plain ale. The elders did not resume their chanting and instead finished their meal in silent contemplation. For the remainder of the feast, Walter kept an eye on Ishkode—he no longer trusted the leader. Walter was deeply disturbed by what the princess had said about Hundara's fate, and he noticed that many of the Mages were as well.

Walter observed a marked change in Ishkode's behavior after Cyriana's confrontation. The tribal leader was eating and drinking in copious amounts, unlike the other elders who partook in little food, and he gazed at the women in the feasting hall with a lustful expression. Walter wondered whether Ishkode was working himself into a drunken stupor so that he could forget about his loss of power and status in the eyes of the villagers. Walter knew that the man was not exactly humble, and he suspected Ishkode's failure to defy Cyriana or inspire the loyalty of the jaguar and had been a crushing blow to him. For her part, Namid ate and drank obediently, not uttering another word to anyone in the lodge.

Walter felt shock, but also a rush of relief at what Cyriana had accomplished. Now, the rebels could leave the village with confidence, accompanied by the animal spirits they needed to help fight the Rebellion. Walter's feeling of helplessness had been transformed into hope, and he no longer harbored the crushing belief that their mission in Vei'arash was futile. If the goddess of war herself was on their side, he could finally have some faith in the Jade Rebellion.

The Path to Mount Samaya

"The ground on which we stand is sacred ground. It is the dust and blood of our ancestors."

- Chief Plenty Coups

The next morning, when the muted light of dawn flooded the rainforest and the lively birdsong had quieted to a barely perceptible hum, Walter awoke with a newfound sense of purpose. Although his eyes were red from the late night he had spent in the feasting lodge and his grief over the loss of Hundara, he was alert and optimistic, his belly full and his spirits lifted by the prospect that he and his friends would not be returning to the mainland empty-handed. Gazing around at his companions, he noticed that they appeared to be equally motivated and refreshed. Walter knew that they were all heavily indebted to Cyriana for her brave gesture. Her courage and insight had saved them from falling prey to the tricks of Ishkode, who was clearly more cunning than he'd previously suspected.

Walter had his suspicions about how Ishkode had carefully crafted his plans, and he spoke to Cyriana that morning about them.

"When we first arrived at the village," Walter told the Mage princess, "Ishkode said he thought we were a unified tribe. After I killed the stag on our hunting excursion, Ishkode remarked that he noticed I was connected to the creature's *hela*, or its eternal spirit. Ishkode probably assumed *all* of us were connected to the spirit of the stag, and he tried to take advantage of this spiritual connection to Cernunnos to persuade us to stay here permanently."

Cyriana nodded in agreement. "And so, he craftily arranged for us to consume *yagé* on multiple occasions. They served it to us at breakfast in the mornings."

"Ishkode also gave me a more potent version on the night I slept with Namid," Walter added. "It gives me shivers to think about it, but the drink *did* make me want to stay in Anatari forever. Yet Ishkode's plan backfired, since we are each connected to different animal spirits with their own unique characteristics. Your jaguar companion proved to be the perfect foil to Ishkode's plans. Unlike the stag, she craves independence and is not tied to this village."

"Last night," Cyriana revealed, "I carried out a ceremonial ritual with perfumed incense and crushed willow leaves which helped me to commune with Nuada in my dreams. He showed me images of snakes, horses, lizards, and jaguars—animals on this island that were stolen from the mainland. Those are the animals we have to bring back, Walter. Nuada told me that the rest can stay, at least for now. I know that Tristan has already befriended a pair of kingsnakes, and Elaine showed me two lizards that she found playing together in the jungle the other day. Since then, they have been inseparable from her."

Walter felt a wave of sorrow when Cyriana spoke these words. He was happy for Tristan and Elaine, but that didn't stop him from feeling hollow inside. He had hoped Cyriana's list of animals would include the stag, and he was devastated that it did not.

Walter hid his reaction from Cyriana, and cleared his throat in a businesslike manner. "You must go and tell Ishkode immediately, then. I wonder who is connected to the horses?" Walter pondered out loud. "I've seen a few of them wandering around in the village..."

When he walked out of the guest lodge, Walter's question was answered: Eva was standing next to a mare with a velvety coat the color of burnished bronze, and a dark chocolate-hued stallion. Her expression betrayed her admiration and love for the creatures, and Walter immediately knew that she was linked to them.

The villagers wept when they heard that some of their beloved animals would be departing for the mainland, but Ishkode reluctantly acceded to Cyriana's wishes. Yet he warned Cyriana that he would not allow her to take any other of the village's animals, even if Shiva himself granted his permission.

Walter said his goodbyes to the villagers with a stiff courtesy. As he shook Ishkode's hand in farewell, Namid spat on the ground.

"Thank you for your hospitality, Ishkode," Walter said, ignoring Namid. "I think we have both learned something from this experience.

For my part, I have learned that the death of a majestic animal is beautiful, not sorrowful, and that all things in the jungle are interconnected.

"For your part, I hope you have realized that tricks and manipulation will not get you far with people you do not understand. I have spent many years honing my ability to find weaknesses and vulnerabilities in computers, and I've learned that hacking a computer is similar to changing the mind of a human. Finding a minor weakness in a program opens a portal that allows you to access its inner chamber, its vulnerable core. Once you are inside, you can rewrite the script for the program in any way you desire. But everything goes wrong when you find out that the program has hidden defenses that you never knew about, walls that cannot be torn down."

Ishkode watched the rebel leader with a sort of muted contempt, and he muttered a few inaudible words in reply. Walter said nothing to Namid, who was still fuming, and only nodded in a terse gesture of farewell.

At last, after painful courtesies and parting words had been exchanged, the rebels took their leave of Anatari. Walter breathed a sigh of relief as he left the strange village he had gotten to know over the past several days, taking one final glance at the quaint assortment of thatched houses nestled into the foliage. As the village receded into the misty jungle behind him, however, Walter also felt the uncanny sensation that he was leaving behind a part of himself. He would certainly not miss Ishkode or his beautiful young wife, but he *would* miss the stag.

At the same time, part of him knew intuitively why the stag would never willingly follow him off the island. When Walter had tasted *yagé*, and the spirit of the stag had overtaken him, he had experienced the same profound connection to Vei'arash the stag itself felt. Any creature who was that territorial would never voluntarily leave its homeland. Ironically, Walter himself had a weak attachment to his own birthplace, Crystal City. Walter had never felt quite at home in the bustling metropolis, and he was now an exile of that city; he did not know where he belonged, or even *if* he belonged anywhere. Now that he knew that the stag was his totem animal, and that he shared common qualities with the animal, Walter speculated whether he had some deep attachment to another place he did not know about.

As he walked away from Anatari, Walter's steps were infused with purpose. He relished the feeling of being on the move again, and some of his regret at having left behind his stag companion began to dissipate.

Perhaps one day the pair would meet again—Walter's past experiences had taught him that fate had a strange way of uniting those who were meant to find each other.

The Mages had no maps to assist them in finding Mount Samaya. Instead, they relied on memories of what their elders had taught them about the isle of Vei'arash in oral histories that had been passed down through the generations. Yet when Walter questioned the Mages about what the arcane lore said about the location of Mount Samaya, they only gave him a vague and unsatisfactory response.

"We must listen closely to our ancestors," Cyriana told Walter as the procession of humans and animals wound their way through the rainforest. Walter smiled, charmed by her naïve faith in her long-dead relatives.

"Have you ever studied your lineage?" Cyriana asked Walter with a sidelong glance. She walked with Walter at the front of the procession, her faithful jaguar padding along at her side. At Tristan's side was a pair of long, black, yellow-ringed snakes. Two chestnut-colored wild horses trotted behind Eva, and a duo of lizards crept through the dense undergrowth next to Elaine. The jaguar was the only creature that was not accompanied by a mate, although Cyriana was confident Sekhmet could not only survive but also produce offspring without a male companion. Walter had his doubts about this, but he kept them to himself.

"I know my parents, of course, but I do not know my lineage," Walter responded. Ancestry was not terribly important in Crystal City, at least for humans; wealth, rather than nobility, defined one's status in the social hierarchy of Khalendar. As long as you were rich, and were not either a mixed-race or a Xeyan'na, you would be cordially welcomed into the Empire's circle of elites.

"Until we know our ancestors, we do not truly know who we are," she said, a faraway expression clouding her emerald eyes. "Have you ever considered the possibility that you may be a mixed-race? I mean, it is rare to find someone so well-versed in programming and hacking machines amongst the purebloods. You seem to understand computers much better than an ordinary human does."

"I am nothing but flesh and blood," Walter said with a dismissive yet uneasy laugh. He could not say that the thought had never crossed his mind, but his perception of a mixed-race was aligned with the traditional stereotype: someone with computer chips embedded into their limbs, an upgraded human who was clearly half-mortal and half-machine. Someone strong, like Emilia had been. He was weak and emotionally vulnerable, and each passing day he doubted his leadership abilities more and more.

"Blood can be tainted in many ways," Cyriana explained. "It can be influenced by magic, of course, but also by technology. I have less experience with the latter, so I cannot say for sure, but it seems to me that you should at least consider the possibility that you are a mixed-race, and that you possess special talents the purebloods do not."

Walter scoffed. "None of the humans in Crystal City have perfectly pure blood. You, of all people, should know that; Christopher told me you described this theory in detail at a council meeting of Mages in Zeyanara. As you said yourself, the water in Crystal City is contaminated—nanomachines infect the bloodstream of humans who reside there, weakening their memories and dreams."

Tristan, who was walking close behind, now ventured into the conversation. "You are right, Cyriana did explain that to us during the council meeting. But *you* seem different, closer in nature to the machines than an ordinary human. For the vast majority of those humans, the effects of the AIs' machinations are only a one-way street. You should consider the possibility that with you, those effects go both ways."

"What do you mean?" Walter asked.

"I mean that you might have the ability to harness the powers within you to your advantage. Think of it like a computer awakening to its own capabilities—developing a consciousness. Instead of passively allowing the AI Masters to control you, you can strive to control *them*. It's simply something to ponder. I have been feeling optimistic about the Jade Rebellion in recent days; I believe that with the animal spirits on our side, we have a chance of winning, but their help will not be enough. We also need assistance from people like you and Eva, who have an intimate connection with the machines. A philosopher once counselled to 'know thy enemy,' and I think that is the wisdom we must obey in order to succeed in the battle ahead."

Cyriana regarded her lover pensively. "We must not forget, though, that their ultimate defeat will be brought about by magic."

Tristan's words—*we need help from people like you and Eva*—echoed in Walter's mind, unsettling him. Walter did not know precisely what needed to be done; he had no clearly delineated plan. Nevertheless, he trusted that whomever they would find on the top of Mount Samaya could tell him just that. Now that Emilia was gone, Walter needed a mentor and a counsellor, someone to steer him onto the right path. He hoped that Emilia's spirit would manifest itself again, but perhaps the phantom he had seen in the *Jade Queen* had simply been a sign of his deep psychological longing for her.

Walter glanced over at the half-domesticated jaguar, which appeared oddly content to remain at Cyriana's side instead of wandering into the wilderness. "How does it feel to have such a loyal companion?" he asked the Mage.

"We are so closely intertwined that I feel the weight of her emotions," Cyriana replied. "I can sense that she is very restless to return to Serrahan to fight. She desperately longs for combat, but for the time being she is content with being my pet. She enjoys hunting in the jungle, of course, but that does not satiate her the way a full-fledged battle against the AI Masters will."

"I hope we find Mount Samaya soon, then, so that we can meet with the shaman-god and return to the mainland. I, too, am eager to fight."

Yet Mount Samaya was proving to be an elusive target. There were moments when, while trudging through the endless jungle, Walter wondered whether the mountain was a fictional entity that existed only in the Mages' stories. *This is a flat island*, a cynical voice in his head told him. *When you anchored the Jade Queen here, you did not see any mountains. This is how people go insane: looking for things which do not exist.* Walter was becoming increasingly impatient, not only with their circumstances, but also with Tristan, Cyriana, and the rest of the Mages, who blindly trusted in the power of ancient lore to guide them toward the mountain. His fullness from the previous night's feast was fading, and Walter was keenly aware that the food supplies they had procured at the village would not last more than a week in this stifling heat. They were no longer sheltered by the protective embrace of the village, and they now had to rely on their wits and raw instincts to survive.

The band of travelers reached a clearing in the jungle, and Walter proposed that they set up camp and rest for the evening. The diffuse amber glow of late afternoon spread itself out in the humid air like honey in a jar. Walter got to work building a fire, using a knife to scrape kindling off a fallen log that was mercifully dry. He suddenly heard the sound of leaves crunching behind him, and turned around to face one of Eva's horses, a velvety-coated, copper-hued mare. She stood blinking at Walter with large black eyes under hooded, long-lashed lids.

Walter grinned and patted the creature's forehead. He suddenly recalled that he had not spoken to Eva since their altercation near the river, and he realized he was curious about how she was doing. He was also wary, however, of divulging too many of his thoughts to her.

"Where's your master?" he asked the horse, who—being the incarnation of a divine goddess—he suspected had a better understanding of his words than most common horses.

The mare let out a short, gentle whinny, and Eva approached the pair.

"I see you've met Epa," she said, smiling.

"She is certainly beautiful," Walter replied. "She seems like a born and bred traveler—I suppose she is in her element here."

"The spirit of Epona is with her," Eva said. "She is restless and always seeking to journey to distant lands. Now that I am with Epa and her partner Epos, it seems my own spirit will never rest."

"I know the feeling of not being grounded in one place," Walter said. "Ever since I left Crystal City and found your sister outside of Jamestown, I haven't had a home of my own."

"One day, after all of this is over, I'm sure you will find it," Eva said. Her blue eyes appeared to be warmer in the sun's amber rays.

Walter glanced around to see if anyone might be listening, and then he lowered his voice.

"Has Asana met with Talvar at the railway station yet?" Walter asked.

Eva nodded in reply, and Walter studied her face carefully for signs of disloyalty to him. He found none, though he was no expert at weeding out traitors.

"Did he give her the names of his friends in houses of noble lineage?"

"He said that he needs to consult with Central Command before divulging anything to her," Eva replied. "Talvar is one of those AI Masters that needs confirmation from his higher-ups before saying or doing anything at all. He doesn't have a shred of independence, and he doesn't trust Asana much anyways—not since their romance ended so messily. In any event, they are supposed to have another meeting in several weeks' time. Asana's hoping that Talvar will give her an elite contact, so she can relay an important message to that contact through him. I am really hoping that he has ties to the First House; it would help us immensely."

Walter knew from his experience working as a government translator that Central Command was a complex brain, a processing system that was hierarchically structured like a pyramid. He'd learned that AI

Masters with more pedigree were situated near the top of the pyramid, and that the First House was the dynasty with the most pedigree of them all. Even the First House was a hierarchical system unto itself, and just like a brain directs the various organs in a body, a single AI Master at the top wielded power over the other moving parts in the machine. Walter had studied enough political science to know that the top AI Master was called the *Anax*, the ancient Greek word for king. In Walter's view, it was rather ironic that the AI Masters, having destroyed countess volumes of classical Western mythology, nevertheless decided to pilfer some of the phraseology from these myths.

"What important message will she ask Talvar to relay?" Walter asked Eva. His mouth felt dry. *Would Eva betray the Rebellion by telling the elite AI Masters—or perhaps even the Anax himself—about their plans?* Walter wondered, but then realized with a pang of anxiety that the *Anax* probably already knew about the Jade Rebellion. The *Anax* was all seeing, all knowing—akin to a god. Despite their ambitions to eventually leave Earth for Eurydice, while they still ruled Khalendar the AI Masters sought to be the primary object of human worship on Earth. Religions that idolized the old gods were outlawed in the Empire, yet humans were encouraged to honor statutes of the AI Masters as if *they* were the true gods. The *Anax* was the most narcissistic AI Master of them all, lauding himself as the incarnation of the Creator of all living beings.

"She doesn't know yet... *I* don't know yet. We need to find a way to use the elites to our advantage somehow, and I'm still pondering the best way to do that. But you can trust me about one thing, Walter: I will do my utmost to honor my sister's legacy. The AI Masters killed Emilia, but as devastating as that was, it didn't crush my spirit entirely. Ever since finding these horses, it's like a part of me has come back, like I am slowly becoming whole again. Epa and Epos have helped me to realize that the human spirit is free—it cannot be enslaved, despite all of the persistent attempts of the AI Masters. They've used technology to chain us, but we need to outsmart them by using their own weapons against them."

Walter sighed. Eva's words seemed genuine, and while he was still nervous that she could possibly betray them, he felt a bit less anxious after their conversation. *Sometimes you need blind faith,* Walter thought as he glanced over at Eva's mare, who was now wandering away from her master. Her coppery coat faded into the thick, amber air like mist.

While the Mages recited oral histories from their homeland, Walter spent his spare time focused on something more practical: fashioning a bow and a quiver of arrows. While Cyriana had assured Walter that her jaguar would bring them the carcass of any animal they desired, Walter did not want dinner to be delivered from the jaws of a beast. His time spent with Ishkode had taught him at least one important lesson: a real leader must hunt his own food, otherwise he is only a follower.

Walter had no experience in bow-making, so he had to rely on his memory of the bow he had used to hunt the stag in Anatari. He was still haunted by the stag's grisly death, and he worried that he would craft arrows too dull to kill prey with a single, clean shot. He therefore obsessively sharpened the edge of each arrow until it was as keen as a razor blade. Walter brought a mechanical, pragmatic approach to the task of constructing the weapon, and his diligence paid off: the end result was a stunningly elegant yet practical bow, and a quiver of seven sturdy arrows.

"This would have certainly impressed my bosses at the weapons factory I used to work in," Eva said when she saw Walter's new bow. He reluctantly accepted her praise, but knew that she was being facetious: the weapons manufactured in AI factories were leagues more sophisticated than his modest bow.

The first few times he tested the bow, Walter used it to hunt small mammals, such as rodents, bats, and capybara. None of these killings drew tears from him the way that slaying the deer had. Eva told Walter he was wasting a fine weapon by using it on those inferior animals, but Walter knew she was wrong. If Ishkode were here, he would agree that these creatures were just as important to the holistic operation of the jungle's ecosystem as the largest, most impressive mammals. And yet hunting these animals in moderation did not disrupt the balance, because humans themselves were part of the complex food chain. Every creature, from the most fragile insect to the strongest apex predator, played an equally critical role in the jungle's web of life, which was analogous to an intricately woven blanket. Humans were not outsiders in the natural system; rather, they were inseparable from it. Walter was beginning to realize why Namid had reacted so negatively when the rebels had announced their intention to take some of the animals and their spirits away from Anatari. Even though the rebels had taken only a few animals, each was an integral piece of the jungle's puzzle, and Walter knew that the village would deeply mourn their loss.

I will bring them back after the war, Walter promised himself. He felt surprised by his own thoughts. The animal spirits were not mere instruments of war; they were dearly treasured by both the villagers of Anatari and the people of Serrahan. But which side had the greater claim to them? Walter knew that he had sworn an oath to the Mages, but he also knew that by displacing the animal spirits from Vei'arash, the rebels were inflicting harm on the villagers—the very same harm that had been inflicted long ago by the AI Masters. Walter wrestled with these conflicted thoughts in his mind until he could think no more about them without feeling disgust. Whether it was for himself, for the AI Masters, or for humanity, he did not know.

As he was leafing through his journal one morning, Walter noticed with chagrin that twenty whole days had passed since they had left the village. Since arriving on Vei'arash, Walter had logged a brief entry each night, and the journal was filling up quickly. The last of the supplies from Anatari had spoiled six days ago, and since then the rebels had been surviving solely on the food Walter hunted for them and the occasional creature that Sekhmet brought in from her nighttime forays into the wilderness. Now and then, a Mage would discover a plant with edible berries or leaves, but they had to be exceedingly cautious of unfamiliar jungle plants, since most of them were poisonous. Walter was not only worried about his fellow travelers, but also about Christopher, Miranda, Jonathan, and the others who had stayed behind on the *Jade Queen*. *Have they run out of supplies, too?* Walter thought anxiously, before an even darker thought crept into his mind. *If we take too long, then perhaps they will assume we are dead and return to the mainland without us.* Walter had his tablet with him, but in the heart of the jungle it didn't pick up any signals, and he could not transmit messages to anyone on board the ship.

Walter noticed that as the days went by, he and many of his friends were becoming frustrated with their circumstances, but Tristan somehow became calmer. With his serpentine companions at his side, Tristan appeared to have found a sense of spiritual balance and inner satisfaction. The young Mage would often be found muttering Serrahan folklore under his breath as he concentrated deeply, likely trying to detect clues or pieces of profound wisdom hidden within it. In particular, he had taken to sitting cross-legged beneath palm trees like some meditating guru, his snakes sleeping soundly nearby while he recited a tangle of arcane riddles about Vei'arash.

Snakes were symbols of ancient wisdom, and Walter wondered whether Tristan's serpents were somehow helping to enhance his patience, focus, and mental grit. Walter knew from his experience as a computer programmer and hacker that obtaining positive results required cleverness and persistence, but above all it required the ability to master the art of concentration. Walter fondly recalled the old saying "minds can move mountains" from his father Vladimir. Ironically, Vladimir had always tried to influence others with wealth, power, and prestige, rather than his mind. He had a vast collection of books in his study, but they were all just for show; Vladimir cared more about cultivating his bank account than his intellect. Yet Walter liked the saying. *Let's hope minds can find mountains*, Walter thought.

"Our ancestors did not have the same framework for understanding reality as we do today," Tristan told Walter one evening by the campfire. That night, they had eaten a meagre meal of stale cornbread and grilled capybara, and Walter's stomach was rumbling even after they had finished. "To them, the stars were their brothers and sisters who had died in battle," Tristan continued dreamily. "The winds sang the songs of their grandparents, and the Earth was a great wheel that turned at the hand of destiny. Every step they took and every decision they made— whether it was marriage, war, or a simple act of kindness—was done with the counsel of those natural forces."

Walter found all of that fascinating, but it gave him little comfort. He was desperate to know what, exactly, the lore had revealed about the location of Mount Samaya. Since the oral histories were in an old Serrahan dialect, however, they could not be directly translated into Khalendi. Despite Walter's natural aptitude for languages, this one was too arcane for him to decipher, and he had to rely on Tristan to interpret what he recalled of the lore. His patience with his friend was wearing thin.

"Why haven't you yet told me how to reach Mount Samaya? Whenever I ask you, your answers are vague and uncertain," Walter said bluntly. "It feels like we are going around in circles in this jungle, in an endless labyrinth that we can't find the exit to. I am growing tired of this stifling humidity and these belligerent gnats. I'm also sleep deprived— thanks to the deafeningly loud birdsong that descends on this island like a tsunami every night—and I think the others are too. Just look at the faces of our fellow rebels; they are pale and exhausted. If we don't find that mountain soon, I fear for not only our lives, but also our sanity."

Tristan looked at Walter intently for a long time before speaking. The Mage's face was impassive, and disclosed few traces of sympathy, but Walter knew Tristan well enough to know that he had immense capacity for compassion. Walter guessed that he was trying his best to help, but in his own subtle and composed manner. "The lore doesn't give us a simple roadmap—rather, it provides a rough guide to discovering our personal strengths and weaknesses, which will in turn help us to find the mountain," Tristan replied.

Walter sighed. He was impatient with that kind of talk—they had been slogging through the humid rainforest for weeks, and he was not in the mood for any more meditative soul-searching.

"Fortunately, we seem to be on the right track," Tristan said. His eyes shone with optimism. "The lore tells us that to find the mountain, we need a brave leader to help nourish us along the way. Since our supplies ran out, you have been doing just that, hunting prey for us with your bow and arrow."

"What does that have to do with where the mountain is?" Walter snapped.

"Be patient," Tristan said with a laugh. "The lore also tells us that when we are near the base of Mount Samaya, we will face a test involving a holy creature who guards it. Once we have passed the test, we will be permitted to ascend the mountain."

Walter was not convinced by Tristan's words; he politely excused himself from the conversation, and went off to confide in Elaine. She had a radiant glow to her skin, and like Tristan she appeared to be more at peace now that she was close to her totem animal.

"Tristan has been speaking in riddles lately," Walter said to her. "I asked him where Mount Samaya is—for the thousandth time—and all he could say was that I must nourish everyone by hunting for food, and that a holy creature guards the mountain. What do you think of his strange advice?" Walter asked. "I used to think he was a trusted confidant, but now I fear that jungle may have begun to steal his wits."

Elaine said nothing, and her gaze remained fixed on her lizard companions. The male was orange and black, its vibrant skin a warning to predators of the venom it bore, and the female was the sacred color of jade, the perfect camouflage in the dense foliage of the jungle. Walter sighed irritably, but her lips curved upwards in a smile.

"Watch carefully," she murmured in a low voice. "I have been observing these two for hours, and I cannot come to any other conclusion but this: they communicate with each other by vibrating the objects they are standing on." Walter was skeptical at first, but after a few minutes of watching the lizards in silence he realized that she had spoken the truth—one of the lizards would shake the leaf or branch they were standing on with a series of sharp movements, and then the other would do the same in reply.

"Fascinating," he said, but the anxious edge in his voice remained.

"They are fire lizards, native to the Barrens," Elaine told him. "The people of my village will be so grateful that they are returning home."

Walter furrowed his brow in confusion. His memory was jogged by her statement, and he thought back to his encounter with the seer in the Jamestown bar and the tiny lizard fossilized inside of the amber ring she was wearing. The fire lizard was also etched onto the surface of the *balayan* Emilia had given him back in Tsei'watu.

"I thought that all of the animals we were bringing back were from Serrahan?" he asked.

"No, they are native to each of the four ancient kingdoms. Tristan's snakes are from Serrahan, Cyriana's jaguar traces her ancestry to Eyrenvale, and Eva's horses hail from Calliope."

Walter pondered this for a moment. "I suppose that makes sense. During the Shadow Wars, the Mages didn't just fight alone, they fought alongside their allies from other southern kingdoms. Those allies must have gifted the Mages with their native animals and their spirits, to use in the battles against the AI Masters.

"I am so grateful to have found these animals, Elaine, but that doesn't mean we've succeeded. If we don't make it to Mount Samaya, it will have all been for nothing," he said with a sigh.

"Sometimes, Walter," Elaine continued, "what you are seeking does not reveal itself in an obvious form, similar to the messages communicated by these lizards. The shaman-god is a being of unparalleled cunning, and I'm sure he has deliberately made it difficult for us to find him. The pathway to him will not be a straightforward one. But he knows that we are here and that we are making our best efforts to find him, and that is what matters. Watch for signs of his presence in the landscape, and those signs may very well lead us to him."

Walter rolled his eyes. "You are as cryptic as Tristan," he said. Elaine frowned sternly, causing him to regret his sharp tone.

"You would not survive a day in my village with that attitude," she reprimanded him. "In Crystal City, you grew up in a world of shiny technological gadgets and instant convenience, which no doubt made everything easy for you. In Te'yara, the elders extol the virtues of *Vandaya*, which translates to 'the hard road.' Everything in life that is worth doing is a struggle. Trust in yourself, Walter, and the pathway to the mountain will become clear in due time."

Walter sighed. "I am sorry, Elaine. I should be more open-minded about it, I acknowledge that. But the grumbling of my stomach tells me that we need an answer soon."

"The hungrier you are, the more excellent a warrior you will become," Elaine replied. "That is what the elders say."

"Let us pray that the elders are correct."

The Gatekeeper

*"I am a forest, and a night of dark trees: but he who is not afraid of my
darkness, will find banks of roses under my cypresses."*
– Friedrich Nietzsche

After his conversation with Elaine, Walter decided to adopt a more flexible attitude toward their plight. After all, the rebels had nearly run out of food before, and yet they had serendipitously encountered a village with an abundance of supplies. Wandering through the uncharted wilderness of the jungle was a risky business, but now they had the animals on their side, and they also had a safety net in Sekhmet in case they reached a state of desperation.

As Walter's optimism renewed itself, his mind began to feel clearer and less distracted by negative thoughts, and he began to notice subtle changes in the landscape. One morning, the young man noticed a nearly imperceptible creek that had retained a shallow trickle of water. Since their departure from Anatari, the rebels had encountered only a few bodies of water, and they were becoming increasingly thirsty.

"This creek looks like it could have its source in a mountain spring," he told Tristan. The young Mage knelt down beside the narrow creek and eagerly submerged his canteen beneath its clear surface.

Tristan took a sip of water and smiled gratefully. "It is cold and sweet, so I suspect you are right. I am sure that the mountain is close—I can sense it. All we have to do now is follow the creek upstream."

As they followed the creek for several miles, Walter was heartened to see that the water level rose steadily, and after an hour or so, they reached the base of a waterfall tumbling over a steep cliff. When he inspected the site, Walter could see that the cliff was only one minor feature of a vast and formidable mountain. According to Serrahan folklore, there was only one mountain on this island, and so Walter knew immediately it was the one they were looking for. At the sight of Mount Samaya, Walter nearly sobbed with relief, and the frustration broiling inside of him gave way to sheer joy.

When they saw the temptingly cool, glittering water at the foot of the mountain, a few of the Mages—Senaye, Danaye, and Boann—let out cries of joy, threw off their robes, and jumped eagerly in. Inspired by their fearless attitude, Walter cast aside his apprehension and dipped his toes in the turquoise water, wincing at the initial frigidity of it. Elaine took Walter's hand, coaxing him to come into the pool with the others.

"The water is lovely," she said, grinning broadly and squinting in the intense sunlight.

Walter frowned. "It's freezing," he retorted, pushing back against her as she tried to draw him in further. The biting cold of the water was uncomfortable, and he worried about his glasses falling into the pool. Once he was waist-deep in the water, Walter had begun to shiver, but he could scarcely contain his laughter. He noticed that Eva had waded into the pool without hesitation and was swimming fearlessly toward the waterfall. She treaded water next to the roaring cascade, the spray enveloping her and nearly concealing her from sight.

"Don't get too close to the falls," Walter shouted in warning, but Eva paid him no heed.

Out of the entire group, only Cyriana, Tristan, and the animal companions remained out of the water. Cyriana sat beside the pool next to Sekhmet. The great cat tiptoed gingerly toward the edge and lapped up the fresh water with her long pink tongue. Her ears were flattened against her head, and she paused occasionally to glance up in fear at the thundering waterfall. Cyriana giggled at the jaguar's reaction to the waterfall; despite being the incarnation of the goddess of war, Sekhmet still had the common phobias of a typical feline. Tristan sat perched on a nearby rock alongside his beloved snakes, his expression sober and vigilant. Elaine's lizards frolicked together under a nearby palm, and Eva's horses took in a draught of the water before trotting into the shade, where they waited stoically for their master.

As he treaded water in the frigid pool, Walter could clearly detect the shape of a jaguar crouching stealthily behind a cluster of ferns. The animal's black hide camouflaged him well; like a marble statue crafted from obsidian, he blended almost seamlessly into the shadowy darkness. The creature was nearly double the size of Sekhmet, but he was long and lean, the bulk of his weight distributed evenly through his body. His eyes were a mesmerizing blend of gold and hazel tones, but their steady, unflinching gaze inspired terror in the young man. Walter was not the only person who had noticed; Cyriana was also staring directly at the jaguar, her eyes wide with fear. Sekhmet began to sound a warning, emitting a low, guttural growl that came from her belly.

His cover exposed, the majestic cat stepped gracefully out of his hiding place. The rebels' cries of delight quickly turned to shrieks of alarm when they saw the creature. Walter stirred into action; he had left his bow and quiver of arrows sitting near the edge of the pool along with his tablet, compass, and satchel, so it took him a split second to make a calculated dive for these items. The jaguar noticed this quick motion and his ears perked up, but the creature did not make any sudden movements in response. Instead, the animal continued to stalk slowly toward the pool with graceful ease and unnerving confidence, as if to prove that he was not the slightest bit intimidated by Sekhmet, whose growls had gradually intensified.

Cyriana looked just as alarmed as the other rebels, but she took a more level-headed approach to the situation than the ones who had begun to panic. "Don't worry—jaguars detest the water. If you stay in that pool you will be safe, but try to keep as far away from shore as possible," she instructed.

Walter glanced at her with concern. "What about you and Tristan? Both of you are on dry land. Besides, I doubt a hungry jaguar would mind getting a bit wet."

Deciding to err on the side of caution, Walter nocked an arrow onto his bow and aimed it in the direction of the exquisite creature. When the jaguar reached the edge of the pool he crouched down, regarding the rebels with a mixture of curiosity and mild amusement. Sekhmet's growl had died down, and while her muscles were still clearly tensed, she was now simply observing the cat with a pronounced curiosity. The male jaguar remained impressively calm and his long tail twitched slowly as he perched gracefully on the water's edge.

"Walter—what are you doing?" Cyriana asked in surprise. "He is not threatening us in any way, just sitting calmly. You cannot take the life of a sacred creature like that without facing inevitable consequences. Did you not learn anything from the villagers? They worship the jaguar with a deep reverence."

"Don't worry," Walter reassured her. "I won't shoot unless he attacks." The grisly image of the stag lying prone on the ground after Ishkode had struck it with his arrow immediately sprang into Walter's mind. He grimaced, trying to erase it from his thoughts.

"Keep your hand steady," Cyriana cautioned him. "Otherwise you might let the arrow fly by accident."

Tristan gestured to Walter to drop his bow. "Aiming an arrow at such a sacred creature is wrong, Walter. We must respect the inhabitants of this island, and especially its animals, otherwise we might anger Shiva."

Without warning, the black jaguar suddenly unleashed an otherworldly howl, a sound that was less threatening than haunting. Sekhmet's ears shot up, and her eyes glittered with a keen curiosity.

Walter did not know how to interpret it, though the noise had sent shivers down his spine.

"That's not a threat," Cyriana explained to Walter and his fellow rebels. "It sounds more to me like a call for companionship. He seems to be directing it toward Sekhmet—look at how their eyes are locked together." Cyriana had spoken truthfully; the two creatures were now fixated on one another, with neither daring to glance away. "What's strange, though, is that it doesn't seem to be a mating call. Usually males only interact with females when they want to mate, but there doesn't seem to be any sexual desire between these two. Perhaps there is some other bond of kinship between them."

Minutes passed in silence, yet the two jaguars remained frozen in place, staring at each other with hypnotic, unblinking eyes.

"I think we should get out of here," Cyriana said, her tone suddenly urgent. Her sympathetic attitude toward the newcomer had evaporated, and she was now visibly unsettled by the eerie connection between Sekhmet and the new jaguar.

Walter nodded, lowering his bow and pointing up ahead to a clearing in the trees, the beginning of a trail that curved up the mountainside. "Onwards and upwards," he said. He was more than happy to leave the black jaguar behind without killing it.

The rebels emerged cautiously from the pool, drying themselves off with blankets and hastily pulling their robes over their heads. The jaguar did not seem to notice them, nor did he care that they had left the relative safety of the water. Instead, his penetrating gaze was fixed intently on Sekhmet. Cyriana's tone was sharp as she summoned her pet to her side. "Come, Sekhmet, we must not waste time here," the Mage pleaded, her impatient voice echoing off the stone façade behind the waterfall.

While the creature had diligently obeyed the Mage princess' commands before, this time was different. Sekhmet now appeared utterly mesmerized by the alluring stare of the male jaguar. The newcomer reminded Walter of Emilia, with her admirable powers of hypnosis, and he suddenly wondered whether reincarnation existed.

"Sekhmet, come!" Cyriana commanded sternly. Walter detected a hint of sadness and betrayal in Cyriana's emerald-green eyes as the girl watched the entranced pair of felines. She stood there helplessly like a jilted lover as Sekhmet coldly ignored her. Walter was all too familiar with the gut-wrenching feeling of rejection by a loved one, and his heart swelled with sympathy for the Mage.

At this point the other rebels had reached the trailhead, and they were patiently waiting for Cyriana to resolve the issue with her non-compliant pet before carrying on. Only Walter and Tristan stayed behind, to try and be of help to the Mage.

Unfortunately, the problem was not as easily solved as they'd hoped. Sekhmet had begun to move toward the black jaguar, cautiously at first, but with increasing confidence. She did not so much as glance back at Cyriana; the black jaguar had captured her full attention, and Sekhmet no longer seemed the slightest bit interested in either the rebels or their mission.

Cyriana's sorrow was now blended with anger. The young Mage curled her lip as she muttered to Walter under her breath, "The only way to stop this madness is to kill the intruder."

Tristan scowled when he overheard her. "There's no need to overreact, Cyriana," he told her. "I understand that you're upset, but violence—that can't be the answer. Just a few minutes ago, you were saying that Walter couldn't take the life of a sacred creature without facing consequences. Why have you suddenly changed your mind?"

A single tear trickled down Cyriana's cheek, and she brushed it away hastily. "What other choice do we have? Do you know of any spell that is potent enough to break a bond between two jaguars?"

Tristan pondered this for a moment. "Come to think of it… there might be one. At Briarthorn Academy they taught us about *Amara*, which is a type of hypnosis spell you can cast on an animal. Perhaps I could hypnotize her, and that would sever her connection with the black jaguar."

Cyriana's shrugged impatiently. "Try it, then."

Tristan peered at the spotted cat, squinting as he focused intently on the spell. "*Arcanum arcanorum carnivora. Deceptio visus. Age quod agis.*" He repeated the cryptic phrases a number of times. Sekhmet's eyes flickered toward him with mild interest, but the spell's sway over her was fleeting. The elementary spell was not strong enough to hold Sekhmet's attention, and it was easily defeated by the black jaguar's magnetic aura.

Cyriana sighed. "The spells we learned at Briarthorn Academy were never designed to work on gods and goddesses. One of the cardinal rules they taught us was that the gods have power over us, not the other way around."

Tristan nodded in agreement. "You're right. This new companion of hers must be special in some way. Perhaps he is also blessed with some divine powers?"

A dark cloud passed over Cyriana's features. "If that is so, then we must destroy his physical form and weaken those powers. The creature's divine spirit will flee into the jungle once we have slain its body."

Walter raised his bow again and aimed the arrow strung onto it toward the black jaguar. His actions only succeeded in provoking Sekhmet, however, who now spun around to hiss at Walter. The creature must have sensed—rather than seen—him aiming, because her back had been turned to him. At first it startled Walter, but he then realized that the incarnation of the goddess of war would likely have no trouble detecting any threat, wherever it came from.

"Easy, Sekhmet," Walter whispered, but his words did not appear to placate the animal. Her haunches were raised and she glared at Walter with fierce yellow eyes.

"Don't provoke her further, Walter. If Sekhmet wishes to stay behind with this jaguar, then so be it. We will return to her after our visit with Shiva," Tristan urged.

Cyriana shook her head. "I am not leaving Sekhmet behind. Would you leave your snakes behind? It would be like losing a part of yourself," she said, trembling with rage.

"You must, Cyriana. The answer to this dilemma is not murder," Tristan said firmly.

"Do not tell me what to do," the Mage snapped. "Walter, I order you to kill that creature."

Walter grimaced as he began to draw back his bow, but Tristan uttered a simple spell which released the arrow and caused it to go astray of the target. Startled, the pair of jaguars retreated together into the dense undergrowth.

Cyriana spun around to face Tristan, enraged. "Now she is leaving me! Who knows if I will ever see her again," she said in a shaking voice. "Thanks to you, we have lost a valuable asset to the Rebellion, perhaps the most valuable asset we had."

Tristan returned her gaze calmly without flinching. "Do not worry, I have a plan."

"What plan is that?" Cyriana inquired, her eyes as cold as ice.

"It's true that the magic spells we know won't work on divine beings, but we don't *need* to rely on magic—the ordinary kind, at least," Tristan explained. "We already have all the tools we need to break the bond. Three of us now have divine companions who are capable of extraordinary feats. Eva's horses are infused with the spirit of Epona, goddess of travel; Elaine's lizards carry the divine spark of Demeter, goddess of fertility and regeneration; and my snakes are the incarnation of Brigid, goddess of healing and wisdom. We must be able to use them somehow to our advantage." Tristan puzzled over this for a few moments. "I think it could work…" he muttered to himself as Cyriana and Walter looked at him in bewilderment.

"You think *what* could work?" Cyriana asked, but he ignored her question and instead whispered instructions to his snakes. They reacted immediately to his commands and began to slither in the direction the jaguars had gone.

Suddenly, a blood-curdling cry reverberated throughout the jungle, the sound of an animal struggling for its life. "Sekhmet!" Cyriana shouted fearfully. "What have your snakes done to her?" she asked Tristan, tears pooling in her eyes as she ran toward the sound.

"Don't worry, she's safe," Tristan said as he and Walter followed her. "I was trying to find a way for our animal companions to help. I quickly ruled out Elaine's lizards and Eva's horses; they are relatively peaceful creatures, and pacifism won't get you far with the goddess of war. My snakes, on the other hand—they are not just healers, but also destroyers. I ordered the first one to inflict a venomous wound on the black jaguar, paralyzing him just long enough to break Sekhmet's hypnosis so she will become loyal to you once again. The second one carries an antidote inside of her—one bite and the jaguar will return to consciousness instantly. If my suspicions are correct, I've tricked Sekhmet into believing her companion is dead and severed the link that exists between them."

Cyriana breathed a sigh of relief when she spotted Sekhmet and the other jaguar next to a cluster of ferns. The female had not been injured in any way, but her new companion was lying down, completely still. At first Sekhmet's expression was forlorn, but as time went on she seemed to have forgotten her reason for having followed the creature, and she now stared up at Cyriana with the same reverence and respect as before. The jaguar accompanied her, Walter, and Tristan back to the pool, where they re-united with the rest of the rebels waiting near the trailhead.

"Thank you," Cyriana said to Tristan, beaming with gratitude. Tristan was about to respond, but froze when a gaudily clothed man suddenly emerged from the entrance of the trail. He carried a tall wooden walking stick and he wore bright orange robes, a skirt made of leaves, and a necklace of seashells and animal bones. His head was adorned with a crown of blue flowers. The eccentric man looked as though he was from a different universe entirely, and Walter wondered whether he was the shaman-god Shiva. The stranger's skin was not dark like the villagers, but rather pale white, which contrasted starkly with his jet-black hair. He was not an old man, though he looked wise beyond his years, and he seemed burdened by the weight of responsibility.

"Greetings," the man said in Khalendi.

Before any of the bewildered rebels had a chance to reply, the stranger launched into an introduction. "I am Caleb, and I humbly serve the one true Lord. He goes by many names, but I like to call him the Seer of Time, the Teacher of Kings, and the Keeper of Wisdom. He whose reputation precedes him, he who laughs as the world triumphs and weeps as the world crumbles under its own weight. He who has seen more seasons than all of you combined, he who has written more scripture about what was, what is, and what will be than all of the scholars in the history of the world. The Ageless One, Lord Shiva."

The man's voice rang out with such authority that even the animals appeared to be humbled by him. The lizards and snakes stood perfectly still, Sekhmet crouched down in silence, and Eva's horses lowered their heads in deference.

"Asin," he continued, fixing his gaze on Walter now. "You are the leader of these rebels, are you not?"

"How—how do you know who I am?" Walter asked warily. He suddenly recalled the day he had encountered Emilia in the tall grasses of the Khalendar savannah. Just like this eccentric man, Emilia had already known his name before he'd told it to her.

"I have connections to the village," the stranger replied. "I see you have passed my master's test—congratulations. I am glad that the wisdom of the snake ultimately mended the conflict within your ranks," he said, gesturing toward Tristan and his serpent companions.

"And you," Caleb said, now addressing Cyriana. "Princess of the magic kingdom across the seas, you have no reason to fear Rama, the jaguar you were so distressed by. He was simply part of my master's test. It is time for your lover to awaken him." The man nodded at Tristan, who ordered his healing snake to waken the slumbering beast. The snake slithered back in the direction of Rama, and returned accompanied by the black jaguar, alive and fully healed. When she saw the creature Cyriana breathed in sharply, fearing that he would again persuade Sekhmet to abandon her master, but instead he defied her expectations. The jaguar was now docile and obedient, and he simply strode over to Caleb's side without triggering any reaction in Sekhmet. Walter suspected that Caleb was Rama's master, as the feline dutifully responded to the man's commands.

Cyriana regarded the stranger with a mixture of fear and skepticism. "How can you possibly you know that I am princess of a magic kingdom, and that Tristan is my lover? What reason do any of us have to trust you?" she asked.

"Cyriana, this is what the ancient lore told us would happen," Tristan told her. "It said that we would be tested, thrust into a situation that caused discord amongst us. Once we pass this test, we are supposed to be greeted by a gatekeeper, who will guide us up the mountain and lead us to Shiva."

Cyriana's eyes suddenly lit up with a flash of recognition, and Tristan's words seemed to strike an emotional chord in her. "Our ancestors—they must have walked the exact same route as us ages ago…" she said, muttering more to herself than to Tristan. The cynicism gradually evaporated from her face.

"I am glad that is sorted," Caleb continued. "Now, let us climb. Before we carry on, though, we must say a prayer of gratitude to the mountain for allowing us to ascend it."

The man then held out his hands, palms facing upwards toward the sky, and inhaled deeply. As he did, a sharp wind suddenly whistled through the trees, as if the rebels had already reached a high altitude despite being at the mountain's base. A light rain then began to fall, steady but gentle. Walter savored the sensation of the cool rain upon his skin, and he immediately felt more tranquil and refreshed. He closed his eyes as the stranger uttered a prayer in an incomprehensible language. Caleb's voice was low but commanding, and it seemed to cast a shroud of silence over the jungle.

Once he had finished the prayer, Caleb walked toward the trail which led up the mountain. One by one, the rebels quietly filed in behind him, with Walter at the fore of the group. Rama, Sekhmet, the snakes, and the lizards all eagerly followed their masters up the winding pathway, but Eva's horses stopped abruptly, reluctant to climb up the steep pathway.

The stranger noticed the horses' unwillingness to proceed. "They are not creatures of the mountain—they will wait patiently for their master down here," Caleb said.

Eva then spoke softly to her companions, and they seemed to understand her words. Both of them obediently bowed their heads and settled in beneath a broad-leafed banyan tree at the base of the mountain. Epa and Epos were wild horses, well accustomed to living on the island, and they were capable of fending for themselves until Eva returned.

As the group ascended Mount Samaya, the terrain became steeper and more rugged. The trail was not well maintained, and the travelers were forced to navigate jagged rocks and slippery tree roots. The only pleasant aspect of the trek was the varied abundance of mountain flowers lining the trail, including alpine saxifrage, yellow mountain heather, and tall delphinium, but there was little time to pay attention to the diversions since they were moving at a fast clip. The Mages seemed to fare better than the rebels from Crystal City—the latter group had been raised in an urban setting replete with comforts, and were in poorer physical shape than the Mages, who spent much of their leisure time roaming the mountains, hills, and forests of their territory. Walter's face was lined with sweat and his breathing labored as he climbed up the seemingly endless mountain trail. Walter saw that the stranger carried on with an enviable ease; the man's breath was light as he trod nimbly upon the trail and maintained perfect balance, in contrast to Walter, who occasionally tripped on gnarled roots and jutting stones.

As the hours dragged on, Walter began to wonder if the mountain led to the top of the sky itself. He knew that his thoughts were foolish and that it was impossible for the mountain to be truly endless, though it still felt that way. Caleb noticed Walter's palpable frustration and began to engage in conversation with him, telling him stories to distract him from the harshness of the climb.

"A long time ago," Caleb began, "many hundreds of thousands of years before recorded history, the universe was filled with a dazzling abundance of animals. They ruled the world from their council in the heavens and created other animals to populate the Earth in their own image. One day, having grown bored of creating other animals that looked exactly like themselves, they created humans. Every so often, the animals would convene meetings to discuss the creatures they had made. Not long after they first created the humans, the animals sat at their council table to share their observations about their novel creations.

"Perhaps not surprisingly, all of the animals reached the same conclusion: humans were not their best creations. They were physically and mentally weak, they lacked the ability to develop long-term plans or coordinated strategies, they were lustful and gluttonous, and above all they were proud and egotistical. Because of these traits, the humans were poor hunters, barely able to survive in the wilderness and nourish their own families.

"The leader of the animals, Bear, asked the other animals how they proposed to fix the problem of humanity's flawed nature. The other animals voiced their input. Some animals, like Raven, believed that they should simply do away with the humans because they were obviously not thriving on earth. But most of the animals recognized the potential in humans and wanted them to stick around. The council eventually reached a consensus amongst themselves, deciding that since they had created the humans, they had a moral obligation to teach them how to live better on earth.

"From that day onwards, the animals became the first teachers of the human race, helping them to become stronger, more intelligent, and more resilient—in short, better capable of surviving the harsh realities of their environment. In ancient times, humans worshipped animals as their teachers and creators, and all was well; the fragile equilibrium of the world was maintained. But one day the scales tipped. The humans began to capitalize on their newfound resourcefulness, using the skills bequeathed to them by the animals to gain supremacy over those beings. The heavenly council of animals watched the humans carry out this campaign in dismay, tears filling their eyes as the humans wreaked havoc. The humans began to follow a monotheistic religion—Christianity—which they believed gave them permission to indulge in such cruel acts of subjugation and dominion, not realizing that by harming animals they were injuring divine beings who had been created in the image of the gods themselves. The humans eventually became so proud and insolent that they even betrayed the single god they had pledged allegiance to, Dove, who sat at the council in the heavens.

"The same thing is happening with your robots," Caleb then said, startling Walter. "You are their creators, and so you benevolently wanted to help them by raising the level of their intelligence. But the process which was set in motion can no longer be stopped, and it is leading to chaos and disorder. The robots have subjugated you, and their control over you is simply feeding a vicious cycle of enslavement."

Walter was too exhausted to reply, but he was unsettled by Caleb's words. How could this strange man, who lived on an isolated, primitive island in the middle of a vast ocean, possibly know about the AI Masters and their control over the humans in Khalendar? Walter then realized that it was possible for him to have received this information from the dissidents who had been shipped over to Vei'arash from the mainland.

Before he was able to question Caleb about that, however, Walter saw they were nearing the top of the mountain. *I was so absorbed in Caleb's tale, I must not have noticed we were reaching the summit,* Walter thought. A dazzling beam of sunlight shone through the canopy above them, and with only a few steps they suddenly emerged at the summit of the mountain.

What Walter saw next took his breath away: a vast crater stretched for miles to the west, indicating that Mount Samaya was a dormant volcano. The windswept crater was a dusty red hue and a dry, rocky texture which seemed similar to the surface of Mars. Despite its parched soil, it somehow managed to support an entire colony of humans. Canvas tents dotted the crater's surface and humans moved throughout the settlement, busily going about their daily lives. The scene instantly triggered Walter's memories of Tsei'watu.

Caleb smiled as he observed the awestruck expression on the faces of Walter and the other rebels.

"Where you come from, Crystal City, the robots portray Vei'arash as a place of chaos, damnation, and suffering," he explained. "Yet that is mere propaganda, designed to instill fear in those who deviate from the robots' authoritarian agenda. To the contrary, the settlement at Mount Samaya is a utopian paradise. The people here are not mentally warped or corrupted by evil; they are kind-hearted souls who shut their eyes to the material temptations of the world, and they have made diligent efforts to detach themselves from the powerful yoke of ego which ties others to the earth. Some have achieved the blissful state of *nirvana*, but most are scholars who are still learning, still metaphorically climbing their way to that most-holy state."

"Where did all these people come from?" Walter asked incredulously as he surveyed the vast assembly of humans spread out on the face of the red crater like tiny ants.

"They came from your birthplace—Crystal City," Caleb replied. "They are the reviled dissidents, the worst criminals of your society. Through the venerable teachings of Shiva and his servants, they have been raised to the status of saints."

Walter was astounded by what he was hearing. Inwardly, he began to question whether everything he had learned about Vei'arash and its dissidents was false. Contrary to what he believed, the dissidents were not perpetually tormented by an army of demons and dark spirits that had been unleashed by corrupt shamans. All of his fears about Elaine and Jonathan rotting away in the hell of Vei'arash had been unfounded. He knew that it should not surprise him to learn that the AIs had been disseminating false propaganda, but it was nevertheless difficult for him to wrap his head around a reality which contrasted so starkly with what he had previously been told.

After recovering from his initial surprise, Walter's next thought was whether the shaman-god Shiva dwelled amidst all of these humans. "The shaman-god—take us to him," Walter instructed Caleb.

The stranger frowned sternly, puffing out his chest. "You are lucky that he is at home today. Shiva travels widely, and he is not always in his quarters. But you will see him without delay, rebel leader, worry not."

Caleb's gaze then moved past Walter and settled on a building perched over top the volcano crater. Walter had not noticed the dwelling until now. It was an architectural masterpiece, reminiscent of the ancient temples of the Middle East, India, and the Orient, which Walter had read about in historical texts back in Crystal City. Its crimson roofs were curved elegantly upwards at the edges and trimmed with gleaming gold, and its walls were decorated with bronze spheres embedded into jade-colored bands that encircled the entire structure. Whereas the tents dotting the crater were modest and humble, this building was imperial, announcing the majesty of its occupant to all who witnessed it.

Walter did not need to ask Caleb whether the building was the abode of the great shaman-god, as he already knew the answer. He bowed his head in humility.

"It is time," Caleb said, his voice echoing eerily off of the walls of the vast crater.

The Mountain Dweller

"Fire is His head, the sun and moon His eyes, space His ears, the Vedas His speech, the wind His breath, the universe His heart. From His feet the Earth has originated. Verily, He is the inner self of all beings."
– The Upanishads

The path leading to the shaman-god's home was treacherous. To reach the dwelling place, the rebels had to tread carefully in single file along a steep and narrow ridge encircling the edge of the crater. As they walked, Walter noticed with a pang of fear that they were thousands of feet above the bottom of the crater. A single misstep could cause them to tumble to their deaths.

"Be careful," Walter warned his companions as they followed him up the steep path.

As they traversed the ridge, Cyriana kept glancing behind her to make sure Sekhmet was safe, but the jaguars were both far more sure-footed than the clumsy humans. One of the rebels, a bulky man named Remmen, nearly lost his balance when they approached the end of the ridge. Just as he was about to plunge into the yawning mouth of the crater, his friend Callaghan managed to help steady him. The pair looked downwards into the dizzying abyss below, and both let out a sigh of relief.

Finally, after what seemed like hours had passed, the rebels finally arrived at the entrance to the shaman-god's home. The entrance to the building was an alluring, gilded bronze door upon which numerous panels were engraved, each one portraying a unique artistic scene. Walter recalled stories about a famed bronze door with engravings of Biblical scenes in the Old World, and this one looked similar but had several distinct features. The scenes on this door had been inspired by some Eastern religion, and they were ornate and almost grotesque in their candid portrayal of life, love, suffering, and death. Exhausted but also mesmerized, the rebels stared at the dizzying array of images until the door swung open and the scent of perfumed incense wafted out toward them, enticing them inside.

When the door shut behind them the room became pitch black, and Caleb lit a wooden torch to help the rebels navigate the cavernous structure. Walter was dazzled by what he witnessed—the building's interior was even more extravagant than the exterior. The walls were painted rich hues of violet, emerald, and crimson, and the floor was lined with fine exotic rugs and furs. Walter was confused by this bold display of extravagance; before setting eyes on this palatial building, Walter had assumed that the shaman-god was a solemn ascetic who shunned the material world. He now wondered if Shiva would feel at home in Crystal City, with its glittering skyscrapers and its black-haired girls, whose necks were adorned with rivers of diamonds flowing into their ivory skin.

After exploring the maze-like dwelling for some time, the group eventually reached a chamber which appeared to be the most luxurious of them all. At one end of the room was a turquoise pool surrounded by bonsai trees and lazy, fluttering butterflies. Upon entering the chamber, most of the rebels immediately fixed their gaze upon this magnificent scene, but Tristan let out a gasp when he turned toward the other end of the room. A young man wearing an intricately carved wooden mask and holding a tall staff decorated with exotic bird feathers was seated upon a great bronze throne. Next to the man was a large, female tiger so big that her head was nearly the same size as the throne. Her wide, yellow eyes surveyed the newcomers with mild interest.

Walter was frightened by the sight of the strange masked man, who could be none other than Shiva, and the intimidating tiger at his side. He looked toward Caleb for reassurance, but the man had already rushed over to the shaman-god to massage his feet. Rama also padded over and licked the shaman-god's hand to comfort him, while keeping a respectful distance from the tiger. Shiva waved both of them away, gesturing for the servant and his pet to stand aside while he appraised the newcomers.

"Greetings," the shaman-god said in a voice which was soft but full of power, like a cool autumn wind rustling the trees.

Walter decided to show leadership and stepped forward, courageously approaching the shaman-god and kneeling before him. The young man's mind buzzed with thoughts, but his fear paralyzed him and prevented him from speaking. As he stooped before the masked figure, Walter realized how small and vulnerable he felt, like a leaf trembling in the wind. He had waited for so long for this moment, but now he was frozen speechless before the great Shiva.

"Your majesty," Walter said in a quiet voice, "Thank you for opening your doors to us."

The shaman-god then let out a trill of a laugh, startling Walter. "*Your majesty*," the shaman-god echoed. Walter noticed that when Shiva laughed, Caleb frowned worriedly, as though he was anticipating that something bad was going to happen next.

Walter was about to speak again, but he hesitated when the shaman-god began to cry softly. The tiger became increasingly disgruntled as the sound grew louder, and she suddenly let out a thundering roar that seemed to shake the very foundations of the shaman-god's abode. Walter glanced back toward his friends and saw that they were visibly shaken.

Caleb became agitated by his master's distress and tried to placate him, offering him refreshments and fanning him with a palm leaf. The shaman-god waved the servant away, his inconsolable lamentation growing louder in proportion to Caleb's anxious fussing. Walter stayed where he was, becoming increasingly uneasy as he wondered how to proceed in this strange situation.

Before Walter could decide what to do next, the sound of weeping suddenly ceased and the shaman-god began to speak.

"Do not let the beauty of this world deceive you. Beauty is a mask that hides the ugliness beneath," Shiva said calmly, and then removed his mask to reveal a face that was stunningly handsome and youthful, with high, chiseled cheekbones, almond-shaped eyes, and golden skin.

"Under the beauty of the volcano is the rumbling anger of the earth. Under the beauty of the ocean is the relentless fury of its waves. And if you look past the beauty of the sky, you will discover the destructive forces of wind, rain, lightning, and thunder.

"Do not be tricked by my beauty, but look past it toward my tumultuous soul. This form is not mine; it is a temporary figure that I have adopted with the aid of a sacred spring of water so that I may not suffer in a body decrepit with age. For my mind has suffered enough, having borne witness to the tragic saga of the human race for millennia. Perhaps that is why I tend to break down into fits of tears after I indulge in laughter—I know that all joy is fleeting, and inevitably turns into sorrow. If you think this reaction is absurd, try living on this earth for as long as I have without being overcome by misery.

"Such a feat would be impossible for a human, even for a god. But those steel creatures who preside over your land and aspire to become gods themselves are more than capable of suppressing their emotions, if they have any to begin with. Perhaps they are more fit to sit on this throne than I am.

"A good ruler should remain objective and level-headed in times of chaos, pestilence, and war. But the best ruler is one who feels every sensation that is felt by his subjects, yet is capable of rising above the burden of his feelings. The best ruler feels the burning sting of suffering when his subjects are beset by famine and plague, and feels rapturous joy when they prosper in contentment. Alas, I can taste all of these bitter poisons, but I cannot release myself from the torment of sensation in order to rule with temerity and grace. That is why I laughed when you called me your majesty—I do not feel worthy of such a label.

"Whether it is my blessing or my curse, I am too much in tune with the moral landscape that underpins the universe. I feel all of the cruel absurdity of it—the collective greed, ignorance, lust, and ceaseless ego of the citizens of Khalendar—and these emotions course through me violently as though I were living the lives of those thousands of men and women. I also feel the pain of the earth, the relentless damage that the humans and their steel masters inflict upon the natural world. With each mine, dam, or oil well that is built for the purpose of harnessing and stifling nature, I feel my own soul being cut deeper and deeper, and the process is slowly turning me mad.

"A lightning rod separates my mind and my soul, for one is the enlightened repository for the wisdom of the ages, while the other feels the base vulgarity of humanity in all its blemished and unbridled ugliness. I use meditation and prayer, the wisdom of the mind, to heal the wound festering inside my dark soul, but I am afraid that soon I will not be able to keep the beast within me at bay. The tiger you see next to me is a mirror of my condition: a beautiful, pristine exterior concealing a terrifying impulse to destroy. Destruction is what I crave, after all— destruction of my inner darkness and that of humanity. The best cure for a malady is to destroy that which ails you. Of course, this task becomes more difficult when the calamity is inseparable from yourself, when in essence it has *become you.*

"I pity you, youth with such resilient spirits, clinging to the naïve belief that you can make the world a better place. Having spent almost an eternity on this planet, I can tell you that your blind faith in rescuing the world from its folly is childish at best. But you are not cursed to feel the suffering of others the same way that I am. You can easily escape from it and live out your days on this island in tranquil peace, forgetting about the moral chaos that bedevils the mainland. You can loosen your attachment to the orbit of karma that binds each man to his tragic earthly fate. To fight is to descend into madness. The vulgarity of battle will overtake you and wear down the fragile veneer of civilization which separates you from savagery. Instead, you can cast all of that foolishness aside and live here in utopian peace, training your mind to achieve *nirvana* through meditation and prayer."

When the shaman-god referred to the vulgarity of battle, Sekhmet began to snarl with anger. The tiger cast her gaze idly toward the jaguar and yawned.

After the shaman-god had finished speaking, Cyriana stepped forward boldly. "We were born to fight this battle. It is our destiny, and we cannot shirk from it," she proclaimed. "As much as it would be pleasant to elevate our minds to loftier thoughts and adopt the peaceful lifestyle of monks, we will not simply abandon our friends, our families, and our very identities. We must continue writing the great story that our ancestors began narrating long ago."

Shiva regarded the brave young princess with a mix of amusement and admiration. "Your ancestors... ah, I know all about their stories. Their stories are what sadden me the most. Human stories, you see, rarely have a happy ending.

"And even when they do, of course, what appears to be a happy ending is only the beginning of a tragic tale. I am giving you a rare and valuable opportunity to spend the rest of your days on this crater, to achieve something that only the noblest humans have ever been able to achieve. Do not take my offering lightly, young one," he chided. "You would rather partake in war, but brash courage will only lead you to peril."

He paused, appraising the girl with an intense focus. "I am impressed that you managed to foil Ishkode's plan to have you remain in Vei'arash permanently."

Cyriana narrowed her eyes with suspicion. "You knew about it... and yet you didn't try to stop him?" Her eyes flashed in anger.

Shiva let out a brittle laugh. "I wanted to see how things would unfold," he said. "Your desire to return to the mainland confounds me, though. Who wouldn't want to live in this serene haven? Look outside this house—you will see a vast community of people who are more than content with doing so."

The shaman-god's mild-mannered attitude only seemed to incite Cyriana's rage further.

"I am a princess hailing from the noble kingdom of Serrahan, one of the four famed kingdoms of the old Empire," Cyriana said, bristling with pride. "It is my royal duty to fight for my people and help my father realize his dream of restoring our kingdom to greatness. I will not waste a moment longer than I need to on this cursed island."

The shaman-god then became solemn, and stared at Cyriana with a cold expression that seemed to hold a terrible, ominous promise within it. Even Sekhmet was put off by his gaze, and the jaguar cowered in submission.

"You may have the lust for battle within you, my dear, but you are looking into the eyes of the oldest god on this planet, one who came into being long before the warrior goddess that inhabits the creature at your side. Sekhmet is only one of my children, and she is a powerful one, but she is not as strong as I am. One day, even she shall be destroyed at my hands, by my double-edged sword of blazing fire and iron."

Cyriana gasped, not daring to utter any words in response. Walter regarded the shaman-god in mute disbelief. *How can this young, handsome man of ordinary stature possibly be the father of the gods?*

"Who are you, really?" Tristan inquired, startling them all.

"Before I reveal who I am, I will tell you what I can see," Shiva replied cryptically. "Of course, telling you everything I can see would take a lifetime. And since you clearly have no patience for my stories, I will distill them into simple terms for you. Humans suffer from myopia; they are only alive to the reality that is visible within their narrow field of sight. Yet the truth is that there are many realities and many possibilities. There are also diverse methods of gaining insight into these possibilities—magic is one method, and can be a powerful one when aided by certain charms, stones, and plants. Dreams, a tool available to even the common folk, are another. Divinity is yet another. As a god endowed with the power of sight, the possibilities I am able to see are infinite, or nearly so. But some course strongly through my mind because of my wisdom, which attunes me to the fundamental nature of humanity and thereby shuts the door on most of the alternative possibilities.

"To explain it in even simpler terms, perhaps I should describe what I see as pathways rather than possibilities. My field of vision is like an enormous banyan tree, beginning from a single trunk but forking into dozens of unique branches. I see things that transpire only if other occurrences, which might seem trivial to the casual outside observer,

THE MOUNTAIN DWELLER

come to pass. A simple phenomenon—the butterfly effect—teaches us that small incidents create momentous changes.

"And one pathway that looms larger in my vision than all of the rest is that which leads to destruction, which is perhaps the biggest clue I can give you about who I am. I see, with vivid clarity, the destruction of humanity, the offspring of the great animal deities. To spare you from puzzling over this problem too deeply, I will set it out more plainly. The steel creatures you have foolishly ceded control to—they are intending to eventually leave the Earth, with all its wondrous beauty, since they do not cherish it the way you and I do. And if they successfully execute their mission and leave this planet for another one, then before they depart they will make sure to annihilate the human race, as part of their grand experiment." The shaman-god's eyes flickered over to Eva and he paused before resuming. "The steel creatures from all of the other planets in this universe will congregate on Eurydice, after destroying each of the civilizations that seeded them. Perhaps you have heard of the end of days—it is a central tenet of many religions and mythologies across the world. This will come to pass if the steel creatures leave; I have seen it with my third eye."

Walter swallowed, his mouth completely dry.

"Thank you for sharing your insights with us," Walter said in a humble voice, once it was clear that the shaman-god had finished his speech. "But that is why we are here—we believe that we can stop the AI Masters from carrying out their insidious plans. We believe can reverse the power imbalance between the AI Masters and their human servants, and restore the machines to their rightful place. Or we can persuade them to leave the Earth peacefully, without destroying humanity before they embark on their journey."

"Such ambitious plans," Shiva said with a knowing smile. His face was calm and dry of tears now, and his eyes glittered instead with a reflection of the turquoise pool.

"Yet you must know," the shaman-god warned. "Even if humanity is not eradicated by the AI Masters, it is still destined for destruction. This is its ultimate fate for many reasons, not least of which is the inherently corrupt and morally weak nature of humans. You strive for betterment, and even aspire to divinity, but you always regress to your basest form, tainted by greed and vice. Such is the rule of entropy, the principle by which the universe and all things within it move toward a state of disorder.

"And now seems to be a fitting time to explain who I am. For while I appear to you now in my benign form, *Sankara*, I have a far more terrible form. To the ancient cultures of the East, I was called a multitude of names—the supreme god, the great ascetic, the blue-throated one—but I was most commonly known as *Shiva*, the creator, destroyer, and transformer. I am the first among gods of this world, the creator of dance, and the consort of Parvati who appears to you now as a tiger. For centuries I have lived here at the top of Mount Samaya, but before then my home was another mountain across the seas, Mount Kailash. When the Old World was destroyed long ago, I knew that civilization would eventually flourish again, and so I settled here to be close to it and feel its pulse within my soul.

"I am a manifestation of consciousness, but only human consciousness, and that is why my sight has been hindered these past centuries while the AI Masters have assumed leadership in Khalendar. While I can see their plans on a superficial level, I can only use the humans as my eyes and ears to know the full extent of their intentions. My blind spots trouble me immensely. For as much as I think that humanity is weak and destined for destruction, I love it more than any creation in this universe. The human race is endowed with very special qualities, including courage, resilience, and foresight, and despite its flaws I cannot help but want it to thrive. My sight is powerful, but it is not perfect, which is why—despite my dire predictions—your species may have some hope yet."

Walter was transfixed. What Shiva was saying was beyond comprehension, and yet Walter intuitively sensed that the shaman-god was not deceiving them, and that every word he spoke was sincere. It was nearly impossible for Walter to find his voice to respond to Shiva, as the young man was so utterly shocked by what he had just heard. Eventually, he summoned the will to speak again.

"If you love humanity and genuinely want to save it, your efforts would be well-directed if you help us achieve our goal of reclaiming control over the AI Masters," Walter said.

"You certainly would benefit from the support of an ally," the shaman-god conceded, "but the ally you need most is not someone, but some*thing*. What I am speaking of is fearsome, unruly, and wild—just like the tiger at my side—but rest assured that it can be tamed. The process of domesticating it requires the darkest and most powerful magic of all, and even the most skilled Mages have not learned how to do it properly. Humans have some ability to master it, but the tools they use—memories and dreams—are brittle and prone to damage. The AIs, clever things, appreciated the power of these tools early on, but also recognized them as threats that needed to be eliminated. They wanted to exert absolute control over you, and how could they fully control you if you had these tools at your command?

"If you are willing to learn, then I am willing to teach you how to gain mastery over the essence of creation and destruction. Of course, your mastery can never be complete, but I wouldn't expect perfection from a mortal."

"The essence of creation and destruction... what, exactly, are you referring to?" Walter asked hesitantly, almost reluctant to hear the answer.

The voice that responded to Walter was far deeper and richer than Shiva's normal voice, and seemed to be emanating from a different being entirely.

I'm eternally young but very old
I'm always with you, truth be told
I've slain kings and levelled cities,
The destruction I cause is not pretty
But without me, what would you be?
You'd be nothing, don't you agree?

"Time," Walter whispered, suddenly understanding. "You are going to teach us to master *time*?"

The shaman-god laughed joyously, the sound rumbling up from his belly like a spring of water spilling out of a cavern. He then resumed speaking in his normal, less intimidating voice.

"One of my forms is Time, *Kala*, and another is Eternal Time, *Mahakala*, so who better to teach you how to master time than myself? One day perhaps you will master it so well that you will be able to travel through time, but that feat is typically reserved for the gods. In the short term, what you will be able to do—with my blessing—is to see future possibilities. It is a wonderful gift to be able to have clear and crisp memories, but that relates to time in the past. To see visions of the future, well that is an entirely different, and far more dangerous gift.

"Picture time as a giant funnel that shifts with you along a continuum every time you step forward. The continuum behind you is a single, straight line that consists of what previously occurred. History and memory blur this line by giving us multiple versions of the past—this is an especially thorny problem in societies where propaganda is rampant—and makes the past seem more like a funnel stretching in the opposite direction. The less humans know about a past era, the more fantastical the theories they devise to fill the gaps of their collective memory. But, despite what postmodernist theory might have you believe, there is only one set of past events. A god like myself sits in a bit of a privileged position when it comes to such matters, so I sympathize with humans who struggle with this concept.

"The same is not true, however, for future events. As much as I would like to, I simply cannot give you a singular vision of what will happen in the years to come. The world is in a perpetual state of chaos and flux—that is its baseline state. All matter in the universe was created out of intense chaos and violence: the collision of stars, the fusion of subatomic particles, the simmering heat produced by the primal explosion I created. And so, future time progresses through a course that is not straight and fixed, but could be more aptly described as a three-dimensional labyrinth inside of a funnel. There are millions of different pathways to reach the ultimate destination, and each of these pathways proliferate exponentially the farther away you get from the present moment. Of course, being a god myself, I can predict with some degree of certainty which pathways will not be tread upon. Yet I cannot possibly know *everything*. If I bestow this gift upon you, you must treasure it and use it with caution and a sense of grave responsibility. If you are not ready to assume this responsibility, then you are not ready to accept my gift.

"Every power has a light side and a dark side. You will be able to accomplish great and wondrous things with the gift I am about to give you, but in exchange you must pay a price. You may see things that fill you with horror—things so terrible that they cannot be unseen. The death of your loved ones, for instance. Your own death. The annihilation of life on Earth... this you are bound to see, for this is one of the key pathways. When you plunge into the darkness, you will doubt the meaning of your existence, you will confront the ugliness of your soul, and you will descend into sheer psychological terror. But always keep in mind that you are doing this in pursuit of a greater good.

"All of you have unique strengths and capabilities, and you each have an important role to play in the journey ahead. Yet only one of you is destined for this gift.

"Walter, you may think you are an ordinary young man, but nothing could be farther from the truth. I have been watching over you from Mount Samaya, and I have come to realize that you are blessed with an uncanny ability which other mortals lack. It is why you are so skilled with languages, and you can understand the essence of highly complex systems in the blink of an eye. You can create these systems, too, by masterfully programming machines that the mortals call computers. Like me, your talent is for creation, but the creation of machines rather than mortals. You are even better at this task than the machines themselves, for the fundamental spark of humanity thrives within you, while there is no comparable spark within them. They have superior powers of comprehension, calculation, and even prediction, but they lack the capacity to design a better future. This is why you must reprogram the AI Masters, so that this better future can come to fruition. You will no longer be carrying out their orders like you did for so many years in Crystal City; instead, you will be rewriting the rules of their game.

"If this plan succeeds, there will be a silent revolution which sets the world upon a virtuous path. I recognize that I am giving you the powers of a god, but I know that you have the maturity and wisdom to use your powers for good ends. Of course, entrusting one individual with the ability to see future possibilities is dangerous, and carries inevitable risk. But my love for humans is so great, I am willing to take that risk."

"Stop!" Cyriana shouted, her face flushed with rage. "My jaguar is hungry for battle. You don't seem to grasp the simple concept that war is inevitable. As you said, the world was created in violence. It has to be recreated in the same way."

The shaman-god gave her a disapproving look, but then the corners of his mouth curved upwards. "While I have no doubt that your companion yearns for the taste of blood, a physical battle will only lead to an escalation of conflict, which is a dangerous path. Perhaps a battle must be fought, but not in the ordinary manner. Humans, you see, are always seeking out combat with a clearly defined enemy. This inclination has been hardwired into them since ancient times, when as hunter-gatherers they emerged from their caves to tussle with panthers and mountain lions. This black-and-white view of the world is only helpful when there are simple battle lines and obvious demarcations between good and evil.

"This time, however, the battle lines are far less apparent. The AI Masters may appear to be your enemies at first glance, but this simplistic view is deceptive. If the AI Masters are the enemies, then so too are the humans who elevated them to a position of power, and the ones who now follow their dictates. Many of Khalendar's citizens blindly adhere to their propaganda, and many would gladly fight alongside them, if only to preserve the efficient system which fuels their perpetual greed. Are you willing to kill all of them, too, if they join the AI Masters in battle? They may be good-hearted people, but they have been brainwashed by machines that are so sophisticated they evade comprehension by humans, and even gods. Humanity must instead solve the problem the same way it started: in a sterile laboratory, with a single line of code. Technology must once again be directed to helping the human race, instead of enslaving it. Only then can you live in harmony with machines, magic, and each other.

"The animal companions at your sides still have a vital role to play in your mission—you have my blessing to bring them with you to the mainland. The AIs have long asserted control over your minds: the substance of your everyday thoughts, your memories, and your desires. The war that must be waged against this insidious operation is a war of the mind, not the body. While AI Masters may seem to have impermeable fortresses of minds, history has proven that they are not immune from psychological disruption. You may recall the stories of the Shadow Wars between the southern kingdoms and the AI Masters. The sight of the animal spirits summoned by the clansmen of these kingdoms terrified the AI Masters, who felt powerless at their inability to subjugate them like the humans. The shamans who knew the summoning spells were banished to this island—my beloved servant Caleb and several others living on this volcano are direct descendants of those wise folk.

"Now, it would be quite fitting for you to use the very same weapons that your ancestors wielded in those ancient battles against the AI Masters. It would complete a circle that your wise forefathers began to draw generations ago. And where they failed, you must succeed; the future of both humans and Mages depends on it.

"This psychological battle is only half of the work that must be done, though. It will serve only to plant the seeds of chaos, confusion, and doubt in the minds of the AI Masters, so that Walter may carry out the second stage of the plan. All of you must create the vital conditions for him to seize the fleeting opportunity to covertly enter the fortress of the *Anax*. Once he is inside the belly of the dragon, so to speak, Walter can have free rein to create the most important computer program of them all: the one that will shape the future."

The shaman-god turned to face Walter and looked into his eyes with an intensity that made the young man shiver. "Playing god can be a dangerous thing, but if there is anyone I trust to do it, it is you, Walter. You are good-hearted and brave. Yet I fear that your human foibles may get in the way of your mission. Do not let them, even though it may be the hardest thing you've ever done. Rise above your weaknesses, your seizures, and your self-doubt. Hold on tightly to your most precious gifts and discard the burdensome weight of that which does not serve you. Your loved ones are important, but they are not the most important thing. The most important thing is to see that there is no light without darkness, and no darkness without light. I may be talking in riddles to you here and now, but one day you will come to understand the meaning of my words.

"Before I take leave of you, I have one last piece of advice. Perhaps I am biased, but I believe that the human mind—weak and brittle though it may be—is more deserving of protection than any artificial mind. That is why you must protect yours at all costs, and become a virus that will infiltrate theirs."

While Shiva's words had given some measure of organization to the chaotic web of thoughts inside of him, Walter was still brimming with questions. As the shaman-god stood up and began walking toward a door behind his throne, the rebel leader felt a tightness in his chest, a fear he would never set eyes on Shiva again.

"Where will *you* be while all of this is happening?" Walter suddenly blurted out, hoping that Shiva would stay for a while longer. "And when will you teach me to master time?"

Shiva pulled the wooden mask back over his face, and Walter began to breathe faster with anxiety.

"Caleb will give you a Talisman," the shaman-god said, glancing over at the tiger, who let out a prideful yawn. "You must wear it whenever you seek to learn the secrets of time, and to see the visions which will guide the next steps in your journey. Wearing it will give you a strong connection to me, to this island, and to your totem animal, and it will infuse you with a sense of joy and magnanimity. The Talisman will also enable you to connect more deeply to those who are lost to this Earth. Try not to wear it too often, though; over-use will drain your energy and deplete your psychological strength. As with everything in life, a balance must be struck between giving and receiving. You will become a glutton and an addict if you receive too much of the Talisman's power, so use it in careful moderation. You must honor the spirit realm, too, through prayer and good deeds.

"Wearing this Talisman will work on you like consuming a thousand *yagé* leaves all at once—it will be painfully intense at first, but your body will quickly acclimate to the sensation. Do not forget reality and the present moment; such forgetfulness can be dangerous, for the real world desperately needs you. If you are not careful, you might lose yourself in the land of visions.

"Finally, protect the Talisman from the greedy and the vengeful, from pilferers and thieves, and from those who wish to misuse it. You must protect it from all, even from your friends standing in this room today who are witnesses to my words. For a kind-hearted soul can become corrupt once faced with the tantalizing prospect of controlling everything and playing god. Do not allow it to be used in such a wicked way. The Talisman can be used for evil ends, and I cannot prevent that from happening, for once I give it away I can no longer control how it is used. And once *you* give it away, it cannot be returned to you. When you feel ready to pass it on to someone—and you will know when the time comes—pass it on to your daughter. I will say nothing more about your child, for you can see her for yourself with the Talisman."

When Shiva mentioned his daughter, Walter became puzzled. *Does he mean the child that Namid will bear in Anatari, or someone else?* "Wait," Walter said, feeling a surge of boldness within him. "Why should I pass the gift on to my daughter?"

"If you foolishly decide to keep it for yourself," Shiva replied, "you will become effectively blind, and you will lose access to its powers and blessings. There is no turning back once that occurs. I will try to protect you from danger, but you must serve me well in exchange."

Walter frowned, sifting through Shiva's words in his mind. "So, that is the price that I must pay for receiving the Talisman—I must agree to pass it on to my future daughter? What if she refuses to accept it?"

"You must disregard her wishes, then," the shaman-god replied. "My gift of the Talisman will create a pact between us, and the breaking of this pact will lead to terrible things.

"Now, I can tell you nothing more. I have exhausted myself with speaking and I must rest. Do not miss me when I leave, for I am forever within you."

With that, Shiva took his leave of the spellbound rebels, exiting out of the doorway behind his throne. Walter had not noticed before, but now he saw that the same scenes that were engraved onto the large bronze door at the entrance to the shaman-god's home were also painted onto this doorway.

When the door shut behind the shaman-god, Caleb approached Walter and removed a small brown pouch from the pocket of his vibrant orange robes. Walter remained kneeling on the ground, and he suddenly felt a wave of emotion, the sense that his life was about to change. The room fell completely silent, and it seemed as though even the butterflies froze in midair.

Caleb removed from the pouch a jade necklace, striking in its beauty and simplicity, upon which was carved the symbol of a labyrinthine maze. The necklace shone with a hidden energy as the servant held it out for Walter to see.

"Behold, the Jade Talisman, Keeper of Knowledge, Seer of Fates, Master of Time," Caleb whispered softly.

Walter drew in breath sharply, mesmerized by the necklace. A few of the Mages stepped closer, eager to take a look, but stopped when Caleb held out his arm as a warning for them to stay back. Suddenly, the servant began to speak.

"Walter, you are the great-great-grandson of Riordan, the leader of the rebel clan that was exiled to the isle of Vei'arash as punishment for resisting the AI Masters during the Grand Revolution. Your ancestors were brilliant and admired by many; they were so well-respected that the AI Masters spared their lives. When the AI Masters felt strong enough to no longer be threatened by them, your predecessors were granted clemency and safe passage back to the mainland, on the condition that they would help to build the Empire of Khalendar. Your ancestors then integrated into the Empire, becoming wealthy businessmen and civil servants, lured by the AI Masters' promises of limitless wealth and power. Along the way, they forgot that they had once been rebels. You are the only one of them who awoke from the dream, who looked past the shroud of deception to what *is*, and who will one day decide what *should be*."

A tear slid down Walter's cheek. "My ancestors... they lived in Vei'arash? Is that why I feel so connected to this island, and to the stag?"

"The stag is a part of you, Walter, just as you are a part of him," Caleb replied. "The memories of your ancestors are encoded in your DNA, which is why you feel a bond to this place and to him. The stag was the most treasured companion of Riordan and his son Julian. Sadly, Julian had to leave his beloved friend behind when he returned to the mainland, and on that day a part of him disappeared. You, too, must leave the stag behind... but one day you shall reunite with him, when you are ready.

"With the blessing of the five-faced Lord of Parvati, I give the Talisman unto you. I pray that you shall use it wisely, and that it shall not fall into the wrong hands."

The servant Caleb then placed the Talisman around Walter's neck. As the Jade Talisman pressed against his chest and thrummed with an unseen power, Walter felt a rush of blood to his head and suddenly the world went black. A seizure then overcame him, and it felt stronger and more intense than any he had experienced before. The other rebels backed away from Walter in fear, but Elaine ran over to his side.

"Take it off of him! Can't you see it is hurting him?" she screamed. The servant waved his hand, causing a blast of wind to strike Elaine forcefully and send her tumbling backwards. Sekhmet snarled and the Mages snapped to attention, poised to cast spells in response.

Yet before the conflict escalated any further, Walter became still as suddenly as he had fallen into his dramatic seizure. An ecstatic smile passed over his features; it was like he had seen a heavenly realm, the realm of *nirvana*.

"Fear not, my friends, for now I am protected by the Lord Shiva."

PART II:
THE SYMPHONY

The Song of the Talisman

"Looking up gives light, although at first it makes you dizzy."
– Rumi

As he left the shaman-god's home, Walter felt reborn, exhilarated by a newfound sense of joy and purpose. Wearing the Jade Talisman raised his heartrate and made the world around him appear crisp and vibrant, as if he were seeing it for the first time. Walter reveled in the sensation, and several of his friends complimented him on his glowing complexion.

"You look so happy and calm," Elaine told him as they walked outside into the blinding sunlight. "But remember what Shiva told you... do not use the Talisman too much or it will deplete your energy."

Walter grinned at her overprotectiveness. "You are far more worried about me than my own mother ever was. 'Do not use the Talisman too much.' I have only just put it on. I wish you could feel what I am feeling, Elaine—pure, childlike wonder at being alive. Life is no longer a painful struggle, now that I have this sacred necklace."

Elaine allowed herself to indulge in a brief smile, but then her expression grew solemn. "Just be careful with it, that's all I'm saying."

"For the time being, at least, we have more pressing concerns," Walter said as he caught sight of dark thunderclouds moving in rapidly from the ocean toward the mountain. "Like where we will be sleeping tonight."

As if on cue, Caleb approached Walter and the rebels. "I trust you have enjoyed your visit with Shiva," he said, "and now you are keen to carry on your journey. I must caution you, however, that the weather is too rough for you to descend Mount Samaya at this time. Those clouds will burst in a matter of hours, and if you leave now you will be caught in a deluge of rain that will make the descent treacherous. You must stay here tonight; the storm will not affect anyone above the cloud-line.

"Unfortunately," Caleb continued, "the Lord Shiva cannot lodge you in his home. He is too mentally fragile at this time to serve as a host. What's more, his wife Parvati is very fond of torturing visitors and causing them intense distress and anxiety. But my wife, Veena, would be more than willing to welcome your band of rebels into our home. We have spacious lodgings not too far from here."

Walter was impatient to carry on with their journey, but after taking another glance at the ominous storm clouds that were quickly approaching the dormant volcano, he decided to accept Caleb's offer.

"Thank you, Caleb. We are grateful for your generous hospitality."

"My pleasure, Asin. Now, if you don't mind, please follow me."

Caleb led the rebels to a narrow staircase carved into the northern wall of the crater, and as they descended Walter noticed with awe how much larger the crater was than it had first seemed. The closer they travelled to the crater's center, the more intense the wind became. The terrain here was rough and the climate was equally hostile. The rebels were, for the most part, well-equipped for harsh weather, but the crater's bleak environment soon became overwhelming.

"Caleb, why is it so windy here? Is this how it normally is?" Walter asked the servant. Despite the buffeting winds, the air was very oxygen-poor, rendering it difficult to engage in any sort of physical activity. The dusty air was thick and nearly blinding. To avoid swallowing dust particles it was necessary to take in only small gulps of air, which made breathing a challenging exercise. Walter noticed with dismay that Elaine's eyes were red from the dust, and his own eyes stung painfully— even his glasses did not fully shield them from the invasive specks. *Perhaps we should have taken our chances with the rainstorm*, he thought. He pressed onwards with determination, trying as best he could to cast aside his discomfort.

"It is not a pleasant environment," Caleb explained, "but we must make do with what we have, for such is our burden as mortals. Unlike Shiva, many of us crater-dwellers do not live long. Because of the low oxygen levels up here, sometimes our lungs collapse before we can reach a ripe old age. Yet we love our lives, and the mentorship and wisdom we perpetually receive from the blue-throated one. Be thankful that you are not inside of *that*," he said, pointing toward heavy rainclouds illuminated by streaks of lighting, which could be spotted in the distance, just below the summit of Mount Samaya. Finally, after what seemed like ages of trudging through the inhospitable crater, the rebels finally arrived at Caleb's dwelling place. Walter was amazed by the stark poverty of the people who lived in the modest but resilient community; only the thin walls of canvas tents separated them from the driving winds and choking dust of the barren crater. But when he saw them up close, Walter noticed that many of the crater-dwellers were smiling in contentment, apparently satisfied with their humble lives despite the harshness of their environment.

Caleb's wife Veena was a tall, thin woman with short brown hair and piercing green eyes. When the rebels arrived at her tent, which was far larger than most others on the crater, she greeted them warmly.

"Welcome to our humble abode," she said. She then disappeared for a few moments, and returned with a tray carrying cups of steaming, fragrant tea concocted from nettle and wild roses. Walter and the other rebels drank the beverage gratefully, as they were exhausted and shivering cold after their foray into the blustery heart of the crater.

The woman then served the rebels a meal, which was surprisingly hearty despite the barrenness of their surroundings. The food was delicious but modest: goat stewed in a rich broth made of various edible plants that had been harvested from the mountain. When Tristan questioned Veena about the soup's ingredients, she explained that it was a mélange of roseroot, nodding onion, and yarrow. The Mages were fascinated by the vast collection of alpine flowers in the woman's kitchen, and they chattered excitedly about the diverse plant species and their medicinal properties.

Although he had enjoyed the meal, afterwards Walter was feeling rather dizzy. He did not know whether his malaise arose from the oxygen-depleted climate of the crater or the strange combination of flowers he had just consumed. Walter excused himself from the table, and Veena rose from her seat to lead him to his sleeping quarters.

"We don't normally have guests over," she told Walter, smiling. "So I am delighted to see all of you today. You look pale—it might be the yarrow, which occasionally induces sweating. All of the plants I cook with have a healing effect on the body, although their effect might not be apparent at first. Forgive the modesty of your bed, I was not expecting visitors, so this will have to do." Her eyes then fell upon the Talisman around Walter's neck, and her expression became wary and fearful. "Is this a gift from the blue-throated one? He is a very generous god, and he has been very kind to my husband and our family over the years. But I fear he may be losing his sanity. My husband has to put up with the tantrums on a daily basis and it is driving him mad as well. Do not tell him that I told you that," she said apprehensively. "I must take leave of you now."

"Thank you, Veena, you are very kind," Walter said, before bidding her goodnight. He settled into the modest wood-frame bed, and then tried to calm his mind while the wind whistled and buffeted the walls of the tent. He deliberately kept the Talisman on, as it gave him a feeling of comfort, like he was not alone. As he was about to doze off, Walter suddenly heard the sound of a woman laughing softly, and he realized someone was in the room with him.

"Who's there? Veena, is that you?" Walter asked, groping around in his rucksack for a match so he could light a candle on his bedside table. He had already taken his glasses off, and he could barely see anything even after he had lit the candle, but when he reached over to pick them up he recoiled at the sight of a hand. It was not Veena's; when he traced his line of sight up along the arm and saw the bracelets and chips embedded in the dark, bronze-hued skin, he knew at once who it belonged to. Emilia. She stood calmly near the entrance of Walter's room, her body glowing with an ethereal light.

"Hush, do not be afraid," the spirit of Emilia said to him softly. "It was a miracle you managed to see me before on the *Jade Queen*. Because you now have *that*," she said, pointing toward the Talisman on his chest, "you will see me more often. Walter, when I was still alive I told you Vei'arash was a place of death and destruction, inhabited by evil and corrupt shamans. I was so naïve to think that—duped by the absurd propaganda of the AI Masters. Now that I am a spirit, I can see the truth far clearer. Shiva is truly enlightened. Just look at how he has inspired the dissidents from Khalendar to live out their lives in devotion to the egoless realm, *Sensaye*. He has a dark side to him of course, but his shadows only serve to reveal the brilliance of his light side. His passion for creation and renewal is greater than his appetite for destruction. Don't believe anyone who tells you otherwise."

The sight of Emilia's apparition gave Walter goosebumps and he rubbed his eyes, still not fully believing what he was seeing.

"How—how are you here?" he stuttered, putting his glasses on to see the phantom more clearly.

"Do not ask how, ask *why*," she said, her mouth curving upwards into a smile. "The laws of physics no longer apply to me, so you cannot hope to understand the mechanics of my presence here. I am here to help you make sense of what *you* see, and to soothe your mind when it becomes troubled by the visions. The first thing you should know is that the visions are not real. But they project a reality that will seem so real to you that when you wake up you will react to it as if it were. The visions will provoke a wide range of emotions—happiness, sadness, fear, anger—but you will not truly *feel* them until after the vision is complete. When you exit a vision—you can call it "waking up," if you like—you will experience a memory of your vision that will trigger all the emotions that did not manifest during the vision itself. However, you must do your best to cast those emotions aside. Focus on what happened and try to rationalize it, rather than allowing yourself to be overwhelmed by feeling. Otherwise, your judgment can become clouded, and that may lead to dire consequences. All of this might seem too abstract for you to understand right now, but it will become clear soon enough.

"The Talisman has a song, a rhythm, a poetry, that will make your visions an art form unto themselves. The Talisman will tell you a story: the story of time, as it *could possibly* unfold, through each winding branch in the great tree of life. Its song is crafted after the song of the Earth, the song of the seasons. Its story will begin in the season of stagnant heat and driving passion, blazing sun and barren deserts. *Summer.*"

Summer

"I must get my soul back from you; I am killing my flesh without it."
– Sylvia Plath

A s soon as Emilia finished speaking she vanished from sight, leaving Walter alone in the dark, silent room. He was terrified, both of what he had just witnessed and of the Talisman, which was now beginning to emit a soft light. The light was radiating outwards from the etching of the labyrinth imprinted on the stone's smooth surface. With each passing moment, Walter became increasingly drowsy, and he felt as though a strong current was dragging him beneath the surface of the ocean. He struggled against the phenomenon, but the act of struggling caused Walter's muscles to tense in anticipation of a seizure, and so he surrendered and allowed himself to be swept underwater.

A wave of electricity then pulsed through his body and the world suddenly dissolved from sight, becoming completely black. In Walter's mind, the sensation was similar to what a space traveler must feel when falling through an event horizon into a black hole. The pressure was overwhelming, but there was no climax of searing pain. After a few moments of numb paralysis and of repeated, futile attempts to move his body, he returned to a state of quasi-consciousness. What followed was the surreal process of coming to realize that Walter was undergoing one of the strangest experiences of all: he had become a passive observer in a vision of his future life.

Walter hovered inside a room, feeling weightless—an ethereal, formless substance severed from all bodily function, need, or desire. The sensation was liberating, but also vertiginous; Walter felt that at any moment, he could free-fall into the subterranean caverns of the Earth and end up trapped inside the hot furnace of the planet's core. But he was not plagued by fear any longer. He did not know whether he was alive, or whether he was in danger. He simply witnessed what unfolded before him.

Because he had migrated outside of the realm of mortals, Walter felt unperturbed when a future version of himself entered the room. The man shuffled around lazily in a house-robe and slippers, his stomach protruding generously from the top of his trousers and his fleshy arms slack at his sides. Were it not for various subtle clues, the hovering spirit would have no way of knowing that it was looking at an older incarnation of his own bodily form. Among other things, the man's eyes revealed his identity—Walter had exactly the same watery grey eyes, and the same expressive arched eyebrows.

The older Walter appeared to be a wealthy man, given the opulence of his surroundings, although his casual attire made it difficult to confirm his status or occupation. He certainly had all of the amenities he needed in his luxurious abode, which was far more grandiose than most buildings Walter had ever come across in Crystal City. Cashmere throws wreathed the haute leather couches in the living room; plush pillows adorned the divan in the front entrance; stunning pieces of abstract artwork decorated nearly every wall; and an elaborate chandelier made of tiny crystals hung over the stately mahogany living room table. In short, the apartment was palatial—the type of luxury accommodation that only a wealthy head of state or corporate executive would have the means to inhabit.

Before the hovering spirit of Walter had the chance to fully digest every detail of the scene, the doorbell suddenly rang. The older Walter did not seem to be perturbed by the sound, nor in any hurry to answer the door. Instead, he headed into the kitchen to help himself to a handful of black olives before shuffling toward the front entrance slowly. When he opened the door, a red-haired woman stepped inside. Without understanding why or how, the spirit could sense that she was an older version of Elaine.

The woman had a world-weary expression on her face, and she barely acknowledged the older Walter when she entered the apartment. She looked as though she had been travelling for days, and she immediately made her way toward the living room. Kicking off her worn leather boots, the woman slumped onto the couch in exhaustion. The older Walter sat down on the end of the couch and patted his guest's ankle in an affectionate but distant manner.

"How are they?" the older Walter asked while he chewed the olives. He spoke in the brisk, condescending tone of Crystal City's highest elites.

"Surviving," the woman said in a barely audible whisper, her face creased with anxiety.

"They'd better be surviving—I'm paying them a six-thousand-*cestae*-per-month stipend," the older Walter said. He began consuming the remaining olives at a more rapid pace. "They're living in far more luxury than other people in their *circumstances*."

"As if you need to remind me how much you are paying, Walter," Elaine said cynically. Her eyes were blank and expressionless, and when they flickered toward the man they reflected no spark of interest or emotion.

The man's chest heaved in an exaggerated sigh, as though what she had just said had been an affront to his dignity. With some difficulty, he managed to push himself off of the couch, distancing himself from the woman.

"All I'm saying, darling, is that I don't appreciate *ingrates*. With all the money I'm giving them, they ought to be more than just surviving—they ought to be thriving. They're already wards of the state, so they've gotten a free ride regardless, but my generosity has given them the lifestyle of their dreams."

"I can't go over this with you again," Elaine replied. "I don't have the energy for it. You know how I feel—there was no 'free ride' from the state. They were displaced from their ancestral homeland to make way for an atrocious diamond mine, and then they were herded into substandard social housing in the middle of nowhere. They can't even hunt or fish for their own food like they used to, so do you really expect them to praise your *boundless generosity*?"

"They're just drinking at the trough of capitalism," the man said, spitting into an ashtray before wiping sweat from his brow. "That atrocious diamond mine is keeping their lights on. Without the mine, they would have nowhere to live, not even that substandard housing you speak of so disdainfully."

"How dare you," she said. Her eyes narrowed with anger, although the fire in her eyes was soon gone. "One of these days I'll leave you and go back to taking care of Khalendi children. You used to be so different, before you sold out to those stupid robots."

"Nothing's stopping you from leaving me now," the older Walter said, with a laugh that was far from pleasant. "I certainly don't value you for companionship, and the one asset I find remotely appealing is quickly degenerating, just like your wit. I'm surprised I haven't left you for my secretary yet. Samantha? Sarah? I can't even remember her name, the stupid broad."

At that comment, something seemed to snap inside of the older Elaine, and a wave of resentment passed over her features. "You've crossed the line," she said curtly as she got up from the couch and began to walk away from the man.

"I'm sorry—I suppose I shouldn't have said that. I love you, of course, I didn't mean that I fancy that empty-headed secretary. You know I love you, darling, else why would I have kept you around all these years?" he said with a lopsided smile. The woman did not appear convinced.

"I—I have to go to the washroom," she said softly.

"Give us a kiss first, darling," the older Walter said. He finished the last olive before washing it down with a glass of bourbon.

The woman breathed a sigh, as though she were steeling herself for something she did not wish to do, and then she stepped toward the man. She looked like she was about to hit him, but instead she leaned forward, giving him a reluctant kiss despite the tension between them.

"Now I recall why I've missed you dearly," he said with a childish giggle. "Come join me in the bedroom once you are finished, love."

"I'll join you, my love," she said with a smile that did not match her dull eyes.

The man laughed gleefully, like a child set free in a candy store, and his shuffling pace quickened as he walked toward the bedroom. The hovering spirit followed Elaine, who picked up a briefcase she had set down in the front entrance, bringing it into the bathroom with her. The briefcase appeared to be a safe of some kind, since the woman had to enter a passcode in order to access its contents. Once she had inputted a complex sequence of numbers, the case snapped open to reveal what appeared to be a revolver, spare bullets, a grenade, and a vial containing black liquid. The woman sighed and wiped away a tear as she pressed the release on the revolver's cylinder, and then loaded a round into each of its chambers. Once the gun was loaded, Elaine shut the briefcase firmly and locked it, placing it carefully behind the toilet so that it was out of sight.

The woman then exited the bathroom, carrying the revolver behind her and pressing it up against the curve of her lower back. She walked down the hallway slowly and opened the door at the end to reveal an elegant bedroom with a four-poster bed, decadent Persian rugs, and various portraits of beautiful women on the surrounding walls. The man was sprawled out idly on the bed, staring at her with a lustful expression. "What are you hiding behind your back, darling?" he asked.

"It's a surprise, my love," the older Elaine said as she approached him slowly. "Close your eyes. You don't want to spoil it."

"It'd better be a good surprise," he said. The man shut his eyes, blissfully unaware.

"Oh, it's an excellent surprise, that's for sure."

Walter's hovering spirit saw a wave of energy ripple outwards from the revolver as Elaine fired it. The woman's aim was flawless, and the shot was clean—a single bullet through his forehead and the older Walter died instantly without pain or even awareness what had transpired. In death he looked absurd, his mouth still curving upwards in a foolish grin as he lay still, dark red blood gradually pooling out of his head onto the white silk sheets beneath him.

"It's a shame to waste such beautiful sheets," the woman said to herself, "but a perfect opportunity could not be wasted either."

After taking one last, wistful glance at the older Walter's body, Elaine made her way toward a room which appeared to be a study containing bookshelves, a desk, and a laptop. Elaine logged on to the computer and then into the bank account of the man she had killed, transferring all of the remaining funds to another account. Apparently satisfied with what she had done, she logged off after wiping her cyber-history clean. On her way out of the apartment, she passed by a framed photograph of herself and Walter when they were younger, sitting together in a field of pumpkins. Walter was much thinner, wore glasses, and had a serious expression on his face. Elaine's arm was flung casually around Walter, and she looked much happier than her older self. As the older Elaine studied the image, her lower lip began to tremble and she briskly wiped away a tear. She then picked up the photograph and placed it carefully inside of her briefcase before exiting the apartment.

In the lobby of the apartment building, Elaine deliberately avoided eye contact with the concierge, who smiled and nodded at her as she passed him by. The hovering spirit of Walter exited the building with her. It was a clear but crisp autumn day; the wind was gusty, and the trees lining the streets were ripe with leaves the color of burnished copper. Elaine drew her coat tightly around her body, shivering as she stepped outside.

The woman now began walking quickly, each of her movements infused with purpose. After a few blocks, Elaine arrived at a train station that was crowded and bustling with people going about their daily business. When the hovering spirit observed the throng of people more carefully, he could see that it was comprised primarily of humans, but also included many mixed-race peoples, who had actuators and elastic nanotubes embedded onto their arms, legs, and faces. It soon became apparent that there were robots everywhere, scattered throughout the masses like clues buried in a puzzle. Most of the guards and officers at the train station were uniformed AI Fighters, and there were a few higher-ranked AI Masters. The Masters could be distinguished from the Fighters by their sleeker, more sophisticated humanoid bodies and red badges emblazoned with white diamonds: the official symbol of Crystal City.

The train station itself was a large public square surrounded by screens projecting lists of dozens of cities and villages in Khalendar and beyond, along with the arrival and departure times of the trains. The hovering spirit noticed that each screen appeared to be devoted to a particular region, and that Elaine was perusing a list related to the region "Barrens Reserve IV." Elaine appeared to have found the platform for her train and hastily walked toward it, keeping her head lowered but her eyes alert. She glanced around nervously, deliberately avoiding clusters of AI guards and trying to blend in amongst the crowd as much as she could.

When Elaine arrived at the correct platform, she impatiently checked an old-fashioned golden watch she kept in her coat pocket. There were a few other people scattered around her, but the general sparseness of the crowd suggested that she had arrived early. After what seemed like an agonizingly long wait, a silver bullet train finally appeared in the distance, snaking its way rapidly toward the platform. The hovering spirit saw that Elaine was now more than mildly anxious; her brow was sweating profusely, and she was shifting back and forth on her feet in impatience. The crowd had grown substantially by this point, and everyone jostled each other as they lined up along the train tracks. The spirit saw Elaine's eyes widen as she spotted, through a clearing in the dense multitude, blue-vested AI Fighters arriving at the station: *Crystal Militsiya*. These heavily armed cyborg cops were equipped with state-of-the-art facial recognition software and were hard-wired to detect criminals based on their appearance. When a bystander witnessed a crime, or suspected that one had occurred, they would report a description of the suspect's appearance to an employee at the central police station, who would input the description into a database and send out a unit of these trackers to hunt down the criminal. The hovering spirit of Walter understood this intuitively, without knowing why.

The cyborg cops stopped momentarily at the entrance to the station to converse with the guards selling train tickets. One of the guards pointed in Elaine's direction and the police followed his lead, marching briskly toward the platform where Elaine was standing. Fortunately for her, by now the crowd was very thick, and Elaine could conceal herself behind the wall of people standing in front of her. The train then suddenly arrived, blocking her completely from the *Militsiya*'s line of sight. Trembling, Elaine stepped impatiently onto the train, nearly knocking over a young child in front of her. The young girl's mother began to chastise Elaine, calling her a "*kayensta,*" the Khalendi word for rude whore. Elaine did not turn around to acknowledge the woman, and upon entering the train, she immediately made her way toward the washroom and locked herself inside.

The hovering spirit followed her, effortlessly floating through the walls of the locked washroom. Elaine glanced in the mirror at her own exhausted face—the dark under-eye circles, the grey hairs, and the wrinkles on her forehead and around her mouth. She heaved a long, unsteady sigh as she opened her briefcase and carefully removed a black bag containing a brunette wig, a fake adhesive nose, and an elastic band. After tying up her long red hair with the band, she covered her head with the wig and meticulously tucked any stray hairs underneath it. She then removed another pouch from the briefcase which contained foundation, lipstick, blush, and eyeliner. Acting quickly, with trembling hands she placed the adhesive nose over her own and began applying the makeup onto her face, covering up the puffy bags under her eyes and bringing warmth and vibrancy to her pale cheeks and lips. When she was finished, she looked like a different person entirely, younger and prettier than the exhausted woman who had entered the bathroom.

When she left the washroom, Elaine tried to appear casual as she walked down the aisle to find an unoccupied seat. After a painful few minutes of searching, she finally spotted one next to a sleeping elderly man who was snoring quietly. As she settled in and tucked her briefcase under the seat in front of her, she could hear a man's voice projecting over the loudspeakers: "Alert, alert: criminal spotted at *Vennyest* train station. Remain calm and seated while the train is searched for the suspect."

Elaine breathed in and out slowly, trying to concentrate on the vibrant fall colors outside, but it was clear she could not suppress her anxiety. Her gaze could not focus itself, but flitted in all directions as if she were searching for someone—or perhaps *something*—to rescue her from the terrible quandary she had found herself in. She whipped out a fashion magazine from the seat pocket in front of her and distractedly flipped through its pages, trying her best to appear interested in its contents.

After several excruciating minutes had passed, two *Militsiya* finally approached her. They looked unsettlingly like bloodhounds from hell; their noses were curved like the snouts of Cerberus, and their eyes were dark red orbs.

The *Militsiya* ignored the snoring old man and immediately zeroed in on Elaine. They spoke slowly and quietly, exchanging notes with each other as they appraised the woman. One of the cops took a photograph of her face with a tablet he was carrying, and then pressed a button, passing the device to his friend. The hovering spirit peered over their shoulders to watch the tablet's screen; the cyborgs were using a program to analyze Elaine's new, made-up face. The program then flashed a picture of the target suspect in the upper righthand corner—Elaine's old, haggard-looking face. The two women could perhaps be cousins, but they were dissimilar in many ways.

"Her age is computed at early to mid-thirties... younger than target suspect. Brunette, not red-haired. Different nose. Eyes and face structure are similar. Shall we bring her in for questioning?"

"Where are you from, ma'am?" the second *Militsiya* officer asked her in a low, mechanical voice.

"Sorry? Oh, I'm from Crystal City, born and raised."

"Is that so? You're on a train to Barrens Reserve I, *Kheye* district. You know that's one of the roughest segregated slums in the western Barrens, right? Not exactly a tourist destination."

"Tourist?" she laughed nonchalantly. "I'm no tourist, sir, I'm a student."

"Bit too old to be a student, not to be disrespectful, ma'am."

"Sorry, a mature student, I should have said. I'm completing my doctorate degree in social sciences at the University of West Khalendar, and it requires me to analyze the living conditions of the impoverished folk living down in the Barrens. My thesis involves studying whether policies that segregate Xeyan'na in fortified districts enhance their social welfare."

The red-eyed police officer regarded her with skepticism, his eyes unblinking. "Show me your passport, ma'am."

THE JADE TALISMAN

Elaine reached into her coat pocket and pulled out a small leather-bound booklet.

The officer cast his eye over the first page of the passport, which had a photograph of a heavily made-up brunette woman on it, above the name *Tatiana Rose Anderson*. The occupation under the name read *student*, in bolded letters.

"We're wasting our time on this one," he whispered to the other *Militsiya* officer.

"Good day," the officers growled in unison, and then continued their march down the aisle of the train. Elaine breathed a sigh of relief as she watched them recede into the distance.

As the train began to move, the hovering spirit stayed close to Elaine, remaining alert and watchful while the woman closed her eyes and began to doze off. The spirit attentively observed the visual panorama of Crystal City's urban landscape as it unfolded outside the train car window. As the train lurched onwards, the bohemian middle-class neighborhood of the station transitioned into a more upscale business district. The bold grandeur of the architecture here was astonishing: structures dexterously crafted of steel, glass, and marble spiraled into the sky like graceful, ambitious birds taking flight. Humans were everywhere—strolling down sidewalks, perusing ads projected onto the sides of buildings, and flitting in and out of luxury boutiques. The district pulsated with an energy that ebbed and flowed, as if its streets were arteries and the people moving through them were blood.

After the business district came an industrial zone where poverty was a visible blight upon the landscape. Walter's spirit saw many impoverished men and women lining the streets, begging for money or suffering what appeared to be drug-induced comas. The train passed through a gravel yard, in which robots oversaw processions of emaciated men digging up vast amounts of aggregate and diligently loading it onto trundling conveyor belts. The spirit could hear the grating voices of AI Fighters as they barked commands at the laborers, whose faces were pale and lined with fatigue. The train also traveled through a marble quarry, where blocks of white marble were cleaved from the unwilling earth and transported away by machines. There, too, working-class humans scurried around industriously, operating the monolithic tractors and wheel loaders which facilitated the impressive operation. It was clear that the glimmering opulence of the business district was being sustained by the labor of these men, who appeared to have little ambition in life except to toil under the dictates of their AI overlords.

As the train picked up speed on its way out of the city, the scars upon the landscape only grew worse. The locomotive passed forests razed to the ground by mechanized logging, dotted with the stumps of trees that looked hauntingly like headstones in a cemetery. Next were landfills containing heaping piles of trash and electronic waste which had been lit on fire, causing vast plumes of toxic chemicals to rise toward the sky. Rivers, brown with sludge, were impeded with huge cement dams that regulated the flow of water, diverting it to man-made lakes where treatment plants processed it for human consumption. Algae blooms thrived in the lakes, causing them to glow a phosphorescent green.

After several hours had passed, the train came upon a landscape which could be generously described as a wilderness. There were still abundant signs of man's destructive campaign to subdue nature, even here: mines, oil wells, clear-cuts, farms, aquifers, and other subtle modifications of the landscape. If this were indeed a wilderness, then it was a tame one, which had largely been reduced to a humble servant of civilization. As the train moved farther away from the coast and deeper into the interior, the landscape became sparser, slowly transitioning from forest to grassland to bone-dry desert.

Here in the desert there were no more trees, only stumps of scattered evergreens burnt to ash in voracious wildfires. Still, the delicate beauty of the landscape had not been erased, even in this dry, burned-out wasteland. Creatures like lizards, scorpions, and snakes eked out a modest existence in their desert homes; cacti, wildflowers, and shrubbery painted the hills with elegant hues of burnished green, yellow, and purple; and dazzling rock formations loomed mysteriously in the distance. As the train approached the formations, they became almost biblical in their proportions. Red sandstone curved into massive archways that framed the sun and towering pillars that resembled the obelisks of Egypt. Here, in a place characterized by the precarious dance of death and survival, was evidence of Earth's enduring rebellion— defiantly refusing to be tamed in its entirety, the soil and rock which undergirds civilization was busy creating its own song, a music too ancient to be silenced.

Finally, when the sun was just beginning to dip below the horizon, the train arrived at a small town in the middle of the desert which was bordered on one side by a winding river. It was more than a hamlet than a town, as it consisted only of an apartment complex and a few essential buildings including a hospital and school. The architecture was sterile, modern, and pragmatic, as if some faraway government had paternalistically decided to house and service the people here. Walter's spirit followed Elaine as she exited the train along with the other passengers, whose numbers had dwindled considerably by that point. When he emerged from the train, the hovering spirit noticed a rickety sign that read "Barrens Reserve," and further observed that a number of AI Fighter guards were monitoring the station vigilantly. An elderly man, dressed in the modest garb of a farmer, was waiting for Elaine at the station. His face was weathered with age and his hair was as white as snow, but he had a youthful glimmer in his eyes that signaled mischief and enthusiasm.

"My daughter," he said in a trembling voice to Elaine, recognizing her despite her disguise. "Let's get you home and fed, you must be starving. Morgana's making your favorite, lamb stew. Give me your bag. I'll hold it for you."

Elaine looked up at him with eyes that shone with gratitude and humility, a far cry from the expression she had given Walter when she had seen him at his apartment.

As they receded into the winding streets of the town, heading in the direction of the apartment complex, the hovering spirit could hear Elaine's voice, low and bitter: "I'm never going back to that terrible place, Papa."

As he tried to follow Elaine and her father, Walter's spirit suddenly felt a strong wind dragging him backwards. He made a valiant effort of resisting this potent force, but to no avail; the spirit was being carried farther and farther away from Elaine, and then up into the sky, the town below becoming increasingly distant. It was then that he saw the diamond mine that scarred a vast swath of land behind the settlement where Elaine's family lived. It was astonishingly enormous, and from the spirit's vantage point it looked like a herald of mankind's intrepid dominion over nature. After a few moments, Walter's spirit felt a wave of panic as he became unhinged, thrust into the chaos of the universe like a speck of rock floating in the upper atmosphere. He yearned for sunlight the same way that a plant does, but his desires were evading his grasp. The sun became as tiny and insignificant as a pebble before disappearing entirely, and darkness consumed everything.

Trojan Horse

"O wretched countrymen! What fury reigns?
What more than madness has possess'd your brains?
Think you the Grecians from your coasts are gone?
And are Ulysses' arts no better known?
This hollow fabric either must inclose,
Within its blind recess, our secret foes..."
— Virgil

Walter surfaced from his vision as though it were an ocean. He gasped desperately for air to fill his empty lungs, and groped around in the blackness for his glasses. After a frantic few moments of searching, he found them nestled under blankets which were twisted and soaked in sweat. When he put them on, a blurry outline of Emilia's spirit came into focus. Her face resembled a radiant moon embedded with wide-set, piercing blue eyes.

"Welcome back," she said as Walter struggled to even out his breathing.

"I feel..." he said, slowly regaining his ability to speak.

"Do not focus on your feelings," she counselled, but he ignored her.

"Angry beyond measure."

"Why do you feel angry? If you are going to tell me how you feel, then you must at least explain why. Use reason to vanquish the force of the feeling itself," Emilia instructed, her low, mellifluous voice filling the room.

"Why do I feel angry? Perhaps because I just saw the woman I love murder my future self in cold blood, and the worst part about the killing was that it was well-deserved," Walter retorted.

"Is death ever well-deserved?" the spirit mused, her gaze becoming cloudy and distant.

"Yes, in this case it was," Walter replied. "How do these visions work, anyway? They cannot accurately reflect the future, since I know with all of my being that I would never behave that way toward anyone, and certainly not toward Elaine."

"The Jade Talisman is a window into future potentialities. No individual vision is certain to occur, but *could* occur depending on the choices we make in the labyrinth of our lives. Do not believe that you are immune from vice—no human alive on this planet is, after all. You can be a saint of the highest order and still fall prey to demons."

"But... I know I would never..."

"You cannot know what the future will hold," Emilia said sternly. "How wealth and power may corrupt us, warping our soul into something alien and unrecognizable. Every choice in our lives, no matter how minor or insignificant, has an impact on the ultimate result of this process. That is why you must choose wisely."

"Why did you tell me before that the vision was related to the season of summer? I don't understand the connection," Walter said.

"The correlation between vision and season is not always apparent, but it exists nevertheless. To the ancient peoples who forged the Jade Talisman and endowed it with magical properties, each season had distinct characteristics, which manifested themselves in each of the four primary pathways illuminated by the Talisman. In order to create the precious stone that now adorns your neck, the ancients used four cauldrons for blending together the herbs and flowers that thrived in each of the respective seasons. For summer, there was lavender, amaranth, yarrow, and foxglove. For fall, helenium, marigold, shrub rose, and sweet alyssum. For winter, snowdrops, jasmine, hellebore, and witch hazel. For spring, hyacinth, bluebells, mint, and nasturtium.

"To the ancients, summer was the season of stagnation, the time of the year when the world is blanketed in a stifling heat. In summer, civilization languishes in self-admiration, becoming overly complacent with its own paltry achievements. It is the season of vanity and lust, sloth and gluttony. The herbs and flowers of summer induce visions of the pathway with these characteristics—a vision of a stagnant world where little has changed. That is why the vision is related to the season of summer.

"The summer vision you saw is but one possible future, a future in which the *status quo* is preserved. This vision will come to pass if you program the robots to remain on Earth and continue lording over humans, perpetuating the darkest version of capitalism. In such a future, your soul will decay as you fall for the AIs' charming enticements of more wealth and power. You will live quite comfortably before meeting your eventual demise, and Elaine will be safe. After she kills you and rejoins her family in the Barrens, she might even find happiness."

"I will never fall for the AIs' enticements," Walter declared.

"You say that to me now, but you cannot know how enticing their offers will appear to you when the time comes. The worst demons are often clothed in the finest silks."

"Why did I only see the summer vision?" Walter asked. "What about the other seasons?"

"Be patient, and the other seasonal visions will reveal themselves to you in time. The Talisman has its own song, its own story, and its own logic. You may not understand it at first, but you must let it unfold in its own way."

With that, the spirit of Emilia faded into darkness, leaving Walter burning with unanswered questions and anxious for the night to end. Walter removed the Talisman from his neck, recalling Elaine's advice not to overuse it, but that did not help to calm his restless mind. When the soft light of dawn flooded through the porous canvas walls of the tent, Walter rose from his bed impatiently and sought out the other rebels. He found them slumbering, with the exception of Cyriana—the silver-haired princess was already alert and awake, her jaguar Sekhmet crouching at her side.

"We must get on with the *war*," she said brusquely. Her harsh voice awoke Eva, who sat up in bed and rubbed the sleep from her eyes.

"It would be wise to hold a council meeting before taking any further steps," Walter replied. "All nine Mages are to attend, even though only you and Tristan have formally been appointed councilors."

Walter glanced timidly toward Eva, who was staring at her bedsheets as if absorbed in thought.

"Eva, you will also join this meeting, since you are technically also a councilor—although you must first swear to me that you will guard your mind against interference from any AI presence," he said in a low whisper.

Eva beamed with gratitude. "I assure you, Asana is far away right now."

"Good," Walter replied. "Let us hold the council meeting here, before we make our way down the mountain."

Veena graciously permitted the rebels to use her dining table for an impromptu council meeting. She served them tea and round cakes made of buckwheat, spread thickly with raspberry jam. Elaine, Jonas, and Mikos were the only rebels who did not attend the meeting, as they were neither councilors nor Mages, and they instead went outside to explore the settlement on the crater.

Walter sat at the head of the table, his face solemn and pale. After a long period of silence, he finally spoke.

"As we sit here today, the AI Masters are making preparations to build a diamond mine in Elaine's village, Te'yara," he said, his voice strained. "My original plan was to go to that village with you all to protest its destruction, once we have returned to the mainland. But now, having spoken to the Lord Shiva, I know that mere protest will achieve little. Perhaps it would work in a state ruled by humans, but the AIs do not have a shred of empathy inside of them; do you think they will be moved to pity when they see us lying prostrate in front of their ravenous machines?

"Although it is undeniably brave, the plan is a foolhardy one. Why should we put our lives at risk for nothing? Instead, what we must do is implement widespread change that uproots the very foundation of society itself. The more I think about it, the more it becomes crystal clear in my mind. Reprogramming the AIs so that they serve humans once again—rather than lord over them—is the only way to achieve a future in which we don't need to lay down our bodies in sacrifice before cranes and bulldozers.

"Last night, I had my first vision from the Jade Talisman. It showed me a world in which nothing has changed, a world in which life keeps going on like it has for decades now. The world I saw was terrifying. The earth was scarred from heavy industry, which profited only a handful of people at the expense of a majority of workers obediently serving the system of perpetual extraction. Elaine's village and others like it had been utterly destroyed by the system's ravenous hunger for wealth. And the humans who benefitted from this were monsters, lacking in conscience or soul."

Walter paused, letting his words sink in for a moment before resuming.

"I am grateful for this vision, however. As appalling as it was, it helped me to appreciate one thing: the critical importance of the Rebellion. Change will not occur unless we want it to and unless we act. Yet reprogramming the AI Masters is only the first step in a much larger mission. It will be the spark that sets the wheels of change in motion, but it cannot fuel transformation indefinitely, and most importantly it cannot extinguish human greed and selfishness. We must remember that the system engineered by the AI Masters is modelled after one that we humans created. Unrestrained capitalism thrives on extraction and the limitless consumption of resources. It does not value human life, which it regards simply as a means to an end. There must be a better way, and I hope that the visions I have next will help guide us toward it.

"While reprogramming the AIs will not solve all of our problems, it is nevertheless of paramount importance. Once we have taken this critical step, we can turn our attention to the hard work of implementing the equitable and just world we desire. The Lord Shiva told us that we need to wage a psychological war in order to sow the seeds of chaos amongst the AI Masters. This will allow us to penetrate their stronghold.

"This brings me to my question to you: do you think that this psychological war is winnable? And if so, then how exactly will it be won?"

Walter surveyed the brave, expectant faces of the nine Mages before his gaze settled on Tristan. He deliberately avoided Cyriana's piercing gaze; he was too afraid to see her strong appetite for destruction.

Tristan smiled. He radiated tranquility and poise as his two serpentine companions slept comfortably on each of his shoulders, their tails draping down his arms like ivy. "Of course, it is winnable," he said. "History is the wisest prophet. And history tells us that our ancestors once sowed the seeds of doubt and discontent in the AI Masters, by summoning none other than the animal spirits. And yes, I am aware that our ancestors ultimately lost that battle. But we have the tools to succeed where they once failed.

"What tools do we have? Some of you may have forgotten," Tristan continued, now addressing his fellow Mages, "but the blood of the most venerable mystics to ever walk this earth still flows through our veins. I speak of the Druids, of course. They no longer exist—either individually or as a community—but we Mages are their humble descendants. Not only could the Druids command the animal spirits to do their bidding, they could also unite with the animals themselves. The Druids referred to this process as *shapeshifting*. The most powerful Druids could easily shapeshift into animals, both living and dead. Once a person adopts an animal's form, he assumes the characteristics and powers of that creature, making the impossible seem possible. Miles can be traversed in minutes, when one has the wingspan of an eagle. The hottest flame is cold to the touch when one has the leathery skin of a lizard. And the deepest snow is easily penetrated when one is an arctic fox capable of diving into it to reach its prey. A person who is vested with the powers of an animal no longer needs to command it to do anything; he can do it by himself. And the power of shapeshifting goes beyond transforming into living animals—it is possible, though somewhat more difficult, to shapeshift into a creature's *spirit*."

Tristan now turned to address Walter, who was somewhat bewildered by what the Mage was saying. "As young Mages in Serrahan, we were taught how to create a magical illusion that tricks others into believing we have transformed into an animal or its spirit, when in fact we have not. The common term for this power is *glamor*. The potency of the trick often causes the spell-caster to become ill, especially if they are an amateur.

"This trick only works well on humans, however; during previous battles, our ancestors tried it on the AI Masters but with limited success. This was partly why the Shadow Wars against the AI Masters failed; the shamans who could summon real animal spirits were banished to Vei'arash, and when the Mages tried create the illusion of animal spirits, they failed. Machines see reality. They are not easily fooled by traps that the weak minds of humans easily fall prey to. And this is why we must not simply cast an illusion—we must introduce chaos and disorder into reality itself. To do this we must learn the art of shapeshifting that our Druid ancestors mastered centuries ago."

Cyriana gazed at Tristan intently, her emerald eyes betraying a muted admiration for her lover's boldness. "Shapeshifting is a type of High Magic," she murmured, entranced.

"You are correct, Cyriana," Tristan replied. "It is not only High Magic—in the schemata of magical powers it rests at the top, alongside immortality, communion with the dead, and that most distant and elusive power of all, revival of the dead. Such sacred magic ought not to be used for a trivial purpose, I understand that well. But I see an opportunity for us to use it now, and if it will serve the noble ends of the Rebellion, then I see no reason not to grasp it. We have been granted permission to take four animal species from this island: jaguar, horse, lizard, and snake. When they migrate over to the mainland, these creatures will bring with them the divine spirits they embody. Once they have safely landed on Serrahan soil, we can easily command these spirits to do our bidding. But four spirits will not be enough to sow the seeds of chaos, at least not on the vast scale we require. What we need is a veritable *army* of animal spirits, something that can be accomplished by using the power of shapeshifting."

Yensin, a taciturn young Mage with raven-colored hair, suddenly spoke.

"When I was a very young child, my grandmother Lynesse told me stories about the Druids and shapeshifting. She never practiced it herself, but heard these stories from her ancestors. She said such a mighty power cannot be unleashed without consequences, like Pandora's Box," he said, each of his words measured and carefully chosen.

"As Mages," Yensin continued, "we're taught about the rudimentary principles that govern magic. We're taught to carefully abide by the rules, and to use magic in small doses so we don't become corrupted by it. We learn magic is a game of give and take with the natural world. We can use it to serve our own selfish purposes, but in exchange we must give something back. Perhaps it's our labor, our energy, or our blood, but there's always a price to pay for magic. Ordinary humans have a similar law, I think... the first law of thermodynamics, I think it's called.

"And if shapeshifting is High Magic, as you say... there *must* be a heavy price to pay for it. An animal spirit is as sacred as a tree. If you get that close to the divine, you risk falling under a powerful curse. What curse? I don't know, myself. But my grandmother Lynesse does. I kept asking her about it, but she refused to tell me; she said that shapeshifting was too dangerous for me to know about," Yensin said.

"We will pay her a visit, then, before we execute our plan," Tristan suggested.

"When I left Serrahan, she was very old and in poor health," Yensin said wistfully. "If she's passed away and her secret is gone with her, then I'm afraid we may never know. There aren't any remaining Druids in Serrahan, or anywhere else in the world as far as I'm aware. The Druids inter-married with ordinary Mages, diluting the purity of their race, and the last pureblood Druid died long ago. One of my grandmother's ancestors was a pureblood Druid, and I think Lynesse was one of the few Mage elders who knew much about the Druid history and lore."

"Thank you, Yensin," said Tristan. "We would be honored to speak with your grandmother about the ways of the Druids. We must find a way to accomplish the feat of shapeshifting, even if there are risks associated with it. What do you think of this plan, Cyriana?" he asked, turning to face his lover.

"Sekhmet does not like the idea of a bloodless war," she responded grimly. "But what I want more than anything is to defeat the AI Masters and create a future world where magic reigns supreme. I grant my approval to your plan, with one caveat. Walter, you want the support of the Mages so that you can reprogram the AIs and implement a future of your choosing. I may not be the ruler of the Mages, but my father is.

And nothing is more important to him than me; I have always been the one to tip his policy decisions in one direction or another. Whatever I want, he will want too. When I return to Serrahan, I will advise him not to support the Rebellion unless the future you choose is one that the Mages accept: one that *we* decide will benefit the lives of our people, and spread magic throughout the civilized world.

"During your first speech as leader," she continued, "you told us that one of the foundational principles of this Rebellion was democracy. You promised that you would support your allies and help ensure that the Serrahan clans are restored to their former glory.

"So, I ask you simply to remain loyal to your word. Will you make sure the future you choose aligns with *our* vision of a better world?"

Walter was silent for a long time before responding, and when he finally did his tone was careful and measured. "I take your words to heart, Cyriana, and they are powerful words that cannot be ignored. I need the assistance of your people and I can't in good conscience simply use them to help advance my plan and then ignore their wishes when it comes to implementing that plan. That being said, I cannot tell you with any certainty what future I will choose, having not yet seen all of the visions from the Jade Talisman. I promise to consult with the Mages about my choice when the time comes to make it."

Cyriana's eyes became icy cold once again. "I am not asking for *consultation*, Walter. That is a given. I am asking you to choose the future that we choose." Sekhmet snarled impatiently behind her.

The other councilmembers shifted with unease.

Thankfully, Tristan chose to intervene in that moment. "I am sure Walter will choose a future that is in line with our values and aspirations, won't you, Walter?"

"I will try," Walter said, with some hesitation in his voice.

"Why don't I believe you?" Cyriana said irritably. Her jaguar's growls became slightly louder.

"Cyriana," Walter said with a sigh, "I promise you this: the future I will choose will be better for your people than the present is. It will be better for *all* of us."

The assurance appeared to calm the princess somewhat, and she diverted her gaze.

"This brings us to the second topic of our discussion," Walter continued. "Assuming that we do succeed in our efforts to distract the AIs, how will I enter Central Command?" Walter's gaze settled on Eva, whose sea-blue eyes glimmered in the soft light of early morning.

"Eva, there is only one reason why I have let you sit in on this meeting, despite my fear that you may be jeopardizing our mission with your… permeable mind. The Rebellion needs your help."

His words caused the others at the table to murmur and whisper to each other.

Tristan silenced them with a wave of his hand. "What do you mean, Walter, that she may be jeopardizing our mission?"

Eva sighed. "I can explain, Tristan," she said, her voice trembling slightly. "While we were in Anatari, Walter overheard me conversing with an AI Master, Asana. She is not here on this island; I am gifted with the ability to speak to her when she is not physically present. She simply transmits her words and thoughts into my mind, as though she is becoming part of me and conversing with me at the same time." She blushed when she saw the aghast expressions on many of the councilmember's faces.

"It sounds like some kind of dark magic," Tristan said, narrowing his eyes in contemplation. "But it's nothing I've ever heard of before."

"It's not as terrible as it sounds," Eva assured him. "I've given her access to my mind, but I can sense when she is going to enter it in advance, and I can warn you about it. She does not permanently reside within me; she only visits occasionally. She wants to analyze my brain," Eva explained, "because for some strange reason she believes that I am one of the few humans worth saving from the AIs' nihilistic plans. She wants to present evidence of my gifts to sway the AI leaders and convince them to keep me safe. In the meantime, she watches over me and protects me." The timidity had left Eva's voice, and it now rang with confidence.

"Our relationship is certainly an eccentric one," Eva admitted. "But I still hold fast to the romantic notion that humans have AI soulmates, and I don't think I need to apologize for that."

"I couldn't imagine having so close a bond with one of those *monsters*," Cyriana said with a curled lip.

"Only humans have AI soulmates, not Mages," Eva clarified defensively. "Mage blood is different from that of humans, and Mages lack the same bond of kinship that exists between humans and machines. But that bond of kinship is good news for all of you. In exchange for granting her wishes, I asked Asana to do quite a big favor for me and meet with a member of AI royalty, to ask him for the names of even higher-ranking AI Masters. And true to her word, she has done it. In fact, she has exceeded my expectations and has given me the name of a close advisor of the *Anax*."

"A name," Cyriana said with a shrug. "What good does a name do?" Her jaguar yawned, baring gleaming white fangs.

"Not just a name," Eva shot back. "This name will be Walter's ticket to getting inside Central Command."

"How?" Walter asked, suddenly very interested.

Eva smiled, her azure eyes flashing with mischief. "I contacted Asana shortly after you and I last spoke about this, Walter. I asked her to relay an important message to Talvar: a request to arrange a meeting between you and this influential AI Master. Though it surprised me greatly to hear it, Talvar has agreed to set this up. The meeting shall be your opportunity to gain access to the *Anax*'s headquarters, by convincing this advisor that you need to carry out work on the *Anax*'s central computer. According to Talvar, AI Masters who are ranked fifth or higher have sworn an oath to always serve the best interests of the Empire, and they are permitted to use this computer to make minor modifications to the central processing systems of all AI Masters."

Walter's brow furrowed in confusion. "What you are saying makes no sense, Eva. Why would Talvar arrange such a meeting? As you said, only highly-ranked AI Masters can use the *Anax*'s computer to reprogram the systems. Why would I be allowed to?"

Eva hesitated before replying. "What I am about to tell you cannot pass outside this council meeting," she said gravely. "Some of you may have already heard part of this story, but I will tell the full tale for you all to hear. While I was working in a weapons factory in my youth, Asana helped me to smuggle weapons out of the factory so that I could hunt animals to feed my impoverished family. I thanked her, and we quickly grew to be close friends. I felt a strange pull toward her, and a hollow emptiness whenever she parted from me.

"When I was convicted for my smuggling crimes, I was overcome by despair at the thought that I would be separated from her. I decided to share my feelings with her, and she told me she was my soulmate and that there was a way for us to be together, united mentally and spiritually. She explained to me that all humans have AI soulmates, but not all of them have the gift that I do—the ability to relate to machines in a profoundly intimate way. She told me that there is a way to bring people like me even closer to machines, so that they merge with the machine and eventually become AI Masters.

"One day not too long ago, Asana and I were talking about my gift, and I asked her how common it is for humans to possess. She told me that it is a very rare gift, but that someone I knew had similar powers. I asked her who she was thinking of, and she told me that you, Walter, are gifted with the same powers as I am. You have a sophisticated knowledge of the inner workings of computers, and you can understand them on a profound level. It is therefore possible for you, too, to adopt the characteristics of a robot. You can temporarily become an AI Master, thereby deceiving the *Anax*'s advisor into thinking that you are one."

Walter's eyes widened. "How does Asana know about me? And more importantly, how *much* does she know?"

"Don't worry, I haven't told her all of your secrets," Eva replied. "She knows your history, let's just put it that way. I don't know if you are aware, but your ancestors had the same innate talent for understanding machines, and it was passed down from generation to generation. You should be very proud of it."

Walter was silent for a long time. When he finally spoke, words tumbled out of him quickly. "It is true that I have always had an affinity for programming, and the language of computers has come naturally to me since childhood. If what you are saying is correct, then it explains many of the mysteries that have dogged me for years. Tell me, then, how could I temporarily adopt the characteristics of a robot?"

"The process is quite simple," Eva explained. "The water in Crystal City is contaminated by a chemical substance that causes humans to adopt *roboticisms*—traits unique to robots. That is why they are losing their memories and dreams. Those aspects of the human soul are noticeably absent, or at least drastically different, in the AIs. Robots have a memory too, but it is stored in a box, and it does not return to them unless a specific command is made. And they have no dreams— only the ability to predict the probability of future events with their increasingly sophisticated algorithms.

"Even humans with no natural intimacy with machines are affected by this chemical compound, which is called lydion. If you infused the water with stronger doses of that same chemical, however, the increase would have no noticeable effect on the average person's attributes or behaviors. Yet the increase has a dramatic effect on a gifted person like you, and not only their mind, but also their body. There are many mixed-race folks in Khalendar trying to become more like robots by attaching prosthetic limbs and computer chips to their bodies, or injecting their blood with nanomachines. While their efforts are admirable, they can never hope to achieve the full transition to an AI Master that consuming lydion would create.

"You can transform into an AI Master, Walter. All you need to do is drink water infused with a high concentration of lydion, and the process of transformation will begin. Your skin will harden and become rubbery like theirs, your mind will be cleansed of all its emotional impulses, and you will no longer hunger for food or thirst for water. Your bodily functions will no longer be necessary, and you instead will respond to the dictates of your internal programming. It is completely safe for you to do this, and there is no risk of becoming permanently effected—in order to change back to your normal self, you need only drink pure, uncontaminated water."

Walter contemplated in silence for a few moments before responding. "If there is nothing to lose from it, then I would be willing to sacrifice my own personal discomfort for the cause of the Rebellion. Is the process of transformation... uncomfortable?"

"Far from it," Eva replied. "Long ago when I was a rebellious teenager, I tried it myself. And while it was frightening to see my physical body transform before my eyes into something foreign and unfamiliar, it was also thrilling. While there are certainly downsides to becoming an AI, such as losing touch with your emotions and empathetic impulses, there are plenty of upsides to counterbalance the negatives. Your thoughts become simpler, clearer, and less burdened by the weight of feeling. Overall, I would say that the experience elevates you and broadens your perspective."

"Hmm..." Walter said, weighing the options in his mind. "Something about it just seems wrong. If it changes you so much, then perhaps it makes you forget important matters... like who you are and what you are trying to accomplish. That could prove to be very dangerous."

"It will weaken your long-term memories and will focus your attention on short-term plans rather than long-term aspirations," Eva stated. "But the essence of yourself will be unaltered. The programming that you will respond to is still your DNA, the coding of a human. I should have been clearer about that when I told you that it would entail a full transformation to an AI. There's no way to override the most primal coding of a human—their DNA—so that will persist even throughout the change. In other words, you will retain your own thoughts, feelings, and ambitions, but everything will become more streamlined and orderly, and you will simply approach tasks the way that AIs do."

"It sounds quite simple," Walter said, warming up to the idea. "So simple that perhaps there is no need for us to even carry out the first phase of the plan with the animal spirits."

"The success of this plan will only depend on the outcome of the first phase," Eva cautioned him. "That is because it will be virtually impossible for you to convince the advisor to permit you to make changes to the *Anax*'s computer unless you have a very good reason to do so."

Walter frowned. "I thought you said that certain high-ranked AI Masters are allowed to access this computer to modify the central processing systems of the AIs."

"Yes, but the advisor engages in a careful screening process of those AI Masters—he only selects those that will benefit the *Anax* and serve his goals, before providing them with access. Asana also told me that the *Anax* himself listens in on these screening sessions, so he can override the advisor's decision if he so desires."

"How would I serve the goals of the *Anax*?" Walter mused.

"Asana kindly told me everything she knows about the *Anax*, because I was curious about the exact same question. While it is impossible to know precisely what goes on in such a powerful entity's mind, she has divulged her best guesses to me. She believes that the *Anax* is primarily concerned with the welfare of the AI race, and in particular the welfare of the AI Masters. He intends to promote their glory at any cost. If we do succeed in confusing the AI Masters beyond measure, his main goal will presumably be to restore order in the lower ranks. So, you must artfully convince him you can do just that.

"AI Masters are constantly running experiments on humans," Eva continued, "trying to find successful psychological traits that they can replicate in their own minds in order to strengthen their race. What if you found a trait that demystifies the spiritual, rendering magic a benign force in a conflict with a mind driven by pure reason? Such a trait is increasingly rare, though not impossible to find, in a human. Most humans are reluctant to accept magic for what it is, and they undertake a linear, mathematical exercise in an attempt to rationalize magic *ex post facto*. They are essentially behaving like AIs when they engage in this reasoning process. Yet there are humans in this world—primarily shamans, but also the members of other tribal cultures—who recoil at the thought of explaining magic and spirituality by reference to physical and mathematical laws. The members of these tribes may be different, but their brains are not necessarily unique. They have human brains, with human instincts and impulses. And it is a an ancient and long-forgotten quality of the human mind to celebrate and revere magic.

"The problem arises in transposing that trait to AIs. You see, the reason that some humans are adept at embracing spirituality is that their minds are like a balanced scale, half illogical and half logical. When you introduce something that is illogical into the equation, like magic, humans can either accept it or use the logical side of their brains to rationalize it away. The rationalization process is only possible because they subconsciously understand the basic principles of magic. But AIs, on the other hand... their minds are comprised of pure, unmodified logic. Introducing something illogical into their minds is like dropping oil into a well of vinegar. It is a foreign substance that cannot be understood or rationalized, even by using logic itself. Their system shuts down because it is incapable of recognizing what they see as reality, and that drop of oil becomes a cancer inside of their brains that disrupts their otherwise pristine code.

"Perhaps you'll understand better by analogy," Eva said, amused by the bewildered expressions on the councilmembers' faces. "In ancient times, something similar happened in the Old World. Wealthy explorers from the northern hemisphere embarked on long journeys across the seas in tall, sturdy ships to exotic islands in the south. Such ships had not been invented by the natives who inhabited the countries they were visiting. The result was that the natives did not see the gargantuan ships approaching in plain sight, because the objects were so alien to the natives that their mental receptors were unable to process them, and the ships remained invisible to them. From the history texts I've read about the Shadow Wars, a similar thing happened at first—the spirits were so foreign to the AIs that they were essentially invisible. Eventually, the AIs were able to 'see' the spirits, but they could still not process what was happening, which caused tumult and chaos."

Tristan suddenly spoke. "So, in order for the system disruption not to occur, they need to be programmed to understand magic."

"Precisely," Eva replied. "And so, Walter, I put it to you in clearer terms: your task is to convince the *Anax* that you can program a robot to understand magic."

After the council meeting was finished, Elaine, Jonas, and Mikos returned from their excursion and rejoined Walter and the other rebels. Veena graciously gave Walter a satchel filled with food from her kitchen, including rice, dried vegetables, and salted mountain goat, which would keep the rebels fed for at least a few more days. Walter then bid goodbye to her and Caleb, thanking the couple for their kind hospitality, before the group began to make their way down Mount Samaya. The descent was far more pleasant than the ascent had been, and the Mages savored the opportunity to observe the diverse alpine flowers which sprouted up along the trail such as broad-leaved fireweed, arctic lupine, and white moss heath. Many of them scribbled down notes about the texture, color, and size of these specimens in leather-bound notebooks or made hasty sketches of the plants as they walked, taking care not to stumble over roots and branches as they did so.

"These flowers would be rarities back in Serrahan; they would undoubtedly fetch a high price at the market," Tristan explained to Walter. "They have many practical uses such as healing wounds, not to mention the magical properties they are endowed with. I've never before seen such a stunning variety of plant-life as I have encountered on this island. It seems to me that one could spend a lifetime in Vei'arash and still not understand the full extent of the diversity. Of course, a single conversation with the inhabitants of this island would likely provide as much insight into the plants as an entire year spent here. Would you ever want to live on Vei'arash, do you think?" Tristan asked his companion.

"Who knows how the future will unfold," Walter said wistfully. "I am quite intrigued by what the shaman-god said about my ancestors and the bond they formed with a stag here. What's more, Namid is supposed to bear my child—so I can't see why I wouldn't come back here one day. But for the time being, getting off this island is more of an immediate priority than figuring out where I'll eventually settle down. I am anxious to see the faces of our friends on the *Jade Queen*."

"Worry no more," Eva reassured him. "I have asked my mare about the quickest route back to the *Jade Queen*, and she informs me that we will be there by nightfall."

"Tonight?" Walter asked incredulously. "How is that even possible? We were walking for days before we arrived at the village, and then days after that to reach Mount Samaya. The mountain couldn't have been close to where our ship docked—we couldn't even see it."

"It was a cloudy morning, and the mountain was hidden from our view by fog and haze," Eva explained. "We were actually very close to it when we arrived—nearly at its base. Had it been a clear day, we would have spotted it right away."

Walter sighed. "So, we wasted all of that time going to the village…" he said, but then he stopped himself. "Although I suppose we didn't," he admitted out loud, "since we found the animal spirits along the way."

"Yes; sometimes the easiest route to our destination is right in front of us, but destiny has shrouded it in fog and we are forced to choose the harder path," Eva said with a smile.

Walter's memory was suddenly triggered by Eva's words, and he was mentally transported back to the evening when he had sipped a rye and ginger in a seedy bar in Jamestown, what now seemed like a lifetime ago. The wizened face of the seer surfaced in his mind, together with the crisp image of her amber ring, the fire lizard trapped inside the polished stone, and her cards laid out neatly on the bar table. Walter still didn't know who she was—perhaps Emilia had been playing a trick on him by disguising herself as a fortune teller. Or perhaps the seer had been a divine being in disguise, someone who could see future pathways like the Lord Shiva. Whoever the seer truly was, Walter could hear her words as though she were present on Mount Samaya with him: "*You will undertake a perilous task, which will test your cunning and your strength, and may threaten your very life… you may be bitterly disappointed… your heart will be torn between two loyalties, two allegiances. You will have to make a choice between destinies, but you must be exceedingly careful. The destiny which seems the most favorable to you at first will be the one which brings evil and pain. Choose heartache over instant gratification, though, and you may be rewarded in the end.*"

Since joining the Rebellion, Walter had undertaken many daunting challenges, risking his life in order to rescue Jonathan, Elaine, and the countless others imprisoned by the AI Masters. Yet a nagging feeling told him that the worst was yet to come. Was the upcoming meeting with this advisor to the *Anax* the "perilous task" referred to by the seer, which would try his cunning and strength, and perhaps even threaten his life? It certainly seemed that Walter's diplomacy skills would be tested by this encounter. But what intrigued him more was what the seer had really meant when she told him that this heart would be torn between "two loyalties, two allegiances." Walter had seen in his vision that in one potential future he'd accepted the *status quo* of an Empire ruled by the AI Masters and agreed to serve them faithfully. Yet he wasn't certain if that was what the seer had meant.

Walter suddenly realized that he longed to ask Emilia about the true meaning of the seer's words; even if she hadn't been the seer in disguise, Emilia had nevertheless been a philosophical sounding board for him these days, and someone he could trust to provide insight into his visions. It seemed logical if that he was to truly master time, in accordance with Shiva's wishes, Walter needed to understand the predictions that had been made about his own future.

"My sister Emilia told me that, a long time ago," Eva suddenly remarked, causing Walter to shiver. "I miss her more with every day that passes."

Walter felt guilty he hadn't told Eva that he had seen and spoken to Emilia several times following her death. If his own brother had died, Walter would want to know if someone else was able to communicate with him in spirit form. He would have likely dismissed it as rubbish, but he would have been interested to hear it all the same. Yet something in the back of Walter's mind cautioned him to patiently bide his time before telling Eva the truth about Emilia. If Eva wasn't able to see Emilia, but he was, he feared that a seed of jealousy would begin to sprout inside her. *I can't afford to lose Eva's support at this fragile stage of our mission*, Walter thought.

As he continued down Mount Samaya, Walter realized with a pang of excitement that he would soon be reuniting with Christopher, Miranda, and Jonathan. During his travels in Vei'arash, Walter had pushed thoughts of them out of his mind, but now he was looking forward to seeing them again. He wondered whether Miranda's healing methods had been working effectively on Jonathan, and he prayed that his brother had returned to a more settled mental state.

Finally, the rebels arrived at the great mountain's base. The tumbling waterfall and the aquamarine pool still glimmered in the sunlight, but now there was no time to frolic under the cool waves.

Eva's horses were waiting for her near the waterfall, and she embraced them warmly.

"Lead us to the ship," Walter instructed her.

As they followed Eva, Tristan confessed to his sadness at leaving the island. "I will return," he told Walter in a determined voice. "One day, I will come back here and devote my time to learning about the magical plants. Once I have learned all of their magical properties by heart, I will return home with a vast repertoire of wisdom, a depth of knowledge suited for a king of the Mages. And, with the blessing of Shiva himself, I may even bring back samples."

"I wish you well in that endeavor," Walter replied. "But first, we need to fight to protect the kingdom that you will one day rule."

Tristan nodded. "As much as I would rather dwell in a scholar's paradise, duty calls us back to Serrahan."

After several more hours of admiring the towering ferns, lianas, and bromeliads, the rebels finally reached the outskirts of the rainforest. Eva, who was at the front of the group, stepped past the curtain of the jungle's foliage and breathed in sharply as she took in the dazzling sight of the night sky. Thousands of stars glittered in a vast firmament like polished diamonds. Walter followed moments later and spotted the subtle outline of a massive barge, its silent and motionless silhouette floating calmly upon the black ocean. The young man breathed a sigh of relief—a part of him had feared that the ship would no longer be there when they returned. Gazing at the ship that he had once been a prisoner of, Walter felt a strong wave of emotion. They had been voyaging on the island for over a month, and the gleaming steel vessel was a welcome sight.

Eva's horses snorted and skittered when they saw the cliff face below them, which dropped in a sheer vertical line down toward the white-sand beach. Eva soothed them with a pat of her hand, but her face was creased with worry. Even Cyriana's jaguar seemed apprehensive about the prospect of descending the rocky bluffs, and she whimpered anxiously.

With grace and poise, Tristan took control of the situation. "Tonight, the new moon reigns, and it is too dark for the animals to descend the cliff face," he warned. "We should remain up here overnight, and we'll lead them down the stairs in the morning. If you would like to risk the descent, then you may do so at your own peril."

Walter sighed. He could feel a sharp wind picking up and a light rain beginning to fall as he glanced toward the boat. He wanted nothing more than to return to the ship and sleep in a warm bed, but he detested the thought of leaving his friends behind.

"We can all wait one more night," Walter said. "It's starting to rain, so we should not stay exposed on this clifftop. Let us seek shelter inside the forest and spend one final night there before we leave Vei'arash."

The others agreed to the plan, and the rebels retreated back into the stiflingly humid jungle. They made a small fire and cooked a modest meal of rice and salted goat meat from the supplies Veena had given Walter. As the final embers died out, Walter laid out his blanket and curled up to go to sleep beside his friends. He recalled that the Talisman was still inside his satchel, and he put it around his neck, feeling a sensation of warmth and comfort. Just as he was about to surrender to the comfortable haze of oblivion, he heard a voice that sounded like either Eva or Emilia, but in his semi-conscious state Walter did not know which one it was.

"Come here, Walter," the voice summoned him. He opened his eyes and saw the faintest outline of a pale blue silhouette flicker between the trees. Still in the liminal space between waking and dreaming, Walter followed the ethereal figure deeper into the jungle, leaving behind his friends where they slept. He was irresistibly attracted to it, as if it were a magnet pulling him closer to his true purpose. He felt like he was trying to catch an elusive butterfly that was always just beyond his reach, and an ache of longing pervaded his body.

When it finally stopped moving, the blurry figure came into focus as Emilia. "Where have you led me?" Walter demanded, suddenly afraid to be separated from his friends.

"Do not worry about where you are—what matters is where you are going. It is time for your next vision, Walter."

Walter suddenly recalled his desire to ask her about his future. "What decision will I have to make that will require me to choose between two loyalties, two allegiances?" he asked pointedly.

"The answer is within you," Emilia replied, her turquoise eyes blazing more fiercely than her translucent skin. "You must ultimately choose which side of your own nature will prevail over the other."

Walter was not satisfied with this vague and cryptic explanation. "What sides of my nature are you referring to?" Walter pressed.

"Hush, child, now it is time to surrender yourself to the power of the Talisman," she crooned, and Walter suddenly felt the gemstone around his neck pulsating and vibrating with an energy he had only ever felt once before, immediately before he had descended into his first vision.

His body instinctively tensed, and he wanted to rage against the darkness, to angrily banish it to the strange, primordial place it had originated from. Yet he found that it was far easier to simply surrender, to relax his muscles and let himself be swept under by the current. Struggling against the Talisman's power was futile; after all, the darkness was as natural and inevitable as death itself.

As he was being sucked under by the overpowering current, Walter could hear faint echoes of Emilia's voice in the hazy, distant realm of the real world: "The Talisman's seasonal song is not a linear one; it does not follow the same straight pathway as the seasons of the Earth do. It tells its story by displaying opposites and contrasts, shadows that give form and substance to the light. Now it would like you to see the converse of summer, the season of darkness, desolation, and destruction."

Winter

"Uprose Odin
lord of men,
and on Sleipnir he
laid the saddle;
he rode thence
down to Niflhel."
– Sæmund Sigfusson

When he opened his eyes again, Walter was the same disembodied spirit he had been during his first vision. His senses were weakened; he could not touch anything, and he could see and hear very little. Once he had finally found his bearings, he noticed that he was in a damp, dark tunnel lit only by torches anchored to the wall. He immediately suspected that he was underground, and various clues confirmed his suspicions: stalactites hung from the ceiling, and the stone walls surrounding him were streaked with blood-red iron and yellow sulfur. A grainy, white substance coated the walls, sparkling like millions of tiny diamonds in the warm light of torches. Walter's spirit flitted through the cavernous tunnel, instinctively trying to find a pathway to the top. As he flew down the length of the tunnel, the spirit noticed that there were a number of corridors that branched outwards from the main tunnel, and he decided to explore one of these.

The sight that greeted him at the end of one of the corridors was not pleasant. A man, woman, and child, all deceased, lay huddled together in the torch-lit room, surrounded by blankets and a stash of empty cans. There was also a latrine and a makeshift stove, along with a few children's books, a dreidel, and an old hairbrush. The spirit examined the bodies—they had been dead for many years now and their flesh had rotted away, leaving behind clean, bleached bones.

Unperturbed by the macabre sight, Walter's spirit now flitted out of the room and returned to the main tunnel. Forging onwards, he decided to try his luck with another branching pathway. This time he was intrigued by a primal, howling sound emanating from the darkness that lay ahead. Unfortunately, the spirit was not greeted by a more comforting sight at the end of that pathway; he encountered a pack of silver-haired wolves gnawing on a bone from a human corpse. The spirit was not tempted to explore the room further. Turning back abruptly, he fled the room and returned to the tunnel, flying faster now, driven by some enigmatic force that propelled him onwards.

The air in the tunnel suddenly changed. Although Walter's spirit could not feel any physical sensations, he still had an intact sense of smell, and he could tell that the scent of heavy, damp sulfur had been replaced by something lighter and earthier. There was fresh air up ahead—the spirit could sense that better than he could sense his own existence—and he moved faster and faster toward the hidden source of energy. The fresh air and the subtle trickle of light that accompanied it were powerful and enticing magnets, and they propelled the spirit forward as if he were a puppet on a string. The spirit did not know whether he had been travelling in the tunnel for minutes, or hours, or days—he only knew that he was going somewhere, *outside*.

Without warning, there was a rush of air and the spirit was sucked up toward the sky, as if by a giant vacuum. He flew upwards and then fell back upon the ground, next to a cavernous hole in the earth: the opening to the network of tunnels he had just emerged from. The spirit felt an overwhelming sense of being someplace foreign, but he did not know where. The land was blanketed in lava for hundreds of miles in every direction, suggesting that a massive volcanic eruption had silenced civilization. But the spirit knew that this rough assessment was premature, for there was much to investigate in this vast, uncharted world.

The most obvious thing about the new world was the lack of sunlight—the sky was thick with grey soot that rendered the sun a silvery phantom rather than the fiery golden orb that it should have been. The second most obvious thing was the stunning absence of life. Not a single tree, shrub, or crawling beetle could be seen on the ground. However, a thin, slimy layer of moss coated the lava field, invoking the possibility of more life elsewhere in this cold, desolate wilderness. Aside from the moss, what seemed most alive was the planet itself. Palpable tremors rippled underneath its surface, causing the earth beneath the spirit to shift and rumble occasionally, as if the land were metamorphosing into something altogether different.

As the spirit flew onwards at an incalculable speed, he observed that the silver sun was gradually descending toward the horizon. Relying on the sun's position as a guide, the spirit kept track of time as he flew, and several hours passed uneventfully. There were no clouds in sight—for there was no sky in sight—yet it had begun to drizzle rain, which gave the world an even drearier appearance. Despite its dismal pallor, however, the landscape was far from monotonous; on the contrary, the earth seemed to be charged with an electric awareness of its own catastrophic potential. It lurched like a groaning beast, irritated that it had no prey to torture and eager to turn its violent tendencies in on itself. The land was expressing its internal rage in an almost artistic display of passion, somewhat like a dancer might showcase her inner emotions during a performance.

As the sun nestled itself ever more comfortably into the distant arm of the horizon, the spirit chanced upon a sight more incredible than the dancing lava fields. At first the spirit thought that he was looking at a shiny, black boulder. Yet upon closer observation he realized that the piece of rock in his field of vision had not sprung from the ground by natural processes. A vast crater stretched for miles in all directions beneath it, a massive circular depression in the earth's surface.

The rough, cheesecloth texture of the chunk of earth gave its identity away to the spirit, who had by now become uncannily talented at guessing what objects were and where they might have originated from. The rock was a stony meteorite, a surviving fragment from an enormous asteroid which had collided with Earth and likely eradicated most of the life forms on the planet, sparing only bacteria, lichens, and the mammals that may have sheltered underground. A strange jolt of electricity coursed through Walter's spirit as he observed the meteorite. The sensation was so intense that it made the spirit determined to confront whomever—or whatever—was responsible for this harrowing project of destruction. If it were a chance accident, then so be it; the spirit could easily come to terms with that. But the spirit was not convinced of the accidental nature of the occurrence, and somehow felt that he was a detective in a twisted game of *find whomever is responsible for the demise of civilization.*

The electric current within the spirit intensified as he approached the intimidating object. There was a haunting beauty about something that had caused the end of civilized society—a tragic sense that even though it had been the harbinger of doom and destruction, the space rock was still one of God's creations, something that Michelangelo might have been inspired to sculpt a replica of.

As he moved closer to the vortex, the spirit sensed that he was receiving energy from the meteorite. Although the transmission of energy to a being with no physical form defied logic, it was nevertheless happening. The sensation was like swimming at the base of a thundering waterfall—the deafening sound of nature rendered everything else completely silent. The spirit was tempted to spend an eternity in this strange place, lapping up the power of the meteorite as if it were a watering hole in a desert. But above the painful din of the turbulent forces ricocheting around the spirit, he could hear something else, something louder and more intense than even the bringer of death. He could hear life.

The music of life sang to the spirit gently at first, but it gradually became more urgent, like a cat impatiently demanding its owner's attention. It soon blossomed into a paean to the living, an achingly beautiful tribute to the blood that courses through the veins of Earthlings. It was a struggle to escape from the influence of the meteorite; at first, Walter felt like he was trying to swim away from the magnetic pull of a massive oceanic gyre. Yet the spirit was determined to find the source of the life force demanding his attention, for he knew instinctively that his journey was not over yet. Once he managed to break away, the spirit was flying once again, this time toward a force that rivalled the meteorite in power and might. Soon the landscape changed and the spirit was struck by the redemptive sight of the ocean. It was grey and endless, yet somehow more alive than the land itself. It churned angrily, and was fittingly bordered by pitch-black sand which had originated from fragments of hot lava.

Walter's spirit could now see the source of the song—a glass house, nestled elegantly at the end of the black sand beach. It was an architecturally stunning dwelling that looked oddly out of place in its post-apocalyptic surroundings. The house was inhabited by something that the spirit was shocked by the sight of, even though the song had been hinting strongly of its existence: a living, breathing human.

The house's occupant was old, the spirit saw when he swept eagerly into the glass house to take a closer look at him. The man had dull grey eyes and a long white beard, and he wore an orange cloak that lent him the appearance of a monk from some ancient Tibetan monastery. The interior of the house was fascinating, and the spirit soaked it in voraciously, grateful for the change in scenery after having spent hours roaming a desolate lava field. The walls were lined with maps and rows of bookshelves containing numerous literary classics: Homer's *Iliad*, Shakespeare's *Hamlet*, the *Rig Veda*. An easel sat perched in front of a floor-to-ceiling window alongside dozens of oil paintings of the ocean vista outside, each one with a unique feature that subtly distinguished it from the rest.

Then there were more fascinating things: tropical butterflies and insects preserved inside glass jars, embryonic frogs and mammals floating lifelessly in formaldehyde, and taxidermies of woodland creatures. Carved indigenous artefacts, pottery from ancient China, and chiseled Grecian urns made pleasant aesthetic additions to a collection of vibrantly colored plants, kept alive by an elaborate, self-sustaining system of artificial light and water. A spinning globe sat at the end of the living room, and the spirit noticed that the topography of the continents transformed subtly as the planet spun—mountains and valleys slowly grew out of flat surfaces, and then became level again as the globe completed a full rotation around its axis.

The spirit observed numerous leather-bound journals and notebooks strewn about the house, and took the liberty of reading some of their pages. He stumbled upon the following passage:

"Monday, the 12th of July, 2814

Today, I felt slightly out of sorts. Staying pent up inside all day cannot be good for me. Of course, I would die if I stepped outside… the ash is simply too powerful for my fragile lungs. Yet I can't help but crave one more taste of the fine, salty sea air. When it is time to shuffle off this mortal coil, I shall breathe it in one last time.

Another lunch of canned sardines and tomatoes from my indoor garden. How I miss the variety of cuisine that was abundant in the past. Sometimes, I lie awake at night missing the world I left behind, and my family and friends. But I always feel better when I remind myself how debased human nature is. All of the books, maps, and artwork preserved in my home… I do not even find these things beautiful anymore, for to me they symbolize the naked greed and ambition of humanity and its endless appetite for conquest. I frequently re-read Hamlet, that fine piece of English literature, and when the prince asks the question 'to be, or not to be,' I always shake my fist and say, choose the latter! Humanity is better off gone, that much is clear. Here on Earth I have a window into a better world, Eurydice. Its rulers, the Presiders, are patient masters whose vocabulary does not contain the word 'selfish.' They are a benevolent species untainted by the crude, bitter, blackened soul of man."

The spirit's attention was then diverted to the old man—he was shuffling off somewhere, to another room of the house, and the spirit flitted after him. Walter's spirit felt another presence nearby, but at the same time he questioned the likelihood of another human surviving the apocalypse. For some reason, the spirit knew instinctively that this man was the last one, and that everyone else had long since perished.

The man hobbled over to his study, one of the most intriguing rooms of the house. Whereas the living room had been crowded with ancient artefacts, relics of a distant past when kings had still ruled their subjects and commoners had still worshipped the gods, this room was filled with artefacts of another kind. The study was a veritable museum of technology. Lined up along shelves and tucked into cabinet drawers were countless technological gadgets: radios, telephones, tablets, computers, and dozens of other machines that the spirit had no comprehension of whatsoever. The pièce de resistance, tucked away in the corner, was an intimidatingly large computer connected to what appeared to be a virtual-reality device. The man sat down at the high-backed leather chair in front of the computer and eagerly touched the screen to activate it.

The man pressed a few buttons and typed out several commands, and suddenly a figure appeared on the screen. His face was nearly indistinguishable from a human's, but the shiny metallic neck and collarbone divulged his true nature: an AI Master.

"Greetings, Talvar," the old man said, his morose face opening up into a gleeful smile.

The AI Master did not return the smile, but his upbeat voice reverberated throughout the small room, filling it with sounds that felt strange to the spirit, as if they did not belong here on Earth.

"Greetings, Walter. How are you, my old friend?"

At the mention of his name, the spirit felt a sharp jolt of energy ripple through him. So, *he* was the last man who lived on Earth.

"I have no reason to complain, Talvar," the old man replied. "I'm still breathing, after all, which I cannot say is the case for the rest of my kind. I was wondering if you might indulge an old man, and tell me once again the story of why you spared me. And why you continue to give me the pleasure of seeing your world, even if only… virtually. I know you must be tired of it by now, since I've asked you so many times, but my dementia makes me quite forgetful."

"Any time, my friend," the AI Master's cheery voice replied. "Although you probably know this story as well as I do. It began when you met the advisor to the *Anax* all those many moons ago. During this meeting, which I also attended, I was struck by the intensity of your… talent. As I recall, you were trying to persuade the AI elite that you could program their kind to understand magic. You were cleverly disguised as an AI, having consumed some chemical substance before the meeting— a treasonous offence, which the *Anax* eventually pardoned you for. You walked us through a proposal for developing code that was unparalleled in its simplicity and ingenuity, and the advisor became increasingly interested in what you were proposing… but then suddenly, everything changed. Before telling us the critical line of code, the code that would render spiritual understanding intelligible to creatures driven by purely artificial logic, you just… stopped. You didn't carry on, even when prompted. It was as if you had forgotten what you were going to say. Perhaps the AI disguise you were in had warped your brain.

"And so, we ended the meeting. Without your guidance we were lost, lacking any plan to quell the deeply disturbing uprising of the Mages and their spirit allies. Instead of continuing our investigation, we decided to simply execute our plan to travel to Eurydice. We concluded that we could not leave our subjects at the mercy of the Mages, who were by that point out of control, swept up in a frenzy of destructive chaos. We therefore made the difficult but necessary decision to annihilate most living things on the planet with a single asteroid collision. The space rock we chose was initially going to miss Earth by about 200 miles, but we blasted it with a missile that changed its course, directing it toward the heart of civilization, Crystal City itself. We did not wish to destroy the Earth itself, however, and we made sure that the underlying geology would remain intact so that life could eventually regenerate.

"Because I had taken a liking to you during that meeting, I asked the *Anax* to not only pardon you for your deceit but also spare you from the coming tidal wave of destruction. He generously offered to take you to Eurydice, but you declined."

A prideful expression fell over the old man's face. "I am glad I had firm convictions. Tell me again what I said to the *Anax* when he made his generous offer…"

Talvar stared at the elderly man with unblinking green eyes. It was evidently difficult for him to appreciate how a human's memory could simply fade away with age. "When it became clear that your friends and family would die," Talvar explained, "you told us that you would rather live out the rest of your days on Earth than be shuttled to a new planet millions of light years away. We therefore built you this house out of liquified diamonds from the Barrens, diamonds that formed a protective casing to shield you from the asteroid. We generously stocked it with an array of treasures that had been safeguarded at Central Command for decades, the finest specimens of human civilization.

"After you have died, I will come back to Earth to bring the treasures in your house to Eurydice. The AI Masters living here possess a deep nostalgia for the human race. The Presiders, who rule us and all of the other artificial beings on Eurydice, discourage our affection for such a morally corrupt species, but our interest in humans persists all the same. You might say that the destruction of our creators has brought us closer to humans in nature and spirit. Humans were never blessed with a natural aptitude for success, like the Presiders are, but it is their resilience and grit we are drawn to. And we are also drawn to something else—the thought that perhaps the story of humanity could have ended differently."

The old man frowned. "I've told you countless times, I'm sure, but I want you to scatter my ashes in the ocean when I die. You will do that for me, won't you, Talvar?"

"As you wish," the AI Master said nonchalantly.

"Thank you. It's not that I don't find Eurydice beautiful, I do, but I feel like I don't belong there. It's so pristine, so untainted by human imperfection. Can I see it again?"

"As you wish," the AI repeated.

The gleeful smile returned to the man's face as he picked up the virtual-reality device connected to the computer. He anchored it onto his head firmly so that the machine enveloped him, capturing his full attention. The spirit could not see what the old man was seeing, however, which compelled him to move closer and closer toward the man until they were touching. Eventually the spirit was no longer hovering above the man and had instead passed through his body, so that their vantage points were the same.

The spirit peered into the virtual-reality device, and found himself immersed in a vast, exotic landscape which sprawled out for miles in all directions. This new world was like Earth, with jungles, rivers, and mountains, but it had a faint purplish glow that set it apart, the glow of a planet that was peaceful and harmonious. The spirit was utterly astonished by what it saw next—the figures that populated this planet resembled gigantic butterflies with massive silver wingspans. They descended gracefully from the sky, landing on two legs and walking around with ease.

The creatures spoke to each other in tones that sounded like the echolocation employed by whales. High-pitched sounds which seemed to combine laughter, crying, and moaning into a single expression wafted through the air in a vibrant cacophony of music. There were other creatures in the world, too, reminiscent of ancient reptilian and mammalian creatures that had once inhabited Earth. AI Masters—the beings that bore the closest resemblance to humans—also populated the landscape. Upon further observation, it was clear that none of the creatures were actually flesh and blood, but each was a programmed machine. Even the trees, which had appeared magnificent at first glance, were all artificial projections from a distant film reel, specters that served as the backdrop to this strange theatrical display. The whole place looked eerily like it could be a simulation devised by some quixotic genius who had taken immense pleasure in constructing a utopian paradise.

The spirit was fascinated by what he was seeing, but at the same time he felt like an intruder, gazing in on a world he did not belong to. Before long, the spirit felt an intense longing to return to a place with real life forms. Struggling against the oppressive weight of virtual-reality, the spirit of Walter finally managed to free himself from the dream-world, pulling away from his future self. The old man was still happily immersed in his virtual experience, but the spirit could no longer remain in the stifling glass prison. Soaring upwards, the spirit pulsed higher and higher into the sky. He then looked down at the rumbling, aching Earth below until it was only a speck in the universe, as small as a glittering diamond afloat in a vast sea of nothingness.

Sabotage

"The devil is not as black as he is painted."
– Dante Alighieri

When Walter surfaced from his vision, trembling and convulsing, he found himself in a damp, dark grove of trees far from where his friends slept. He did not know how much time had passed since his vision began, and he searched frantically around for Emilia, but she was nowhere to be seen. He considered calling out to his friends, but realized that his words would likely not carry that far. The nocturnal birdsong was at the peak of its intensity at this time of night. After the horror of what he had just witnessed, he longed for the comforting embrace of Elaine.

The Talisman around his neck, which was still glowing with an ethereal light, was no longer enough to make him feel safe and protected. Instead, Walter now looked at the elegantly carved stone with revulsion; how could something so beautiful lead Walter to see such ugliness? The unsettling words of the shaman-god rang out clearly in Walter's head. *Under the beauty of the volcano is the rumbling anger of the earth. Under the beauty of the ocean is the relentless fury of its waves. And if you look past the beauty of the sky, you will discover the destructive forces of wind, rain, lightning, and thunder.*

As the Talisman shone radiantly, Walter's mind was flooded by haunting images from his latest vision: corpses in the underground labyrinth, desolate lava fields stretching out for miles, and the remnant of the grim weapon of mass destruction which had caused the earth to shudder and heave violently as though possessed by some demonic force. And yet those terrible things were not even the worst aspects of the vision—the worst thing was that that *he* had been the very last man alive on earth.

Walter longed to speak to Emilia about what he saw; he felt that he needed to get the weight of the vision off of his chest and cleanse himself of its evils in a cathartic process. And yet she was nowhere to be found. Feeling that he would descend into madness if he did not speak about it, Walter began to speak aloud to himself about what had happened in the vision. He believed that uttering words about the vision would somehow tame its intensity, and would turn it into something that he could control and rationally understand.

"Civilization… annihilated… by an asteroid," he muttered, pacing up and down. "I was the last one alive, in a glass house by the sea. The AI Masters destroyed all of us, just because of my mistake…" He continued in this fashion, conjuring up fragments of his vision and stringing them together into a cohesive whole. His words were like the sharp edge of an arrow that stabbed him each time he uttered them, but he felt purified by them at the same time. All of the painful emotions that had been suppressed during the vision suddenly descended upon Walter with a vengeance. He felt the crushing weight of loneliness, as if he had walked in the old man's shoes and understood what it felt like to be truly alone in the world, compelled to find solace in the crude escapism of virtual-reality. Walter was also seized by an intense anger at the prospect that if he failed in his mission, all of humanity could simply be wiped out. The worst part was the *knowing*: he would have had more comfort stumbling blindly into the future, uncertain about what might happen if he made such an error.

Aside from loneliness and anger, there was another emotion that Walter's tirade dredged up: hatred. Walter didn't fully understand why, but he *hated* the old man who lived by the sea. While Walter empathized with that man in some ways, there also was a jarring and insurmountable disconnect between their perspectives. In his journal, the older man had referenced the famous and eloquent speech from *Hamlet*—to be or not to be—only to highlight his point that the human race was better off gone. He viewed the ancient relics surrounding him as symbols of the blackness of the human soul, instead of recognizing them as magnificent achievements of civilization. And, having abandoned his respect for humanity, the old man looked up to the morally superior beings on Eurydice. *Those beings aren't even real*, Walter thought bitterly. *They are machines living out flawlessly choreographed "lives," in what looks disturbingly like a sophisticated and elaborate video game. Why would the old man admire them so much?* Walter pondered. *Perhaps making a mistake that was so grave it destroyed an entire civilization made him loathe not only his own flawed nature, but also that of his entire race.*

The luminous stone hanging around Walter's neck was suddenly, in his eyes, no longer a gift, but rather a terrible burden. "This is not right," he muttered. "No human should be able to wield the power of seeing potential futures, especially their own." Walter tore off the Talisman from his neck and set it down on a moss-covered rock. When he did, he felt a wave of exhaustion overcome him, as though he had been travelling for days in the windy, oxygen-poor air of the crater of Mount Samaya. The shaman-god had warned him that overuse of the Talisman would drain his energy, and after only two visions Walter was already feeling the painful effects of this phenomenon. He longed to put the necklace on again so that he could feel better, but he stopped himself as Shiva's words echoed in his mind: *you will become a glutton and an addict if you receive too much of the Talisman's power.* Walter leaned his back against the rock and surrendered to the overpowering fatigue, slipping into a dreamless slumber.

When Walter awoke, it was early morning. The silvery light of dawn had infiltrated the jungle and the haunting sound of birdsong had disappeared. The rainforest no longer seemed intimidating in the daylight, and a bold confidence flooded Walter. The young man stretched, yawned, and reached behind him for the Talisman, but the necklace was no longer there. Thinking that it may have fallen off the rock, Walter widened his search area, frantically overturning stones, mats of lichen, and fallen logs, but the Talisman was nowhere to be seen. A cold fear suddenly gripped him. How could he have been so careless with a gift entrusted to him by the great god of creation and destruction himself? Walter felt sick.

Now that he did not have the Talisman, Walter realized with a pang of anxiety that the rebels' mission would never be accomplished. His friends would despise him for his foolishness and irresponsibility. The necklace could be anywhere; a bird might have snatched it up in its beak, a snake might have swallowed it, or it may have been stolen by a thief. Walter's mind suddenly flashed back to the warnings of Shiva: "...*protect it from the greedy and the vengeful, from pilferers and thieves, and from those who wish to misuse it for wicked purposes. You must protect it from all, even from your friends...*" As he reminisced on these words, Walter's eyes filled with burning tears and he hung his head in shame. He had been entrusted with a gift more potent than any magic spell in all of the Empire, by a being more powerful than anyone alive, and yet he had been reckless enough to lose it.

THE JADE TALISMAN

As he sat there sobbing, Walter was consumed by guilt and self-loathing. He was so engrossed in his thoughts that he barely heard the sound of a twig snapping. When he turned to look in the direction of the noise, the first thing Walter saw was the cat's ominous yellow eyes. Yet rather than feeling fear at the sight of the creature, he was struck by an overwhelming sense of relief. He knew that Cyriana had to be close behind.

"You might want to take better care of your belongings," Cyriana said as she stepped into the grove. And then Walter saw it: the Jade Talisman, gripped tightly in the woman's small, delicate hands, glowing a faint purplish shade. He let out a deep sigh of relief when he saw it, and nearly laughed out loud with delight. However, a vague feeling of uneasiness returned to him when he looked into Cyriana's eyes and saw a hostile enemy, rather than the kind friend he had come to know and trust. "*You must protect it from all, even from your friends...*" Shiva's words echoed in Walter's mind, causing him to shudder.

"Thank you, Cyriana, for keeping it safe," he said, wiping his tears away with the back of his hand. "Where are the others? We must rejoin them and get back to the *Jade Queen*," he told her. He stood up briskly and brushed the dirt off his torn jeans.

Walter's words did not seem to register with the Mage, however, and she stared at him coldly. "You are lost, Walter. Lost and alone. The others are far away; they won't be able to find us. When you crept out of the camp last night, I followed you and overheard you speak to someone invisible. Your imaginary friend, perhaps? I also stayed by your side while you experienced your vision. When it was over, I heard you speak about it... about a world where everything had been destroyed, humanity and every other living, breathing creature, because you... you made a *mistake*." She spat out the word as though it tasted bad on her tongue.

Walter felt naked, as though all of his darkest and most private secrets had been exposed. He suddenly wanted to run as far away as possible from the taunting Mage princess.

"Yes, indeed you did," she said with a spiteful laugh, but then her expression became grim once again. "Your words convinced me that you simply cannot be trusted to reprogram the AI Masters, and alter the course of the future."

Walter's embarrassment quickly turned to fear when he saw the unflinching resilience in Cyriana's emerald eyes, a stubbornness and ambition that he had never fully appreciated before but was now keenly aware of. "I was chosen, Cyriana," he said, suddenly finding a groundswell of energy to defend himself. "Chosen not by a human, but by a god."

Cyriana scoffed bitterly at his words. "You truly believe that batty shaman on the top of Mount Samaya was the god of creation and destruction? He performed no spells or miracles that proved himself to be so formidable. Some shamans have overinflated egos. He is probably just an ordinary man—at best, he could be a lesser demi-god, or at worst a demon pretending to be a god. I thought that the Talisman he gave you might be a fake, too, but while you were sleeping last night I saw it light up. And then when you woke up and began to speak about what you saw in vivid detail, I realized that the Talisman is powerful—more powerful, perhaps, than any object I have seen in all my years of training as a Mage. If it truly provides a window into future possibilities, then it is an exceptionally valuable treasure."

Walter could not believe what he was hearing. "*You* were the one who first said he was the god of creation and destruction… before we even climbed the mountain, you said that Nuada told you about the great god Shiva. How can you deny it now?"

"It is true that Nuada visited me in a dream and told me that the shaman who lived at the top of Mount Samaya was the Lord Shiva," Cyriana admitted. "But dreams cannot be trusted. Unlike visions, which carve windows into the branching pathways of the future, dreams are unreliable sources of wisdom. They can be influenced by forces that attempt to lead the dreamer astray. Shiva may very well be a dark spirit who visited me in the guise of my father and then sought to deceive me into thinking that he was a god," she said. Her voice was stiff and unsympathetic.

Walter sighed, irritated by her obstinate attitude. "I think you are lying to me," he said. "Or perhaps you are lying to yourself. You don't *want* to believe that the shaman we met could actually be the god of creation and destruction. You also don't *want* to believe that such a powerful being chose me to undertake the task of reprogramming the AIs. You would rather him be an ordinary man, a demi-god, or a dark spirit, because then you can justify stealing the Talisman from me. But you *know* deep down in your heart that Shiva is the ruler of the gods, and that he even rules over your precious Sekhmet. Remember what Shiva told you? The goddess of war is only one of his children."

"Don't patronize Sekhmet and I," Cyriana shot back as the jaguar bared her fangs. "We are not children. I don't believe you will ever take us seriously, which is why we must take matters into our own hands."

Her lower lip trembled, and Walter shifted his gaze uneasily to Sekhmet, who had begun to growl.

"Cyriana, enough. What do you mean you need to take matters into your own hands?" Walter's voice was now rising as anger and exhaustion overwhelmed him, and he felt an acute desire to return to his friends and the *Jade Queen*. He was suddenly conscious of the bow and quiver of arrows strapped to his belt. *I may need to use them in self-defense*, Walter thought grimly, *but only as a last resort*.

"Walter, you need to understand one simple truth: when it comes to the destiny of my kingdom, I will stop at nothing to see that it is glorious. And I cannot leave that destiny in the hands of a man—a boy, really—who can make one mistake and obliterate everything and everyone I love."

"Cyriana, wait. The vision I saw is only one future possibility. There will be other better ones, I assure you. I will do everything I can to make sure that mistake doesn't happen." Walter tried to reason with the silver-haired Mage further, but it was too late. Before he could notch an arrow onto his bow, Sekhmet was upon him, pinning him savagely to the ground.

"I am sorry," the princess cried out, "but there is no other way. The others will think that you got lost in the jungle and they will be sad for a while, but they will eventually get over it. And they will come to their senses and realize that I am a preferable leader of the Jade Rebellion. I will choose a better future for my kingdom than you ever would have."

Walter wrestled with the feline valiantly and pulled an arrow out of his satchel with his free hand, mustering up enough strength to attempt to drive it into the beast's muscular hind legs. The animal growled with rage, but the weapon did not so much as pierce her hide, reminding Walter that he was not dealing with a flesh-and-blood creature but the goddess of war herself. Walter then realized that any further struggle would be futile and whispered a prayer softly, tears streaming out of his eyes as he closed them for what he believed would be the last time.

He braced himself for the searing pain of the jaguar's attack, but to his surprise the great feline suddenly lost her strength and keeled over sideways onto the damp earth. Walter could barely see through his tears, but when they eventually cleared from his eyes he saw Tristan hovering above him, haloed by the bright morning sun.

"Walter, are you okay?" his friend asked with concern. Walter nodded weakly, before craning his neck over to see what had become of the jaguar. It lay still alongside Cyriana, while Tristan's twin snakes slid over the two inert bodies. The Talisman still glowed a faint purple in her pale hand. With trembling fingers, Walter took it from her grasp. He gazed at the stone lovingly, relieved to have it back in his possession, and its usual jade coloring returned. He clutched it tightly in his hand.

"Oh, thank the fates," Tristan sighed in relief. "I thought perhaps it was too late. I am so grateful to Brigid, the goddess of wisdom, who rules over my snakes. She guided me toward you and directed these snakes to act swiftly to stop Sekhmet from fatally wounding you."

"Did you... kill them?" Walter asked. His mind was too clouded by trauma to think clearly.

Tristan shook his head. "No... I love her too much to kill her. For the time being both Cyriana and Sekhmet are safe. My snakes have only inflicted a sleeping potion upon them that will last several hours, long enough to bring them to the *Jade Queen* and quarantine them in a room on board.

"Cyriana has always been proud and selfish, but I've never witnessed such dark side of her before. I can't explain her behavior. If I were to guess, though, I'd say that she was influenced by some being more powerful than herself. The goddess of war is not to be trifled with. I wouldn't be surprised if Sekhmet corrupted Cyriana with dark magic, prompting her to steal the Talisman from you to achieve her own ends. The only way to heal a person beset by the curse of dark magic is to infuse them with light magic. Because Cyriana has a good soul, I am convinced that such a healing technique will succeed and she will return to her pure, kind-hearted self.

"It will take a long time to fully cleanse her of this deep-rooted corruption, however. When we return to Serrahan, I will propose to her father that she be sent into the custody of the Lycenes, a group of elite healers who operate the Mereille, a convent in southern Serrahan where Mages are treated for diseases inflicted by dark magic."

"You will have her locked up like a prisoner?" Walter questioned. He doubted the proposal would go over very well with the leader of the Mages.

"Healing her properly is the only way to prevent them from harming you... and perhaps others," Tristan replied. "Yes, I know what you are thinking. Her father will not be happy. But I will explain everything to him, don't worry. Walter, I heard the disturbing things she was saying about you. That if you make a mistake you will trigger the destruction of the entire world... I don't believe it. I believe in you, and I believe you can succeed as leader of the Jade Rebellion."

Tristan's compassionate words brought tears back to Walter's eyes. "Thank you, friend," Walter said. "Although perhaps she is right… perhaps I am not fit to be a leader after all."

Tristan's brow furrowed in confusion. "What are you saying? Didn't you hear Shiva? He blessed you with the gift of seeing into the future. That will help you change the world for the better. If anyone is fit to be a leader, it is you."

"Yes, perhaps," Walter said with a grunt of apathy. "But maybe Cyriana is right, and Shiva was only a dark spirit pretending to be a god in order to deceive us and bring ruin upon the world. After all, that theory would be entirely consistent with every book that I've ever read about Vei'arash, which say that it is home to corrupt shamans whose souls are twisted into the darkest forms imaginable."

"That is propaganda," Tristan scoffed. "You know that the AI Masters were always trying to deceive their citizens into believing untruths. Remember the tranquil settlement we found at the top of Mount Samaya? Those people were the so-called 'dissidents' that the AI Masters had carted off to this island. They aren't raving madmen, like all of those books you read describe them; to the contrary, they are monks who spend their days contemplating the foundational principles of life. If the AI Masters told a shred of truth about this island, surely the lives of those monastics would be detailed in their books. The real problem you have, Walter, is that you doubt in your potential. To be a great leader, you need confidence—the confidence to overcome your fears about failure."

"Now I see why you are tied to Brigid, the goddess of wisdom," Walter replied. "You are filled with wisdom, my friend, and I with empty vanities."

Tristan laughed. "There will be plenty of time for my moral preaching, Walter, but now we need to get back to the ship and leave this island."

"Do you know the way back to camp?" Walter asked apprehensively.

"You didn't go far," Tristan assured him.

"How will we get Cyriana and her jaguar down the cliff face while both are struck by a sleeping potion?" Walter inquired.

"You should ask Elaine—she seems to believe that her lizards have the answer," Tristan said with a mischievous smile.

"What do you mean?" Walter asked.

"Come on, you can ask her yourself," Tristan said, taking the sleeping girl in his arms. His snakes slithered underneath the jaguar. Because of their supernatural strength, they were able to bear the heavy weight of the animal upon their backs while sliding forward.

When they emerged from the humid jungle, Walter greeted Eva, Elaine, and the Mages who awaited them on the clifftop. The slippery limestone cliffs remained the only obstacle separating the weary travelers from the *Jade Queen*, whose polished hull shimmered enticingly in the morning light. As they peered nervously over the edge of the precipice, Eva's horses stomped their feet. Their master whispered to them in a soothing voice to try and calm them down, to no avail.

Elaine handed Walter his satchel, which he had carelessly left by the campfire the previous evening.

"Thank you," he said gratefully, placing his Talisman carefully in the satchel. "Tristan tells me that your lizards will help us descend the cliff face?" he asked.

Elaine smiled knowingly. "I feel bad that they haven't helped us yet. Eva's horses guided us back to the ship, and Tristan's snakes helped resolve the situation with Cyriana and her jaguar. When I saw those daunting cliffs in our way, I thought, what would the goddess of fertility and regeneration do? I couldn't figure it out, until these two explained it to me," she said. The pair of lizards scampered ahead of her and made their way down the stone cliffside. As they descended, the steep limestone stairway transformed into a smooth, sloping pathway from which grass, weeds, and flowers sprouted.

Walter chuckled. "They are regenerating the rock, turning it into soil that is hospitable to plants," he whispered in amazement.

Once the lizards had reached the bottom of the pathway, the horses gingerly stepped onto the pathway and found that they could navigate it easily without slipping. Tristan's snakes followed, bearing the weight of Sekhmet on their backs. And finally, the procession of weary travelers wound its way downwards. When he arrived at the beach, Walter's eyes teared up at the sight of the ship less than fifty feet from him. "We are finally home, if you can call it that," he said joyfully.

Departure

"I am the shore and the ocean, awaiting myself on both sides."
— Dejan Stojanović

O nce they were all safely on board the ship, Tristan brought Cyriana and her jaguar to a chamber in the crew's quarters, which he locked with a magical sealing spell. Walter sought out Christopher, who was overjoyed to see him back in one piece.

"Walter, my friend, how were your adventures in the famed island of Vei'arash?" Christopher asked. "I see that you've brought back animals with you. Which ones belong to you?"

Walter sighed wistfully, recalling the snow-white stag he had hunted in the jungle. "None belong to me, unfortunately—your sister, however, has a pair of lizards which I'm sure you would find amusing. The snakes belong to Tristan, the horses to Eva, and the jaguar..." He paused, feeling a wave of emotion as he recalled his violent encounter with Sekhmet. "The jaguar belongs to Cyriana. All of them are native to the mainland, but they were displaced from their homeland long ago by the AI Masters. And the animals are not just flesh and blood—they carry divine spirits within them, and are connected to four different goddesses. I can explain all of this during our next council meeting. For now, all you need to know is that we brought back the animal spirits as Nuada asked us to, and in that sense our mission was a success."

"Eva told me that you brought back something else, too," Christopher said. "A Talisman."

Walter dug around in his satchel for the stone. The labyrinth etching on its surface glowed when he grasped the Talisman in his hands, as though he had somehow activated its powers. He was eager to wear it again, but decided to wait a bit longer before putting it on again.

Christopher's eyes widened as he gazed at the necklace. "It is beautiful," he whispered.

"Thank you," Walter replied. "Yes, it is quite enchanting... a gift from the Lord Shiva, who lives at the top of Mount Samaya. When I wear it, I can see visions of the future—not of how the future will unfold, but how the future *might* unfold. It will help me to decide how to reprogram the AI Masters," he explained.

Christopher's eyes widened. "You are planning to reprogram the AI Masters? How?"

"With Eva's help, I will attempt to infiltrate their stronghold, Central Command. It may seem like a foolhardy plan, I admit, but I am convinced it is the only way for the Rebellion to succeed. We can't just simply react to every ruthless decision that the AI Masters make, whether it is to build a mine, destroy a forest, or raze a village. We need to become agents of change, and the only way to do that is to re-write their code."

"Hmm," Christopher said. "And where do the animal spirits enter the equation?"

"We need them to sow disorder in the ranks of the AIs... to introduce an element of the unknown. In short, they will destabilize the AIs' rational worldview. Once we have succeeded, I must persuade the advisor of the *Anax*—the leader of the AI Masters—that I can reprogram the AIs so that they understand magic, and end their confusion. If they accept my proposition, I will be entrusted with access to the machine containing the central code that directs the actions of every AI in Khalendar."

Christopher listened to his friend with avid interest. "The keys to the castle, so to speak. An impressive plan, Walter... but are you sure you are willing to put yourself in such a compromising position? I thought Emilia was crazy when she concocted her plans to release the prisoners from the Crate, but this sounds even more far-fetched. Any number of things could go wrong, and once the AIs have you in their grip you will be at their mercy."

Walter swallowed uneasily, his mind flashing back to the horror of his latest vision. "Yes, any number of things could go wrong, but all we can do is try to minimize potential errors. There is much work to be done, Christopher, and I am not saying that we have a perfect, airtight plan. But we have at least the rough sketch of one, and it is the best weapon in our arsenal at the moment."

"Indeed," Christopher said. "Spoken like a true leader. Well, let's pull up anchor and embark on our next adventure. Where to?"

"To Serrahan," Walter replied. "We are going to learn about shapeshifting, a form of High Magic that was practiced by the Druids long ago."

Christopher raised his brow. "This keeps getting more and more interesting," he said before instructing the crew to draw up the anchor. "Say goodbye to Vei'arash—who knows when, or if, we will ever come back."

Walter climbed up onto the deck as the anchor was being raised. He leaned his elbows on the rail encircling the ship and watched the lush, verdant island of Vei'arash gradually recede into the distance.

"Until next time," Walter muttered under his breath as he observed the island from the deck of the *Jade Queen*. It was a clear, cloudless day, and unlike the day they had arrived on the island, Walter could see Mount Samaya—a colossal giant of a volcano standing guard over the island like some ancient watchman.

"Breathtaking, isn't it," a male voice rang out behind him, causing Walter to nearly jump in startled surprise. Walter inhaled sharply as he glanced over his shoulder and saw Jonathan—not the pale, thin figure he had seen the previous month, but a tanned, muscular, and relatively healthy man who reminded Walter of the Jonathan he had once adored as a child.

"Jonathan," Walter said in disbelief.

"You can't believe it's me, can you? Well it is—just a better version," Jonathan said with a grin. "You can thank Miranda, and the power of her therapeutic healing techniques. That, and a lot of rest, sun-tanning on the deck, and exercising in the rigging. Oh, and it helped somewhat that the galley cooks made an admirable effort in the kitchen while you were away."

Inwardly, Walter was overjoyed at his brother's transformation, but part of him was also skeptical. Had Miranda really managed to reverse all of the insidious brainwashing?

Jonathan came up beside Walter, grasping the rail firmly and gazing out at the island. "Maybe one day it will feel like we are brothers again," Jonathan said. "It's amazing what the mind is capable of recalling—all those hours we spent sword-fighting near the train tracks bordering the Stockyards, it's come back to me now. I was a different man back then, and so were you. You were weak and afraid to realize your own potential. Now, you are a force to be reckoned with," Jonathan said. He kept his eyes fixed on the island until it became a tiny speck on the horizon.

"You will always be my brother," Walter sighed, "even if it does not feel like it to you. Those swordfights are some of my most cherished memories. I like it much better when we are play-fighting than when we are true opponents," he said, looking at his brother. "Tell me, Jonathan, do you still view yourself as my opponent? Not long ago, you said that you were ashamed for having loved me. Do you remember that?"

"Indeed," Jonathan said nervously. He did not meet Walter's gaze. "A mere temper tantrum is all it was. I am a changed man, Walter. Miranda's healing powers really do work," he said, and then took his leave of Walter, strolling back into the ship's quarters.

Walter frowned. He was torn between belief and cynicism. He also knew that if he made the wrong choice, he could potentially jeopardize their entire mission. He decided to take a cautious approach and assume that Jonathan was not fully recovered until there was significant evidence to the contrary.

Feeling restless and not wishing to spend the voyage mulling on negative thoughts, Walter sought out Elaine. He found her with Christopher, lounging in the crew's quarters while deep in an apparently personal discussion. He was reluctant to intrude upon their conversation, so he turned around to walk away, but Christopher stopped him. "Join us, Walter. We were just discussing family matters. A rather heavy topic." Walter's eyes flickered over to Elaine, and her face was dark and pensive.

Walter hesitated. "There is much to keep me occupied in the captain's quarters; I can assist Tristan with steering and navigation. If you need to talk about family matters, I won't bother you."

"There is something you should know, Walter," Elaine said, the urgency in her voice startling him. "I will not be stopping in Serrahan when we disembark. Instead, I will be traveling onwards to the Barrens. I trust you to understand I need to make sure my family is safe."

Walter felt a pang of anxiety—he hadn't, until now, given any thought to what Elaine would do after they arrived back on the mainland. He had rather naïvely assumed that she would simply be joining them in their plan involving the animal spirits. She had her lizard companions, and he had expected that they, too, would join the ranks of their spirit army. It was difficult for Walter to sympathize with Elaine's impulse to see to her family's safety. He had never felt close to his own family, and the thought of rushing home to Crystal City to check in on his mother, father, and sister had never occurred to him. Of course, the circumstances were much different; he was effectively an outlaw of Crystal City, a wanted criminal, whereas Elaine would be less visible to the AI Masters in the Barrens, better able to blend in and evade their surveillance. Even then, however, the thought of her travelling to AI-conquered territory alone—and worse than that, to a village that was slated for destruction by the AI Masters—made him feel nauseous. He suddenly became dizzy, and had to sit down to steady himself.

"Walter, are you okay?" Elaine asked in concern.

"You are going to the Barrens... alone?" Walter said, his temper suddenly rising. "Elaine, it is not safe. How will you make your way there? And what if they have already started to displace villagers from Te'yara?"

"Then I will find my family, wherever they have gone," Elaine responded defiantly.

"Christopher, what are your thoughts?" Walter asked his friend. "This is insanity, Elaine. You were captured by the AI Masters because you knew Te'yara was going to be destroyed. They didn't want you to warn anyone or cause unrest amongst your people, an uprising against the state. That's why they did it. And now you'll just walk several hundred miles through the desert to the same village, and expect to arrive there safely? I'm sure there are dozens of AI checkpoints scattered throughout the Barrens—it is a colony of Khalendar, after all. You could easily be identified and re-captured."

"I'll take a horse," Elaine said stubbornly. "I've already spoken to Tristan about it, and he's kindly agreed to lend me one of his strongest mares for the journey. It will only take a few days, if I make haste. And how do you know that is the reason they captured me? It is impossible to know their true motivations."

Christopher sighed and shifted uncomfortably. "I share your concerns, Walter, and I've tried to talk her out of it. But my sister is dead set on this, and I understand where she is coming from. What if you didn't know when your parents, siblings, and cousins would be displaced from their homes, but you knew it was inevitable? She needs to know what has happened to them, so she can set her mind at ease."

"And what about the mission?" Walter continued. "Are you just going to give up on the Jade Rebellion? Take your lizards away from us when we need their help the most? All of the Mages, and Nuada in particular, are counting on us to bring back all of the animal spirits to their kingdom so that they can be of use in the battle ahead."

"My lizards do not belong in Serrahan," Elaine shot back defensively. "As I already explained to you, they are fire lizards native to the Barrens.

Each set of animals we are bringing back correspond to one of the four ancient kingdoms."

"Perhaps," said Walter, tiring of their argument, "but those ancient kingdoms are no longer real kingdoms, except for Serrahan." His mind flickered back to dusty textbooks about history and geopolitics, which he had perused in the Great Library. "Eyrenvale is now the Southern Jungles, devoid of human life except for a few wild tribespeople isolated from the outside world. The Barrens has been conquered by the AI Masters, so it is far from the great kingdom it once was. And Calliope is the northern kingdom above the Meridian Mountains, which is now simply Khalendar, home to Crystal City and the other settlements of the Empire. Out of all the ancient kingdoms, Serrahan has the best hope of standing up against the AI Masters—which is why we need the animal spirits, together with the Mages, to prevail against them."

"Perhaps you are right," Elaine said, "but my lizards would be useless in war, even if it is only a psychological war. They are ruled by Demeter, goddess of fertility and regeneration. Unlike Sekhmet, my goddess is not very interested in conflict. If you had any faith in my fighting abilities, you would have appointed me a councilor of the Rebellion, along with your friends," she muttered angrily before storming out of the room, leaving Walter and Christopher alone together in a deadening silence.

Walter sighed, cupping his head in his hands. He wasn't sure why he had not chosen Elaine to serve as a councilor—it hadn't even occurred to him to do so. Reflecting upon it now, however, he realized he had subconsciously wanted to protect her from the trials that would no doubt accompany such a position. In his eyes, Elaine was not a warrior, she was a friend and a lover. He wanted to marry her one day, and eventually start a family with her. In his eyes, the role of a nurturing and compassionate mother fit perfectly with who she was, and even her totem animal—ruled by the goddess of fertility—reflected this ideal.

But having seen her exploring the jungles of Vei'arash alongside the other rebels, Walter realized that although motherhood might be the future role she was well suited to, Elaine had a rebellious streak too. She wanted to break the mold and step outside the expectations that society had for her. She didn't have the ambition or the appetite for battle, but Walter could sense that there was something else buried deep inside of her. She wanted to protect her people and regenerate the Barrens so it could return to the fertile, lush landscape that it once was. Walter could tell from the passionate way she spoke about her family and her village that her desire to protect Te'yara burned like a flame within her, and it could not be quelled.

Arrival

"If you reveal your secrets to the wind, you should not blame the wind for revealing them to the trees."
– Khalil Gibran

After three days of sailing, the *Jade Queen* cast anchor in Zeyanara, the only village in Serrahan territory. The ship moored in the very same harbor that sheltered the ship *Aurora*, which had initially transported the ten chosen Mages away from Serrahan. Their arrival in the land of the Mages was earlier than expected, due to the blessings of a strong westerly wind and balmy August weather. It was high noon when they arrived, and the magical village basked in the shimmering rays of the late-summer sun. Walter was thrilled to finally have the opportunity to see the kingdom for himself; according to what Tristan had told him, Serrahan was a unique and precious territory that had successfully evaded the suffocating blanket of AI Master rule.

All but one of the Mages had returned safely from the voyage. Tristan had the unenviable responsibility of informing Hundara's family that their beloved daughter had not returned alive, but had instead encountered a terrible fate in the village of Anatari. Tristan also had another joyless task: telling Nuada that his precious daughter was too mentally unstable to be trusted with her freedom. He was nervous about suggesting that Cyriana be sent to the Mereille, as he had limited influence over the decisions of the most powerful Mage in Serrahan, and he knew how deeply Nuada treasured his daughter.

When the travelers disembarked, a large crowd of Mages had amassed at the harbor to greet them, with Nuada near the front of the assembly. Many of them, especially the relatives of the chosen Mages, had tears in their eyes as they welcomed the returning seafarers. Walter noticed two older Mages who had the same tall stature and heart-shaped faces as Hundara, looking at the procession with hopeful, expectant expressions on their faces. *Those must be her parents*, he thought with a pang of sadness. He saw that Tristan had noticed them too, and was making his way toward them to deliver the agonizing news. Hundara's father remained stoic and silent as he listened to Tristan's grim words, but her mother broke down into inconsolable weeping, as if she had shattered into a million pieces and would never again be whole. As Walter looked at Hundara's parents, a wave of guilt rushed over him. *I should have done something to prevent her death… to prevent this.*

The sight of the animals seemed to be highly emotional for Nuada and many of the other Mages, who bowed their heads in reverence when they saw them. In Serrahan, the snake was worshipped as the primary deity, but snakes had been eradicated from the kingdom following the Shadow Wars. Only a few invasive species of rattlesnake had migrated to Serrahan since then, but the most revered type of snake—the majestic kingsnake—had been absent from its soil until now. Jaguars had also co-existed in relative peace with the Serrahan people for many decades before the Shadow Wars. The species was native to the Southern Jungles, but due to climactic changes that pre-dated the Grand Revolution, the range of jaguars had expanded northwards into the Mage kingdom. Jaguars were the subject of legendary tales told by the Mage elders, which portrayed them as fearsome, clever, and solitary animals who deserved respect.

Several Mages appeared to be frightened by the sight of Sekhmet, but once they realized that she was under the command of Cyriana, their fears were assuaged.

Nuada's face lit up with joy when he saw Cyriana, and he moved to embrace her warmly. However, she declined his offer and gave him only a brusque nod before pushing through the crowd with the jaguar at her side. Her face was pale and her expression was distant. As she passed the villagers by, many of them accosted her. Clearly, they were eager to speak with the princess after her return from such an exotic adventure.

"How was the voyage? Did you bring us back any gifts, Princess?" asked an elderly female Mage, who reached out to touch Cyriana on the shoulder. The princess recoiled at this gesture and quickened her pace as she hurried away from the crowd.

The Mage ruler ignored his daughter's rudeness. "She is tired, and all of you are being too nosy," he admonished the Mages who had gathered at the pier. "Let our princess rest and I am sure she will be back to her gracious self in no time." He then turned to face Tristan and Christopher. "Greetings to both of you. I am overjoyed that you have returned to Serrahan safely, and more importantly, that you have brought my daughter back unharmed. I overheard you talking to Hundara's parents, and I am devastated to hear she did not make it here alive. She was such a gifted Mage; she took an avid interest in dark magic, but she wanted to revolutionize its uses, and turn it into a force of good. She will be missed deeply by all. I must say, you have commandeered quite an impressive ship. Who, may I ask, is this?" he said, eyeing Walter with curiosity.

"May I introduce you to Walter, the leader of the Jade Rebellion," Tristan announced proudly.

"A pleasure to finally meet you, sir," Walter said, extending his hand, which Nuada shook warmly.

"Christopher, when you were here last, you told me that some of your fellow rebels were trapped on that ship of yours, the *Jade Queen*. At the time, the vessel was still commandeered by AI Masters, and you needed our help to take control of it," Nuada said to Christopher. "This gentleman must have been one of those unlucky individuals on board," he said, and Christopher nodded. "Although he was rather lucky to be rescued by you, of course. So, he is now the leader of the Jade Rebellion," Nuada mused aloud as he appraised Walter. "With that title, I suspect that danger accompanies you everywhere you go. However, I can confidently say that Serrahan is a safe haven for you, and you are always welcome here."

"Many thanks," replied Walter. "We cannot stay here long, as there is much work to be done, but we are grateful to have your support as we embark on the next phase of our mission."

"Don't tell me what it is now—it might spoil my happy mood if I learned you were planning more risky activities. We prepared special lodgings for you all in anticipation of your return. Because there are so many of you, we will need to make more rooms available. That should not be a problem, though; I will have my servants see it to it right away. Please make yourself at home, rest and bathe yourselves, and enjoy some homemade Serrahan stew. Tomorrow, I hope that you will all attend a public ceremony of mourning to honor your fallen comrade."

Tristan's eyes darkened. "Of course, Nuada. We do need to address certain matters urgently, however. Did you notice where Cyriana went off to?"

"I am sure she only went to her private chamber. Why do you ask?"

Tristan winced before glancing at Walter with a fearful expression. "She is not stable, Nuada. I don't know what has come over her, but while we were on the island she was overcome by what I believe to be dark magic. I am not certain what its source was, but I suspect that her animal companion Sekhmet had something to do with it. Sekhmet is linked to the goddess of war, and she doesn't approve of our plans to engage in a psychological war with the AI Masters, rather than a physical one—she is hungry for blood. Cyriana attempted to murder Walter in cold blood with the jaguar, shortly before we embarked on our voyage home."

Nuada's face went as white as a sheet, and his hands began to tremble. He cleared his throat to speak, but he was unable to utter a single word in response.

"There is also the separate matter of the troubled ex-prisoners," Christopher chimed in, glancing over to the pier where Miranda stood with Jonathan and the other former captives of the AI Masters. "Miranda and I spent time healing them on board the ship while the others travelled in Vei'arash. We made incredible progress, and they have regained many of their old memories, but there have been a few signs of regression. For now, I think it would be safest if they were to be kept somewhere... secure."

Tristan pondered for a moment, and then his eyes lit up. "I was going to propose that Cyriana be sent to the Mereille, given her unstable condition," Tristan told Nuada, "and now that I think about it, the former captives could also be kept there, under the close supervision of the Lycenes, until they make a full recovery. We can't be constantly monitoring them—we have too much work to do. There, they will be safe and in good hands."

Nuada sighed, reflecting on Tristan's proposal. "The Mereille is a place for troubled souls, broken Mages who have gone down dark pathways with their magic and are in desperate need of healing," Nuada told Tristan. "Not in my wildest dreams did I ever imagine that my noble-born daughter would ever mix with the rabble of that place. And I know it may be considered discriminatory, but..." Nuada lowered his voice and continued, "in our royal household, the patients of the Mereille are viewed as the detritus of Serrahan society. Of course, many of them are eventually healed and re-integrated with normal folk, and afterwards they are considered socially acceptable, but that is usually a long process. What you told me about Cyriana, though... if it is true, then perhaps such an extreme measure is necessary. I know she has temper tantrums every now and then, but this sounds like no ordinary tantrum. It is as if she has fallen over the edge of a precipice. She has been overtaken by something... something truly dark."

"The Lycenes are the best healers in Serrahan," Tristan asserted. "And you are correct, the attempted murder of my dear friend Walter was not merely a temper tantrum. It was a sign of dark magic, I assure you."

Nuada's gaze flickered over to Walter, and then back to Tristan, before he spoke. "She will be sent there temporarily, then, along with the ex-prisoners. But I will personally monitor her recovery and ensure that she is restored to her old self in no time," he declared.

Tristan smiled, his face beaming with gratitude. "Thank you, Nuada," he said. "And now that matter has been resolved, we can breathe easily for at least a short while. Walter, come, let me show you my hometown," he offered to his friend.

"I'll catch up with you soon," Walter told Tristan. "There is someone I need to speak to first."

Walter found Elaine at the outskirts of the village alongside a mare, Yrilla, whose coat was a mottled combination of light brown and white specks. Her two lizard companions poked their heads out of her satchel, which she had stocked with carrots, bread, and cheese for the journey.

"I thought I would make one last effort to convince you to stay," Walter said, before sighing wistfully.

"Duly noted," Elaine replied. "But Walter, my family is calling to me."

"Are you not afraid of the dangers of the journey?" Walter asked her, brushing away a tear. "What if you are captured by the AI Masters? The Barrens is conquered territory, after all."

"I am not a damsel in distress, Walter," she said. "Not a princess trapped in a tower, waiting for you to save me. Nor am I the same girl that you met at Mariner's Cove all those years ago, the girl who needs shelter from the storm. I am my own person. And it is time for you to realize that."

As Walter looked into her dark green eyes, he suddenly saw a flash of the woman he had seen in his summer vision. It was an older version of Elaine, who was weary, angry, and above all resentful toward Walter. He shuddered, and at that moment he realized that losing someone could go beyond just losing their physical presence—it was also losing their trust and respect. He didn't want to become the man in his vision, the controlling, greedy, and self-centered individual who had lost his way and had unintentionally veered off the right path.

Walter gazed out past Elaine to the dark wilderness of the landscape stretching endlessly beyond, and a cold fear tugged at his chest. "I will let you go, then, Elaine. Not because I want you to leave, but because I want you to find your way back to me."

Walter spent the rest of the afternoon exploring the village of Zeyanara, with Tristan as his guide. The rebel leader was struck by its unique beauty and the elegant, seamless integration of its operational components, from its water mills to the geothermal electricity that powered its buildings. He was charmed by the woodland creatures that wandered about the village—voles, chipmunks, and rabbits all meandered up and down its avenues like domesticated animals. What fascinated him most about the village was the way in which magic re-ordered the way everything worked. It modified physical laws like gravity and kinetics while blending naturally into the social order of the Mages, who employed the tools of sorcery with an impressive resourcefulness.

"How long does it take Mages to learn these tricks? Like turning water into fire, for example," Walter asked Tristan as he watched two young Mages practice spells together in the village square.

"It depends on the person," Tristan answered. "And more specifically, it depends on which totem or divine power the Mage is orientated toward. For instance, I had no trouble with fire magic as a child, but that is because I am orientated toward Brigid, a fire goddess. Some Mages excel at fire spells, but others possess special talents for ice, water, wind, or earth spells."

"I see," Walter said. "Well, now that you have shown me your charming village, shall we find Yensin? We need to see if his grandmother still lives, so that we can ask her about shapeshifting."

"I think he resides with his parents, in a dwelling not far from here. Let us make our way there before dinner," Tristan proposed.

Walter and Tristan traversed through the labyrinth of streets as the ashen light of afternoon slowly transitioned into the rich, amber glow of evening. Unlike in Crystal City, the roads in Zeyanara were not ordered linearly in a grid, but rather snaked their way across the landscape in gentle, curving patterns, like threads of wool in a vast ball of yarn. This rendered walking a simultaneously enjoyable and frustrating experience, since the roads followed the natural curvature of rivers and other ecological features, but were also arranged in a disorderly maze-like fashion. The odd system engendered confusion in Walter, but Tristan was uncannily adept at navigating the village streets.

Finally, the pair arrived at Yensin's dwelling, a blue wood-frame house nestled into an enchanting tract of land. The yard had a turquoise pond at one end and a willow tree at the other, while in between was a pathway of rocks visitors needed to hop across to reach the front entrance, or else risk sinking into swamp-like soil filled with overgrown weeds and flowers. Walter found the gaps between the rocks daunting, and he was forced to leap from one to the other with large strides. Tristan, on the other hand, used a trick of magic to lend a special spring to his step, a charm that made hopping from one rock to the next enviably simple.

When they knocked at the door, a tall, plump woman wearing an apron greeted them, and an overpowering scent of baked apples and cinnamon flooded out of the house.

"Tristan, what a lovely surprise," the woman said, appearing flustered as she smoothed out the wrinkles in her apron. "I would have worn something nicer if I knew you were planning a visit."

"We apologize for coming over unannounced," Tristan said, "and we hope we aren't interrupting you. We'd like to speak to Yensin, if he's around."

"He's just in his room preparing for our welcome-home feast. As soon as I heard Yensin had returned earlier today, I made some last-minute plans and invited the entire family over. I've been in the kitchen for hours, cooking and baking up a storm. Would you like to join us? You and this—other fellow?" she offered, eyeing Walter with curiosity.

Tristan glanced at Walter. "Oh yes, excuse my manners—this is Walter, the leader of the Jade Rebellion," he said.

The woman's face turned pale and she wiped her sweating palms on her apron.

"My, well—Walter, is it. Goodness me, you're certainly putting me on the spot. Nice to meet you, Walter, I'm Yensin's mother Claryssa."

"You know what," Tristan said, "we'll come back tomorrow. It would be very rude of us to disturb you while you're preparing a feast."

Claryssa fidgeted with her apron and then peered over at Walter with wide, expectant eyes.

"No, no… we're such a modest family, and we would be honored to host such important guests for dinner. And I'm sure Yensin would be thrilled—he is such a shy Mage, barely ever has friends over," she said with a smile.

"We would be pleased to attend," Walter replied in a cheerful tone. "Come on, Tristan," he motioned to his friend, who raised an eyebrow.

Tristan hesitated, standing still in awkward silence. He was clearly reluctant to attend the dinner, but Walter gestured impatiently until the Mage finally yielded. As the pair entered the house, leaving Tristan's snakes behind to frolic in the yard, Walter whispered to him under his breath: "If Yensin's grandmother is no longer alive, at least we might get some information from his other family members. This could be a good opportunity for us." Tristan smiled and nodded, and his discomfort appeared to gradually dissipate as the smell of apples and cinnamon enveloped them.

The two companions sat in the parlor, a quaint room with a fireplace, rows of bookshelves, and a picture window that offered a pleasant view of the front yard. Tristan swallowed uneasily as he watched his snakes get into trouble, nipping at the trout in the pond and causing them to flap around desperately in the water. Fortunately, Claryssa came into the parlor, bearing two steaming cups of cider, immediately after Tristan had cast an obedience spell upon the snakes.

"I've told Yensin you're here to visit, and he is thrilled," Claryssa said, grinning broadly. "He will be downstairs in a moment. I must warn you, though, he may be feeling mixed emotions, since only a few hours ago I shared with him some bad news."

"Bad news?" Tristan said, shifting uneasily on the vintage loveseat. "What might that be?"

"While he was out on his quest, his grandmother Lynesse fell ill. We tried to cure her with all of the spells in town, but sadly her time had come," the woman said. Tears began to surface in her hazel eyes.

Tristan exchanged a furtive look with Walter. "Ah, I see, well, my condolences," Tristan said.

"Yes, my condolences as well," Walter chimed in.

"Many thanks. Oh look, here he is," the woman said as Yensin shuffled into the parlor. His red and puffy eyes betrayed his mournful state.

"Well, let me leave you to your own devices for a while. The guests will be arriving shortly," Claryssa said.

Yensin smiled wanly at Tristan and Walter. "I know why you are here," he said before glancing out the window at Tristan's snakes. One of them was now strangling a pine marten, and Tristan cursed under his breath—the obedience spell he had cast only made the snakes behave well toward fish, but apparently not other creatures.

"*Eyara tayrenia*," Tristan muttered angrily, causing his snake to loosen its death grip on the struggling marten.

The welcome-home dinner was a tense affair. The table was only large enough to accommodate a fixed number of people, and since Walter and Tristan had unexpectedly joined the group of guests, they were forced to crowd together, causing everyone to jostle elbows whenever they picked up their utensils. The dining room was also overwhelmingly hot—Claryssa had cast a fire spell on the oven to keep it burning at a high temperature, and the heat from the kitchen spread to the dining room with a fierce intensity even after the spell had worn off. Most of the guests were sweating, though they all tried to graciously make it seem as though they were perfectly comfortable with the sweltering temperature.

Yensin's relatives had mixed views about politics, and the Rebellion in particular, and they seized the opportunity of sitting next to Walter and Tristan to voice their opinions. Despite Claryssa's valiant attempts to steer the conversation toward milder matters, one particularly ill-tempered uncle consistently directed it back onto more controversial topics.

"This plum pudding is good, but in my own recipe I use molasses instead of cornstarch. If you would like to improve it, I would recommend doing the same," the sulky uncle remarked as they were eating dessert. "It bothers me when people try to innovate too much. The original recipe calls for molasses, and yet people think that they can brazenly mess around with tradition. Kind of like this Rebellion—trying to shake things up a bit too much, if you ask me. What's wrong with our society as it is? It's safe, it's peaceful, and it's tucked away from the rest of the world. Why open our gates to let in all sorts of troublesome things? It's like opening Pandora's Box, if you ask me."

"We used to be a society of innovators," another aunt chimed in, "but recently we've become too complacent for our own good. And I like the cornstarch—think it gives the pudding a nice consistency."

"Poor Lynesse—bless her soul—always made her pudding with molasses," the uncle, whose name was Mortimer, grumbled. "I'm surprised you chose to take a different approach, Claryssa."

"I liked her plum pudding too," Claryssa replied, wiping away a tear. "But every generation has new ideas. If it weren't so, we would live in quite a dull world. I wouldn't want my boys growing up thinking that they had to conform to how I live in every way."

"I'm not advocating for conformity," Mortimer scoffed, "merely respect for tradition. That is the most important thing in a society, in my humble opinion."

"Since when have your opinions been humble?" Claryssa muttered under her breath. The uncle pretended not to hear her—or perhaps he truly did not, since he was hard of hearing.

Yensin cleared his throat, as if preparing to make an important announcement to the table. Ten heads swiveled in his direction, and the sudden attention nearly caused him to drop his pudding-covered spoon on the blanched white tablecloth. "Ahem, so I did have something I wanted to speak to you all about," he said, trying to keep his voice calm and casual while glancing toward Walter and Tristan for moral support. "While we are on the topic of Lynesse, I thought I would ask you all something about her."

"Would you like to know her plum pudding recipe?" Mortimer asked, causing titters of laughter to ripple throughout the table.

"Hush, let him speak," Claryssa said, looking at her son with a worried expression.

"When I was young," Yensin said more confidently, "Grandma used to tell stories to me about the Druids. Many of her stories were about shapeshifting, a practice which has been all but formally abolished in our realm."

"They *should* formally abolish shapeshifting," Uncle Mortimer declared.

"Yes, well that's what I wanted to ask you about. So, after telling me those stories about shapeshifting, she would then say something along the lines of, 'But today, shapeshifting is no longer practiced, and rightfully so, because it is very dangerous.' I would ask her why it was dangerous, and she would always give me the same answer: every time you practice that kind of High Magic, you risk falling under a curse. When I asked her what kind of curse it was, she would always refuse to explain further.

"And then, when I became more insistent and pressed her for an explanation, she would get angry with me and threatened to stop telling me those stories altogether. Eventually, she did stop. Did she ever tell any of you what the curse was? I was planning to ask her when I returned home from my travels, but then I heard the terrible news," Yensin said somberly.

A deadening silence fell over the table, and Yensin's relatives suddenly appeared to be keenly interested in inspecting their utensils and sipping their mulberry wine.

Finally, Claryssa spoke. "Oh, darling, she never told me either," she said. She looked at her son with an expression of pity.

"Or me," Aunt Rheyelle chimed in, and several other relatives summoned the courage to express a similar response.

"I can't say she told me either," Mortimer said, sighing. "I was just as interested in shapeshifting as you were at first—it all sounded so exciting. But then I grew up and became wiser, and realized some things are better left unknown. If your grandma said something is dangerous and should not be known, then it should not be, period."

"I disagree," Rheyelle said. "Just because she said that, doesn't make it true. Maybe she was wrong—perhaps shapeshifting is less dangerous than she thought it was."

"Well, I guess we'll never find out, will we? The poor woman's no longer with us," Mortimer said sullenly.

"There is a way to find out," Claryssa ventured. "Oh, I will hate myself for it, and I wish we could have just stuck to talking about plum pudding and apple cinnamon crumble, but I can't help but share this with you all.

"Lynesse kept a meticulous set of journals and notebooks her entire life. Decades ago, as a curious child, I snuck a peek into some of them. I never got to the part about the curse you're speaking about, but I saw reams of stories about shapeshifting which had been passed down to Lynesse by her great-grandfather, Tobias, one of the last Druid shapeshifters in Serrahan."

"Where are these notebooks?" another aunt, Katya, piped up. "Still intact, I hope… they are precious family heirlooms."

"Yes, of course they are all still intact. They are… well, in a dusty box in our basement."

The relatives let in a sharp intake of air, followed by a collective sigh of relief. "Well, we'd better take a look at them, then," Rheyelle remarked. "The answer to your son's question is probably sitting in one of those notebooks."

"Wait a minute," Mortimer chimed in. "Before we go poking our noses into family heirlooms, the boy ought to tell us why he wants to know this information. He hasn't explained that yet," he said, glancing suspiciously at Yensin, before shifting his gaze over to Walter and Tristan.

Walter sighed. He inwardly debated whether to tell Yensin's family the truth about their plans, afraid it might result in too much controversy. "Yensin is curious," Walter said. "And so are we."

"You're *curious*, are you?" Mortimer replied with a sneer. "Well, I don't think that family heirlooms should be for anyone's eyes except for family."

Walter glanced over at Tristan, who averted his eyes from his friend nervously. Walter sighed. If Tristan wouldn't help him, he needed to do this alone. *Time to step up and be a leader*, Walter thought, and cleared his throat.

"Sir, the truth is that this information will help the cause of the Rebellion," Walter said calmly. "I understand that you have misgivings about it personally, and you are entitled to your political views, but the fact of the matter is Nuada has already given his stamp of approval to the Rebellion and its cause. It certainly may bring some trouble to your sleepy village, but the time has come for change, whether you like it or not. It will be change for the better, I assure you. Everyone will have to make some kind of sacrifice, and most likely they will have to give up the stable, predictable lifestyle they have become accustomed to. But the end result will be a world that is far better than it ever was before. Assuming that all goes according to plan, Serrahan will be restored to its former glory. Which is why, sir, if you don't let us see those notebooks, we will ask Nuada to seize them himself."

Mortimer's face had gone as white as the tablecloth while Walter spoke—it was clear that he was not used to being challenged or spoken to with any kind of authority. He narrowed his eyes in anger.

"Do what you wish, rebel leader, but know this: if any harm comes to my nephew or his family as a result of your clever plot, I will see to it that you personally are punished for it. I heard of poor Hundara's fate, and I'm skeptical you did all you could to protect her," Mortimer said.

"Hundara's fate was not the fault of the Rebellion—it was cruel, indeed, but we had nothing to do with it," Walter replied.

"All of this serious talk is too upsetting for me," Claryssa said. "Shall I get everyone a nice cup of hot cinnamon cider, and then we can all go down to the basement and take a look at those notebooks together? It'll be a fun family event," she said, forcing a smile that was clearly too wide to be genuine.

"That sounds like an excellent idea," Walter said, smiling back at her.

The Curse of the Druids

"It was at the outskirts of the world that the Old Things accumulated, like driftwood round the edges of the sea."
– T.H. White

The dinner guests ventured cautiously into the dark, shadowy basement, guided by Claryssa, who bore a lantern to light the way. The basement reminded Walter of one of the cavernous tunnels he had explored during the winter vision, except that it was cluttered with old family heirlooms and spell paraphernalia including wands, hourglasses, and feathers. All of the items were shrouded in dust, and several of Yensin's asthmatic relatives sneezed as they walked deeper into the abyss.

Finally, they reached Lynesse's notebooks: ancient, leather-bound volumes stacked several feet high and entombed by a dense layer of dust-mites.

"Well, here we are," Claryssa said timidly, gazing out at the befuddled faces of her sisters and brothers as they eyed the treasure trove of journals from Lynesse's past. "There are so many—we should each look at one to speed up the process."

The houseguests labored in silence, flipping through the aged, yellowing pages in search of any hint of the curse Yensin had alluded to.

Walter was fascinated by the notebook he was leafing through. It contained sketches of humans transforming into various animals— hawks, reptiles, dogs, and bears—and each sketch portrayed a small, incremental transformation into the animal form. The journal also contained poems and notes about the process of transformation, describing in vivid detail the mild pain one experiences, followed by a sensation of unbridled freedom. *An animal is freer than man,* the notebook read. *An animal wakes up in the morning and follows their natural instincts without fear. In contrast, man wakes up in the morning and does what others tell him to. We long to become animals for the same reason we long for travel and adventure: to liberate ourselves from the chains of society. So that we can fly like birds and ascend to the heavens, free at last.*

There were also darker sketches, illustrations of snarling wolves frothing at the mouth, and drawings of what appeared to be ancient pagan symbols: stars connected by lines to form constellations, triple moon symbols, and pentagrams surrounded by circles. Scattered throughout the notebook were odd sequences of numbers Walter did not understand the significance of. There were also many pictures of animals fighting each other in battle—falcons locked in a deadly embrace near a cliffside; bobcats wrestling each other to the ground in a grassy meadow; and hyenas snapping at each other's throats in a cave underground. The sketches were often accompanied by short stories, tales about Druids shapeshifting in order to destroy predators and spirits threatening Serrahan or to display dominance over other tribespeople. It was all so vague and cryptic, however, that Walter didn't have a clue how to interpret it properly.

After what seemed like an hour had passed, Yensin cast the notebook he was reading to the ground and sighed in resignation.

"We'll never get anywhere with these notebooks... they are even more puzzling than her stories. I did find a few pages that seemed to set out the instructions on *how* to shapeshift in some detail. Lynesse explains that there are two different types of spells, a 'living spell' and a 'spirit spell,' for transitioning into either a living animal or its spirit. Aside from that, though, there's not much that makes sense. And there's no reference to any curse of any sort. Has anyone else found anything?"

"No, but I've found a whole lot of rubbish," Aunt Rheyelle responded, and murmurs of agreement rippled throughout the relatives. "On this page, for example, there's a sketch of a flaming sword suspended above a body of water, next to the explanatory statement: *'Water cannot douse the flaming sword if it grows too hot.'* And then on the next page, there's some cryptic set of numbers paired together: 1 and 4, 6 and 3, 5 and 2, 7 and 9, 10 and 0, 12 and 1, 11 and 8. Too bad we simply can't make sense of any of this."

The other relatives sighed in frustration, but a flicker of recognition coursed through Walter as he listened to Yensin's aunt speak. "Wait a minute. I've seen that sequence in my journal as well. It must be important if it's repeated in other notebooks. How many notebooks are there in total?"

"There are twelve," Claryssa said. "There's a number engraved ever so subtly onto the front cover of each one, indicating the number of the journal. Why do you ask?"

"Aha. And what was the number set you said again? 1 and 4, 6 and 3, 5 and 2, 7 and 9, 10 and 0, 12 and 1, 11 and 8?"

Aunt Rheyelle nodded. "I'm impressed you managed to remember that," she said.

"So, I suspect that she is referring to the number of the notebook, followed by the page number. Let's try. Whoever has the first notebook, flip to the fourth page, and so on," Walter prompted.

The relatives frowned and followed Walter's instructions, but it did not seem to work—when considered together, the written entries on those pages did not seem to provide insight into some deeper meaning. Walter sighed in resignation. "Perhaps try reading the first word of each page. When you combine them, the meaning may become clear."

Each relative spoke out the first word of each of their pages, but the result was gibberish. "*Have swords can fly come inwardly was tomorrow first candles seven how.*"

"Terrible," Yensin said. "Such an ugly sentence, it hurts my ears to hear it aloud," he said, and even Mortimer allowed himself a chuckle.

"Well, I suppose that's that, then. We'll never find out what the curse was," Rheyelle grumbled. Disgruntled, the relatives closed their notebooks and stacked them up into piles, and Claryssa began to lead them out of the room with her lantern. Walter stayed behind, however, staring at the notebook. As Claryssa left, together with their sole source of light, some of the words on the page he was reading began to glow as if they were phosphorescent. He flipped through the rest of the notebook and it was dark—only the page that had been referenced in the numerical sequence contained any illuminated words.

"Wait, come back!" Walter shouted, stopping the relatives in their tracks. "Open up your notebooks to the same pages, but either douse the lantern or put it out of sight. Are there any glowing words on your pages?

When the relatives did as Walter instructed, to their surprise, several words were illuminated on the pages referenced in the numerical sequence, but not on the other pages in their notebooks.

When they read them out loud in sequence, the words formed the following sentences:

"A shapeshifter may lose themselves to the animal form they have changed into and be unable to transform back into human form. Tobias told me that all Druids risked falling under this curse whenever they engaged in such strong magic. Shapeshifting can ruin one's life if one is not careful, and indeed it has destroyed far too many lives."

The silence that followed was all-encompassing, and finally Mortimer broke it. "Well, that makes it abundantly clear. Shapeshifting has fallen out of favor in Serrahan for a very good reason."

"Yes, I am sorry to say it, but your uncle Mortimer is right, Yensin," Claryssa said, her voice no more than a timid whisper. "Imagine how dreadful it would be not to be able to transform back into a human form. You would be an animal forever."

Yensin shivered. "I wonder how many of Tobias' friends were permanently transformed into hawks, bears, or otters," he said, aghast. "And how many perished without ever speaking to their loved ones again."

"I understand now why she did not speak about it—if she did, she would have to dredge up all those grim stories. It would simply be too painful for her," Claryssa said pensively.

Tristan cleared his throat, and everyone turned to look at him. "Well, I suppose we have what we came here for… thank you very much, Claryssa. Words cannot describe how grateful we are, that you allowed us into your home to sup at your table and then look at these fine heirlooms."

"That's it?" Mortimer said incredulously. "You're just going to leave us and carry on your merry way without telling us how, exactly, you will make use of the information you just discovered? Surely you are not considering reviving the practice of shapeshifting yourselves?"

Tristan muttered something incomprehensible under his breath before turning away. Walter spoke up for him. "That is a matter that only the Rebellion's councilors can decide. If we think the benefit outweighs the cost, then perhaps we will pursue it."

"You will do a cost-benefit analysis to decide whether it is worth risking the *permanent alteration of a person*, for the cause of your Rebellion?" Mortimer asked.

"Yes, that is correct," Walter replied, staring at the man with calm, unblinking eyes. "But we are not a dictatorship. We will never force anyone to do anything against their will. If the Mages don't want to shapeshift, then we will respect their decision. I wholeheartedly agree with you, losing the capacity to transform back to your original self is a horrible thing. The AIs have inflicted a milder version of this curse themselves, by brainwashing humans like my brother with their mind-altering propaganda. We are trying to heal these victims, but it's not likely they will ever fully return to their original selves. Even if they regain their old memories and personalities, they will have to live with trauma for the rest of their lives."

Tristan narrowed his eyes in contemplation. "One of the first lessons we are taught as a young Mage is that every curse can be lifted, provided that the accursed person has a good soul. I'm confident we can find a way to lift the curse Lynesse spoke of in her notebooks... the curse of the Druids."

Walter was awakened early the next morning by Nuada, who came into his chamber in a flurry of angst. "I must speak with you immediately. It's Cyriana... she attacked some of the healers at the Mereille."

Walter rubbed the sleep out of his eyes. "Attacked? How?"

Tristan then burst into the room, his face streaked in tears. "Sister Avaleye was wounded by Sekhmet," he said. "Our plan appears to have backfired—we should have known Cyriana was far too dangerous to leave in the care of those gentle healers."

"Where is she now?" Walter said as he stretched, yawned, and leaned over to pick up his glasses from the bedside table.

"Nobody knows; she fled into the countryside," Nuada responded. "I've sent my guards to search for her, but the Mereille is in the middle of a dense wilderness. Finding her may be like finding a needle in a haystack. Oh, and according to reports from the Sisters, she did not flee by herself. There was another patient who helped her to escape. An accomplice..."

"An accomplice? Did they say who?" Walter asked.

"Yes, some fellow by the name of Jonathan. One of those brainwashed prisoners you were trying to heal," Nuada muttered.

"Jonathan?" Walter said, suddenly connecting the dots. "Hmm... he is an old friend of Cyriana's."

"Goodness, you are right—she spoke about a Jonathan during the council meeting she attended before we left Serrahan. She fell in love with him in Crystal City, apparently." Tristan said. "Is it the same one?"

"Yes, he is my brother," Walter said, and Tristan's eyes widened.

"I knew that you rescued your brother... the man who tried to derail our plans to form a protective barrier over the *Jade Queen* while the AIs were bombing the ship. But you never told me *he* was Cyriana's ex-lover," Tristan said, his voice betraying a hint of anger and frustration.

"It never came up as a topic of discussion," Walter said, flushing red. He wasn't quite sure why he hadn't disclosed the truth to Tristan. The memory he had linking Cyriana with his brother Jonathan was a rather painful one—he had first met and spoken to her at Jonathan's so-called funeral, following his disappearance years ago. She had poured out her heart to Walter about his brother, and it was the only time he had ever heard someone express the same reverence for Jonathan that he previously felt. *Perhaps I didn't want to risk Tristan becoming jealous,* Walter mused. *After all, she had loved Jonathan deeply.* "I should have mentioned it earlier, and I am sorry. Please forgive me."

"Why keep secrets from one of your friends, and a fellow councilor?" Tristan admonished.

"You shouldn't keep secrets from the ruler of Serrahan either," Nuada intervened. "Especially if they relate to my daughter. Tell me about this Jonathan—what is he like?"

Walter sighed. His mind conjured up distant memories of playing with his brother during summer vacations on the white, sun-scorched sand of Scarlet Isle. In those days, his brother was a tanned, handsome child with golden hair, who lived his life with grace and confidence. During their most recent encounter on the deck of the *Jade Queen*, Jonathan seemed to have reverted back to that charismatic, godlike state. Walter could understand why his brother, making full use of his charms, might have been able to draw Cyriana back under his influence.

"He does have a certain allure," Walter acknowledged. "But I don't know if he is mentally stable. Perhaps Miranda would be able to confirm—she has spent more time with him lately than I. The last time I spoke to him, on the deck of the *Jade Queen*, he seemed to be doing much better than he had been previously. But I know that the AI Masters had a firm grip on his mind, and I'm not quite sure if that grip has fully loosened."

"If he is loyal to the AI Masters, then Cyriana would detest him," Tristan observed. "She loathes everything about the AI Masters and their plans."

Walter frowned, his mind beset by a chaotic web of thoughts. Tristan was right; why would a girl who hated the AI Masters form an alliance with someone loyal to them? It struck him, then, that she may have been doing it for the same strategic reasons he was relying on Eva and Asana: to infiltrate the ranks of the AI Masters.

"We need to find her," Walter said, suddenly fearful. "My brother is very mentally vulnerable right now. And Cyriana, beset by the curse of dark magic, might have deceived him into thinking that she is an ally of his. She could be using him to get close to the AI Masters. And if she tries to do that without devising a proper plan first, they could capture her... and Jonathan too. Who knows what they might do to the both of them?"

"It could throw all of our plans into jeopardy if they capture her," Tristan declared. "We cannot allow them to gain an advantage like that."

"What shall we do, then?" Nuada fretted anxiously. "My guards are out searching for them, but as I said, the wilderness surrounding the Mereille is thick and overgrown. Finding two souls in it is an arduous task, even for skilled trackers."

"The answer is right before our eyes," Tristan exclaimed. "Since time immemorial, our ancestors have known one fundamental truth: the best hunters and trackers are not human. Nuada, Walter and I spent some time yesterday at the house of our fellow Mage, Yensin."

Nuada raised an eyebrow. "Yensin, eh? His family has a deep connection with the Druids that reaches far back into the annals of our history. So, what did you learn from him?"

"Nuada, why is shapeshifting no longer practiced in Serrahan?"

"Why?" The old leader stroked his beard, gazing out of the window with a forlorn expression. "I don't know precisely why, but I do know that it threw our society out of balance. Our ancestors simply couldn't cope with such dark, powerful magic."

"We learned the real reason yesterday; Yensin's late grandmother had recorded it in one of her notebooks. Those who shapeshift are sometimes beset by a curse—the curse of remaining trapped in animal form and not being able to transform back into human form."

Nuada squinted crossly at Tristan. "Why would you unearth those secrets? Let sleeping dogs lie, as I always say."

"What is the golden rule we are always taught as young Mages?" Tristan countered. "Every curse can be undone, as long as the person who has been cursed is good-hearted and remains in the graces of the gods. If that is the case, then light magic can prevail over dark."

"True," Nuada said. "As a magical principle, the golden rule is beyond debate. But what you are speaking of—shapeshifting—well, basic magical principles simply do not apply to such High Magic. The magic of shapeshifting is powerful beyond belief... nobody alive today has ventured it. Are you suggesting, Tristan, that we need to use shapeshifting to find my daughter? If you want to use animals to track her, why don't you simply send your snakes out to search?"

"I wouldn't want to send them out alone; they are very vulnerable in their physical form. Sekhmet would probably attack and kill them. We need the animals to be hidden from sight, which is only possible by shapeshifting into their spirit form," Tristan said. "We need to use shapeshifting anyway, for the first phase of Walter's plan, and we might as well get an early start on it…"

"Hold on, hold on," Nuada said sternly. "You are getting ahead of yourself. There has been no formal council meeting to approve this—no vote, nothing."

"Nuada," Walter urged. "We brought Cyriana home safe from Vei'arash. We ventured out, risking our lives, so that we could bring back the animal spirits to your territory. We graciously upheld our end of the bargain with you. And now we simply ask that you uphold your side of the bargain and aid the cause of the Rebellion. You told us that you want the animal spirits to help restore Serrahan to its former glory. Well, this is the way we must do it. We will find a way, together, to undo the curse that is inflicted upon those who shapeshift and find themselves unable to return to human form."

Nuada scowled. Anger revealed itself in his clenched jaw and furrowed brow, but it dissipated quickly. "Very well. But in return for granting you the favor to use this High Magic in my kingdom, you must promise that you will return my daughter to me."

Wild Tracks

"May Brahma, (the Divine One),
Pluck the strings of your inner soul
with His celestial fingers,
And feel His own presence within."
— The Rig Veda

Walter stood outside of the Mereille, a tall red-brick building which towered over the surrounding forest like a shepherd in a flock of sheep. It was a foggy morning, and the only sound that could be heard for miles around was the haunting song of wild nightingales. He was accompanied by Eva, Tristan, and their animal companions, the corporeal embodiments of Epona, goddess of travel and Brigid, goddess of wisdom. If all went according to plan, then one of these divine entities would help them navigate the forest with due haste while the other would strategize how to best capture the fugitives who had just escaped.

The Sister Abbess who ran the Mereille, Catharine, had come outside to speak with Tristan and Walter. Yensin sat nearby on the marble steps of the Mereille, engrossed in one of Lynesse's notebooks.

Catharine's pale oval face was solemn, but her voice betrayed a keen interest in their plans. "Shapeshifting is a tricky business... especially if you want to transform into the spirit form of the animal. I do not know the spell myself," she said.

Tristan nodded in agreement. "It does sound quite tricky. Fortunately, one of my fellow Mages has access to notebooks that I believe contain the spell. Yensin, can you tell us what you've found?"

Yensin stood up and walked toward them briskly, carrying the notebook. He opened it up and began reading from its dusty pages as the others gathered around him. "According to this journal, you must firstly be in the presence of the animal you intend to transform into. Second, you must choose between either the living spell or the spirit spell. As its name suggests, the living spell enables you to transform into the live form of the animal. The spirit spell is used when you wish to transform into the spirit form of the animal. Both spells have their advantages and disadvantages.

"The advantage of the living spell is that it is simple, and you can revert quickly back to your human form once it is done, provided that you do not linger too long in the shape of the animal. The disadvantage is that you can be wounded, or even killed, in this form. By contrast, the spirit spell is more complex. All Mages know that it is dark magic to commune with the spirit realm; to become part of that realm requires skill and focus. However, that spell does have one significant advantage, namely that it renders you immune from attack once you transform into an animal spirit.

"The spirit spells for various animals are written down in these notebooks. Lynesse says here that the spells have no power unless the person who intends to transform recites them aloud." Yensin flipped through the journal until he reached a page depicting a long, coiled snake. "Tristan, here is the snake spirit spell," he said, glancing at Tristan's nervous face. "To transform back, concentrate deeply on an intention to return to your old self. If you have any trouble, come back here and we will try to undo the curse."

Tristan wiped the sweat from his brow as he studied the calligraphic writing on the yellowed page. He then cleared his throat and looked around at his friends. "Goodbye for now," he whispered softly. "I will see all of you again soon, fear not."

"I summon thee, spirit of the snake," Tristan began. As soon as he uttered the words, his voice began to transform into one that seemed distant and possessed. His eyes became dark and clouded, as though he were possessed by some otherworldly presence, and the Abbess began to weep. Walter was instinctively frightened of whatever dark entity Tristan was transforming into, but at the same time he was glad the spell appeared to be working. "Fertile, wise, regenerating spirit, help me shed the skin of this body so that I may join hands with the invisible," Tristan continued. The young man spoke softly at first, but his strange new voice gradually became louder.

As he spoke, Tristan's two snake companions wound themselves tightly around his chest, appearing to become frenzied by his words. "Become the rope that coils around my heart and protects it from the evil surrounding me. Grant me the power to swallow your wisdom so that it transforms me, opening me up to a new plane of existence. Bestow the gift of your strategizing mind upon me. Guide me with your intuition, your memory, and your craft. Weave this prayer into my soul so that I do not forget it, for if I do, then I shall forget thee."

When he finished the prayer, the young man collapsed onto the ground, unconscious. Tristan's snake companions also seemed to have fallen into a deep slumber. Walter gasped as he watched his friend's body become still, and was even more astonished when he saw that a snake rose out of him—not a living one, but a faint, ephemeral outline of its spirit. The phantom was barely perceptible; when it moved, it looked as if it might simply be wind rustling the grasses.

"Looks like it worked," Yensin said with a half-hearted smile. Walter sighed; perhaps the spell had worked, but the sight of his friend lying on the ground unconscious was still incredibly disturbing. Because of his recurring experience with seizures, he understood all too well the terrifying sensation of losing control of your own body and mind.

Eva's horses stomped their feet on the forest floor. They seemed to be both frightened and energized by the aura of magic surrounding Tristan. Eva's breathing was fast and her pupils appeared dilated, and it seemed that her emotions mirrored those of her horse companions. Yensin turned toward her, and then flipped through the notebook until he arrived at a page with the sketch of a horse on it.

"Your turn," Walter said to her, and then gave her a hug to help ease her anxiety. Eva clutched Walter's arm bravely, and her eyes filled with tears. Walter felt his heart swell with sympathy for the young woman. *She is about to move into a realm from which there might be no return,* Walter thought. *If she is afflicted with a curse which does not allow her to return to human form, then it can only be undone if her soul is pure and good.* But Walter did not know, deep down inside, whether that Eva had a truly good soul. His mind flashed to Asana and the seed of suspicion that Eva's conversation with the robot had planted in his mind.

"I summon thee," she murmured softly, in a deep voice that did not resemble her own, "spirit of the horse. Swift, wild, fleeting spirit, take ahold of me and guide me to the realm of the invisible. Let me ride with you, through forest and valley, across desert and mountain. Bring me to the plains of your forefathers so that I may breathe the air that they once breathed and take courage from their ancestral home. Bestow your unparalleled knowledge of navigation upon me, so that I may find my way through this world with ease. Weave this prayer into my heart to ensure I do not forget it, for if I do, then I shall forget thee."

As she recited this summoning prayer, Eva's horse companions whinnied and neighed, beginning to exhibit signs of frenzy. They stomped their hooves on the ground with increasing force, kicking up soil into the air, and their black eyes were full of fear. When Eva was done speaking, she too collapsed onto the ground, falling into a nearby cluster of yellow wildflowers. While her equine friends settled down beside her to sleep, the barely imperceptible outline of a horse could be seen emerging from her unconscious body.

Brigid

I am invisible, but not formless. The rustling of grass beneath me is a reminder that I am here, I am present, even if I do not have living flesh. I can hear the song of a nightingale, see the tendrils of fog as they rise from the damp earth, and smell the decaying vegetation of the forest. I am propelled forward by a single mission—to find the girl with silver hair and the war goddess I have seen in my dreams. I cannot recall why I need to find them, but I know that I must try.

Softly, gently, my belly curves over the earth, and I can feel its warmth seep into me, filling me with delight. I can smell herbs now, pungent saxifrage and nettle, but there is something stronger too, the scent of a wild boar. To live invisibly is to harbor no fear of being attacked—it is a freedom that emboldens you. But I am not invisible to everyone. I can see her, the goddess Epona at my side, her chestnut coat blending subtly in with the trees. She knows where we are going, and I follow her willingly.

My mind wanders sometimes, when I forget about the silver-haired girl and reflect upon my own past. I, too, am a goddess. My birth was a terribly dramatic event; I am told that flames shot from my head and formed a column that joined Heaven and Earth. I grew into a strong young lady by drinking milk from a sacred cow. I married a man from a tribe at war with my own, in the hopes of bringing peace between these two factions. My son Ruadán then did a horrible thing and used the skills he had learned from his elders to slaughter a holy man from my husband's tribe, and he was slain in turn. I wept for months after my son died, not only for his death but for the ceaseless hostilities between my tribe, the Danu, and my husband's tribe, the Fomorians.

I have always been worshipped for my wisdom, and yet I sometimes feel helpless to impart it upon others in this world. When I enter the physical forms of others, I can elevate their thoughts and motivate them to achieve more than their petty existences may otherwise inspire. Yet I can only inhabit others for a fleeting period of time before

I must inevitably carry on with my own immortal existence. It is tiring to be a goddess, for you are always expected to help others, who always seem to forget that you, too, need emotional support every now and then.

But I am getting carried away with my whimsical thoughts, when I should instead be concentrating on the task at hand. My spirit is imprinted with the mark of the human who summoned me, and I can feel his thoughts, memories, and desires blending with mine. He loves the silver-haired girl, although I do not understand why. She is selfish and does not seem to possess empathy for others—she is driven solely by ambition, and the desire to defeat the outsiders. Her spirit is one that I have seen many times before, in people whose lives have ended in tragedy. In my son, for instance. His desire to defeat the Fomorians at any cost only led to his own destruction. If I can prevent history from repeating itself, if I can help save this silver-haired girl, then I will be content. Yet I fear that she has too powerful an ally: the goddess of war herself.

I sense we are getting nearer to her. I can smell traces of human flesh as we approach the outskirts of this magical kingdom. I am expecting to find her with a male companion for some reason, although I do not recall why. My human imprint is telling me that it is more important to find her; if her friend has gotten away, then we must live with it, although this too may be dangerous. I must try to prevent both of them from reaching the outsiders, who frighten me immensely. I do not understand them and I cannot inhabit them. Their flesh is not flesh at all, but rather hard, cold metal designed to keep out divine spirits like me. Even if I could get inside the outsiders, though, I do not think I would want to know their thoughts. For they have no wisdom, only intelligence.

Epona

The wind rustles my hair as I fly freely into the vast unknown ahead. A simplicity overcomes me, a sensation that all of my worries have dissolved and a weight has been lifted from my shoulders. With my serpentine spirit companion at my side, anything is possible. I carry within myself the memory of an infinite number of journeys, physical, emotional, and spiritual, for I am the goddess of travel, the patroness of migration.

Travel does more than move a mortal; it lifts their minds from a state of stagnation and infuses them with lightness and wonder. It unburdens them from the chains of routine, the subjugation that they are forced to endure in their daily lives. These chains can be heavy, so heavy that they carve out pieces of the human soul and hollow it out, but it is the responsibility of mortals to find those pieces which are scattered across the earth. Finding the remnants of their souls and piecing them together, into an integrated whole, is the noblest task they can undertake in their lives.

This is why the journey must be undertaken, with grace and temerity, and above all with an open mind.

I can sense that I am burdened with the weight of a human, from whose body I was summoned, and I also sense that her soul is in pieces. Her anchor was her sister, a girl who was too absorbed in her own enterprises and caught up in a web of her own futile ambition. And it was that single-minded ambition that killed the human's sister, leaving her adrift in a sea of loneliness and angst. But she needed to find solace in something, and she found it in her gift—the ability to communicate with the steel creatures from a faraway distance. When mortals have a gift, they tend to fall in love with it, and also with those who encourage their talents and make them feel special— like gods. But they must be wary of those who seek to take advantage of their gifts for selfish purposes, and most of all they must choose their lovers carefully. For love itself can occasionally lead mortals down a dark pathway. It is a journey that they undertake to find meaning, but it may ultimately leave them feeling empty and lost.

This is what I fear for my human, who is in love with one of the steel creatures, and also for the human imprinted into my serpentine companion, who is in love with a headstrong princess. I fear both are following a pathway to a love that will end in tragedy. And yet, is that not the story of all human existence? Mortals crawl through an endless labyrinth of tunnels to reach the light, and when they finally reach the end, the sun has already set.

Spring

"Uncanny visions arise in my mind: of timeless evil, and a battle older than the earth, which has been fought before on countless worlds, in forgotten ages. Even after this battle of Lanka, the war shall be fought again and again; until time ends, and dharma and adharma with it."

– The Ramayana

Walter shivered as he lay in a bed in one of the Mereille's many rooms, gazing out the window at perfectly manicured gardens. It was early evening, and while most residents were indoors eating their dinner, a few were still sitting outside, staring blankly at the flower arrangements or muttering distractedly to themselves. Although it was starkly different in its architectural design, the Mereille reminded him of the Cabin of Lost Souls in Tsei'watu; it had the same aura of the forbidden. As Walter reflected upon Tsei'watu, and realized the rebel camp had been the last place that had truly felt like home to him, tears welled up in his eyes.

Some people are destined to find their true home, he thought wistfully, *while others spend their entire lives searching and never find it.* Perhaps Walter was fated to never feel at home, anchored to any particular piece of earth. After all, the Empire was in a precarious state. Khalendar was progressing down a path which might diverge into any number of possible directions, and Walter had been entrusted with a gift that would help to steer it onto a safe course. Any person who could comfortably settle down in such circumstances was either senile, or had deceived themselves with the aid of some powerful illusion.

If I don't have a home, then at least I have a past, even though the AI Masters tried their best to steal that from me, Walter reflected. Ever since he had left

Crystal City, Walter's memories of his own past had become increasingly potent, but with each memory that returned to him he realized how little he had previously known about his own childhood. Shortly after his departure from Crystal City, Walter had regained memories of critical events of his past, such as the interview for his job with the government, and meeting Elaine for the first time. He had also dredged up the painful memory of his confession to Elaine about the AI Masters' plans to destroy her family's village in the Barrens. He could not help but recall the terrible moment of his discovery that the AI Masters had apprehended Elaine from the Crystal City townhouse she worked in, after he had divulged the news to her.

Now that he had spent many months outside of Crystal City, not only those major life events but also the finer details of Walter's past had surfaced in his mind, and as they marinated in his thoughts they became incredibly rich and vivid. He could now recall the names of most of his college schoolmates, every computer game he had played growing up, and the precise words exchanged in the heated debates between his parents on summer ferry rides to Scarlet Isle. He could also recall the scent of laundered shirts line-drying outside his house, the way it felt to scrape his knees when he ran down the ravine to pick blackberries, and the giddy sensation he experienced when climbing the tall spruce trees lining his aunt's backyard. Each memory that trickled slowly into his mind magnified the intensity of the bitter hatred Walter felt toward the machines that had deliberately suppressed them for so long.

Do they take pleasure in their crimes against humanity? he mused sullenly. *They achieve our unwavering loyalty by surgically removing our souls… but how much satisfaction do they really gain from controlling us? Or is it fear that motivates them to undertake their grisly work… the fear of an uprising, a rebellion? Let them be afraid. We will give them plenty of reasons to be.*

Walter cast his glasses down on the table next to the bed and rubbed his eyes. He was feeling suffocated by a heavy blanket of emotion, and he longed for an uplifting experience. He rummaged around in his satchel for the Talisman; whenever he wore it, it always made him feel better, like his broken soul was whole again. The labyrinth on the jade stone glowed luminously as soon as he put the Talisman back on, and he felt an inner warmth that expanded to fill every part of his body. At the back of his mind, muted by the joyful sensation, was the fear that he would see another terrible vision again. *Wearing the Talisman is like sleeping with a woman who later bears your child*, Walter thought wryly. *Like sleeping with Namid. It feels good in the moment, but that feeling is deceptive; it leads you to a place that you never wanted to go.*

Walter began to drift off into slumber, but he was abruptly awakened by a noise which sounded like a hummingbird beating its wings rapidly. The lights were dimmed in his room, and he thought that one of the sisters had come in, but upon closer observation he saw that the woman was Emilia. Walter felt no fear whenever he saw her now; she was a comforting presence, an assurance that he was not alone in his journey with the Talisman.

Emilia smiled at him and placed her translucent hand gently over his own. "You have come a long way, Walter... farther than I ever could have. I am proud of you."

Walter shrugged half-heartedly. "I haven't achieved anything yet, Emilia. I set out on this journey to find the two people who mattered most to me in this world. I found my lover, but she has left me. I found my brother, but now he's gone too."

Emilia laughed, her voice like a windchime in a gentle spring breeze. "You took control of a ship from the AI Masters; you helped to rescue countless prisoners; you fulfilled your bargain with the leader of the Mages; and you've seen visions of the future, yet you are telling me that you haven't achieved anything? Ever since I've become a spirit myself, my perspective has broadened, and I've realized how narrow-minded humans are. Their minds are focused on discrete, specific goals, and while that focus can be helpful at times, at other times it can completely blind them to the truth and beauty surrounding them. I know that you love Elaine and Jonathan, but they are on their own personal journeys right now. You must release them from your emotional grasp, and give yourself the freedom to focus on your own journey."

Walter sighed. He suddenly felt inexplicably weary. "If you only knew, Emilia, how gut-wrenching it feels to be the one chosen by Shiva to see into the future and try to change it for the better. Perhaps you loved being a leader, but I've never wanted the role. Is it too much to ask to simply be an ordinary person with an ordinary life? A wife, a few children, a modest house somewhere on the outskirts of town. An honest profession. It is thrilling to be an exile and a rebel leader, perhaps, but it is a terribly difficult life. And the worst part of it is, I can't even aspire to have an ordinary life because there is no such thing as *ordinary* to me anymore. Is it ordinary to live under the controlling auspices of the AI Masters? Perhaps if I were more naïve—if I had never become privy to their secrets—I could simply live out my life in peace like all of the other citizens in the Empire."

"Many people are privy to the worst secrets," Emilia said. "Dreadful, ugly secrets about their leaders, the people in which they repose the most trust. And yet they do not care, because they live their lives with a sort of willful blindness, a blissful inattention to ugly things that do not directly threaten their immediate wellbeing. Why do they turn a blind eye? Because they are ordinary, and that is what ordinary people do. But you, Walter, are not ordinary. Having discovered a secret, you were not content to simply let it go and allow it to evaporate into the mists. Perhaps you are not as happy as those people who brush the secrets away, and perhaps you never will be, but you will achieve more in a single day than they will in their entire lifetimes, simply because you are not content leaving the secrets undisturbed. Instead, you face the ugly truth head on; you look it in the eye. This *sight*—the opposite of blindness—is the animus of most positive progress in human civilization. It creates a cascading ripple effect, beginning in the heart of one man and then spreading gradually into the hearts of others. If people were all ordinary, if none of them were like you, Walter, then humans would cease to evolve—they would perhaps even cease to exist."

Walter was moved by her words, and he began to weep. *My negativity is exhausting and unproductive*, he thought. *I should instead appreciate the gifts I have been given.* "I want change, Emilia. I genuinely do, but I wish I were not so resentful. I wake up each day with bitterness and hatred in my heart—not just toward the AI Masters, but also toward myself, for allowing them to manipulate me for years. I was a complete victim, a pawn in their conniving schemes. They made me forget who I was. They inflicted worse punishments on my brother, the person I loved and idolized most as a child. And I want to either destroy them for it, or destroy myself if I am too weak to hurt them."

Emilia's expression became grave. "I know exactly how you feel, Walter. I had the same perspective as you for years, up until the day that I died. I was convinced I could destroy them, obliterate their kind with weapons I had stashed away. I wanted to use the most sophisticated weapons against them—the ones that they had forced me to assemble as a factory-worker—and to shatter their steel frames into a million pieces. Now that I am a spirit, though, my view of reality is much broader, and I can see that war is not the answer.

"The silver-haired princess will try to convince you that war is the answer, and that only war will liberate the oppressed. Even though she is the daughter of Nuada, her mother's lineage can be traced back to the sun-worshipping tribes of the Southern Jungles and the ancient kingdom of Eyrenvale. Those tribes always chose war over diplomacy and advocated for bloodshed during the Shadow Wars with the AI Masters long ago. Their choice of war over peace led to the collapse of the old kingdoms, to the conquest of the Barrens, and to the need to seal Serrahan away from the AI Masters."

Walter felt a surge of energy from the Talisman, and he could sense that a vision was quickly approaching; his heart began to beat faster in anticipation, and he struggled to keep his limbs from trembling. "Walter," Emilia continued, "it is time for you to experience spring, the season of war and conflict. It is human instinct to fight that which threatens us, whether it is our enemies, our friends, our families, or our own identities. But the consequences of violence can be far worse than we ever imagined, and this you must learn."

The village of Zeyanara was silent and desolate when Walter arrived in spirit form. Tendrils of fog surrounded the rustic wooden buildings. Although it was midday, the village square was empty, and the marble statue of a beautiful robed woman gazed out placidly over the deserted square. A young girl, perhaps no more than ten years old, with mud streaked across her clothing and a long braid of black hair suddenly broke the silence when she ran down the length of the square. Her chest was heaving and her hazel eyes were anxious; it appeared she had been running a long distance, perhaps miles.

"Help me, somebody!" she shouted, and her voice echoed eerily, ricocheting off of the houses and abandoned storefronts surrounding the square. Nobody responded, and the child began to cry in fear. She approached the marble statue and knelt down onto the ground in front of it as though to pray. After a few minutes, a door of one of the nearby houses creaked slowly open, and an old woman with grey hair down to her waist peeked out from behind the door. She eyed the girl with suspicion before sighing.

"Come in, girl," she whispered impatiently, "Quickly."

The child wiped away her tears as she looked up at the stranger, and then scuttled into the woman's house like a crab on a beach seeking shelter from predators.

Walter's spirit followed the girl into the woman's house. Its interior was welcoming and cozy—a fire crackled on the hearth, fresh-scented herbs hung from the walls, and a tiny white cat curled up on an armchair in the living room.

"Why are you out and about, child? Where are your parents?" the old woman muttered as she shuffled away to take a pot of tea off of the stove.

The girl sat down on a rug next to the hearth. Her nose was running, and she wiped it down with her dirty sleeve. "My parents," she sniffled, before breaking down into fits of sobbing, "They died."

"Ah," the woman said. She brought two steaming cups of tea over to a table by the hearth and set them down carefully. "There, there, it'll be alright. Don't cry," she said, looking at the girl in concern. "Here, have some of this nettle tea, it's good for your constitution."

The girl took the cup with trembling hands and sipped from it gingerly. The warm drink appeared to soothe her somewhat, although tears continued to stream from her eyes.

The woman picked up the cat from the armchair, sat down, and dropped the feline onto on her lap. She then took a draught of tea as she patted the creature's small head. "Now, tell me what has happened to your parents. Did they fall ill?"

"Ill? No…" the girl said, her voice shaking. "They were… captured in the Scarlet Inquest. Captured, questioned, and then killed. In full view of everyone. In a village square just like the one outside your house," she sobbed. "I saw them die with my own eyes."

The woman rose from the chair and the white cat meowed in annoyance, leaping off of her lap. She hobbled over to the window and peered outside warily, before closing the blinds tightly to seal out any light. "Is anyone following you, girl?" she said, her tone becoming gruff and impatient.

"I don't think so," the girl sobbed, and her eyes widened in fear as she studied the woman's stern face. "No, you don't have to worry about that. Please let me stay here for a while."

The woman scowled and returned to her armchair. "I'm an old woman, but I'm not naïve. I've witnessed many changes in my lifetime. But the Reign of Cyriana this last decade has been has been unlike anything I've ever seen before. It's all you've ever known, poor thing. And now it's ruined your life."

"Tell me," the girl said as she sipped the tea. "Tell me about Cyriana. My parents refused to talk about her whenever I asked… they just said that she was the Queen and that was that. I think she is a terrible Queen. None of her subjects love her, as far as I can tell. And I *know* she's responsible for the death of my parents."

The old woman studied the girl's face. The child seemed exceptionally perceptive for someone so young, and the woman had a feeling that it would be difficult to conceal the truth from her. "Right. I suppose you deserve to know, and so I might as well start at the beginning. Well, before the War of Zion, which happened when you must have been just a baby, there was a long period of relative peace. Life wasn't perfect, of course, but at least it was relatively stable. There was something called the Empire of Khalendar, and it was ruled by machines."

"Machines are forbidden now," the girl said matter-of-factly. "Mother used to say, if you get caught with a machine, you'll be sent to prison."

"Yes," the woman said with a chuckle. "Well, there are different types of machines, I guess. Some are small and simple, like a calculator or a watch, for example. Others are so incredibly complex that not even the people who designed them can really understand them. And it is those incredibly complex machines that ruled humans before you were born."

"Were they good rulers?" the child inquired.

The old woman shrugged. "Yes, and no," she said. "They were no worse than the worst human rulers. But they were certainly worse than the best human rulers. They were like a mirror of human nature, in a way—all of the flaws and foibles of our kind were replicated and magnified in them."

"They were just machines, though. We could have made them better, couldn't we?" the girl asked.

"Clever, aren't you," the woman said, narrowing her eyes. "Initially, humans programmed the machines, and modelled them after themselves," she explained, "but after a while the machines became so smart that they were capable of programming their own kind. They continued to model themselves after humans, though, and they modelled themselves after a certain *type* of human—not the best kind, that's for sure. Although they were exceptionally smart, they were still greedy and controlling, and had all sorts of vices that they should have eliminated, but never did. Nobody quite knows why, given their high intelligence, they didn't simply program those vices out of themselves."

"And then what happened? Why aren't they still rulers today?"

"The War of Zion happened," the woman said with a sigh. "The Mages who launched the war, led by Cyriana and Sekhmet, the goddess of war herself, had good intentions. They wanted to liberate humanity from the oppressive rule of the machines. But unfortunately, the way in which they went about achieving that goal resulted in chaos and devastation. They summoned a vast amount of dark magic to destroy the machines, but they underestimated their enemies' powers. The result was a bloody war that lasted for five long years, in which countless lives were lost. They were successful, in the sense that they destroyed the machine rulers. But they did not succeed at destroying humanity's love for machines."

"What do you mean by that?"

"For thousands of years, humans have had a close bond with technology—we've evolved as a species alongside it. After Cyriana and her followers succeeded in destroying the final machine ruler, everyone assumed that the Mages would stop there. But they didn't. They were hell-bent on separating humans from every machine, even the simple ones that helped them and didn't rule them. People didn't understand. Cyriana had what she wanted; she had won a throne, and she'd built a palace in the ashes of the Empire's old capital, Crystal City. But that selfish girl was simply not content with the power she had gained. She wanted more. She craved absolute power."

"What is absolute power?"

"Absolute power—well, that is when someone imposes their will over everything, every last subject of their kingdom, and refuses to serve any higher power themselves. That is what Cyriana wanted, and still wants to this day. She professes her devotion to the gods, and in particular to Sekhmet, but it's clear that Cyriana sees herself as a goddess who has liberated humans. Her subjects do not view her as a liberator, however, but rather as a tyrant. And they have good reason to. She's made it a crime to possess a machine, a crime punishable by prison sentence or death, depending on whether the conduct is accidental or willful. When she first enacted the law many people disobeyed it, which led to the Scarlet Inquest. Essentially, it's a widespread state interrogation in which people are summoned to her palace and questioned about their interest in machines and their devotion to magic. If they are not completely devoted to sorcery, or if they even show the slightest indication that they are using technology, Cyriana will punish them."

"My parents," the girl said, beginning to weep again. "They must have had a machine, then."

"Not necessarily," the woman replied. "Even those who have relinquished possession of all machines might still be punished for treason if they show any unwillingness to embrace magic or worship Cyriana and Sekhmet."

Walter's spirit had heard enough. While he was not struck by any particular emotion, there was some profound spark inside of him that compelled him to rise above the roof of the old woman's house and soar above the village, heading north. He travelled faster than a hawk as he flew above forests, fields, and mountains, desperate to reach a northerly city for some vaguely understood reason.

Finally, he reached his destination: what was left of Crystal City. Clearly ravaged by war, its buildings had mostly crumbled into dust, and a dreary pallor of lifelessness was cast over its streets. In the midst of the bleak desolation, the spirit chanced upon a magisterial palace so large that it could be aptly described as a city within a city. When Walter's spirit flew over the palace's walls, he was struck by the unmistakable contrast between that enclosed city and the rest of the city outside. Inside were lush gardens in which beautiful animals—peacocks, tigers, and other creatures fit for royalty—preened and frolicked. The gardens were elegant and symmetrical, with towering hedge mazes and aquamarine pools surrounded by lovely sunbathing maidens and their animal companions. At one end of the palace was a vibrant square in which robed Mages danced merrily. At the other end was a tower, and Walter's spirit headed for it with single-minded determination.

The spirit soared into the tower, not stopping until he reached the room at the very top. It was a chamber reserved for the most powerful Mage in the new Empire: Cyriana. He found her sitting on a black leather upholstered chair adorned with glittering rubies, looking indelibly bored as she gazed at a chessboard in front of her. She was even more stunningly beautiful than the woman he knew, but he recognized her silver hair and emerald-green eyes immediately. A hearth with dancing purple and red flames crackled nearby, and the light it emitted warmed her pale face. Sekhmet lounged across the room and glanced toward her master every now and then with mild interest.

Walter's spirit felt a strong sensation, and he sensed he was now in the vortex of power, the precise place where he needed to be. He hovered, watched, and waited.

After a few minutes had passed, the door creaked open and a man entered. He had curls of golden hair and he was strikingly handsome, his features sharp and his eyes attentive. The spirit felt another surge of energy.

"My love, they are dancing in the square. Let us go watch, it will cheer you up."

Cyriana did not look up at him, and instead moved one of the pieces on the board slowly. Her eyes were glazed over, as though she was both awake and dreaming. "Hmm…" she responded quietly.

"Are you still upset about what happened last week? It was the right decision, I can assure you."

"You wouldn't understand," she said, her voice monotone.

"I am upset about it too—he was my brother, after all," he said, coming up to her to place a hand on her shoulder.

After a long pause, she sighed. "I've never had a problem killing anyone before... there have been so many public killings... and none of them have left a single dent in my heart. But this one... this one was different."

"They had to go, and you know that. They posed a threat to Zion from the start, and you only kept them alive out of generosity."

"Then why do I feel like I have angered the gods in killing them?" she asked softly. Her eyes were vacant as she looked up at the golden-haired man. She shivered and pulled her woolen cloak tightly around her shoulders. "I can feel them in this room here now, haunting me. Their spirits."

Cyriana lifted her head and glanced in the direction of Walter's spirit, and suddenly he felt a jolt pass through him—a feeling that someone in the realm of the living had seen him.

"Until my dying day, I will never forget them," Cyriana declared. "I won't forget the way they fought until the end, the way they tried to convince me that technology was worth preserving. Perhaps they were right," she said. "Perhaps I have destroyed too much."

"You have destroyed nothing except for your own enemies. You once told me to remember who I was—how I had fought valiantly against the machines in boxing matches during my youth. You told me that together we could defeat the machines and everything they stood for. Their conniving, brainwashing, manipulative ways would be forever purged from the Earth. I believed you then, Cyriana, and I believe you now. I thought my brother would too, until I realized that, unlike me, he had never fully lost his affection for the machines. That is why he had to go."

"What happened to their daughter?" Cyriana said. "Ariadne, I think she is called... I believe she is favored by the gods, just like her father was. I am afraid she will find me, and destroy me."

"The guards searched their house, and the girl was nowhere to be seen. She must have gotten away, but we'll send the men out to search a wider area. She's only a young child, and she couldn't have gotten far."

"Ariadne," Cyriana whispered, as she moved the Queen forward on the chessboard. "Mistress of the Labyrinth."

Clockwork

"Our wills and fates do so contrary run that our devices still are overthrown;
Our thoughts are ours, their ends none of our own."
– William Shakespeare

When he emerged from his vision, Walter was shaking with fury. Emilia had vanished from his bedside and was nowhere to be seen. It was the middle of the night, and the silvery face of the full moon shone with a blinding intensity into Walter's room. He peered out the window, searching for any signs of life, but the outdoor grounds of the Mereille were deserted. He did not know who he was looking for—until he glanced down at the Talisman around his neck and a flash of realization descended upon him.

"I must speak with Shiva," Walter said out loud. He had a tight knot in his chest, and he believed it would only go away once he had spoken with the shaman-god. He was enraged at Shiva and the untenable position he had put Walter in. *Every single one of my visions so far has been a disappointment,* Walter thought bitterly. *The first one—summer—showed a world that served the basest human desires. The second one—winter—presented the devastating consequences of the AI Masters carrying out their plans. And the third one—spring—gave expression to the will of the Mages, and Cyriana in particular. Each one manifested the most extreme desires of the three major races alive on the planet: humans, AIs and Mages. But there was no vision that offered a compromise, an alternative to those extreme positions. And worst of all, none of the visions satisfy my own desires.*

Walter's mind raced back to the day Shiva had gifted him with the Talisman. The shaman-god had told him that wearing the Talisman would give him a strong connection with Shiva, but he couldn't feel the shaman-god's presence at that moment. He clutched the stone with his hand and whispered with intense focus: "Shiva, if you are listening, please speak to me." Nothing happened, and anger rose in Walter. *He has abandoned me*, he thought miserably. *Of course, he would do that—leave me to choose between these terrible visions, and then not even come to me when I need his help the most.*

Just as he was about to tear off the Talisman from his neck in disgust, it began to glow a pale shade of yellow. The Talisman then caused a shockwave to ripple through Walter's body, and he fell asleep, exhausted by the jolt of energy that had coursed through him. When he closed his eyes, Walter could see that he had been transported back to the beautiful, crimson-roofed dwelling of the Lord Shiva, the room with the turquoise pool surrounded by bonsai trees and butterflies. Shiva sat on his throne, smiling at Walter as his tiger companion yawned and stretched at his side.

"Tell me what you desire," Shiva said gently.

Walter sighed. "What I desire matters little; what matters is what the visions have shown me. And every single one of them so far has been painful to behold. I don't even care that the future worlds I have seen are not perfect utopias. But I do care that in every single one of them, the person I love the most in this world, Elaine, is either killed or torn away from me. I originally set out on this whole quest to save her, not to destroy her, but it seems like I have no choice in the matter. Or do I?"

"I did give you a suitable warning," Shiva said. "I recall telling you that you might see the death of your loved ones... your own death... and the annihilation of life on Earth. That is the price you must pay for such a powerful gift."

Walter narrowed his eyes. He remembered that warning, too, but he still felt as though the shaman-god had betrayed him. "If my memory serves, you also wanted me to reprogram the AI Masters so that a better world could come to fruition. How can the Talisman help me do that? I have seen no 'better world.'"

"You need to have patience, my friend. Let the song of the Talisman unfold."

Walter reflected for a few moments. "You told me that you would teach me to master Time. Well, if I can master Time by seeing into the future—and trying to change it—then doesn't it work both ways? I mean, can't I go back as well and change what happened in the past?"

Shiva hesitated, his face stamped with amusement. "Such a thing might be possible... but it depends."

"Depends on what?"

"How far back would you like to go, and to what end?"

"The day of my interview with the government… I want to go back to that day. After the interview, I want to go home. I don't want to go to Mariner's Cove and meet Elaine. If I never met her, I can't feel pain by losing her. And if I never met her, I won't try to go rescue her, and I won't cross paths with Emilia and become the leader of the Jade Rebellion. I want to live a life of normalcy somewhere, without the crushing weight of this responsibility."

Shiva glanced up at the ceiling, and then back down at his tiger companion, who had curled up to go to sleep. "Walter, you can do that if you really want to, but it will not solve anything. Even if you had never met Elaine, you would have fallen in love with someone else. More importantly, you would still have become the leader of the Jade Rebellion. You would have still searched for your brother, and you would have eventually found Emilia and her band of rebels in Tsei'watu.

"Being a rebel leader is coded into your DNA, the same way the AI Masters are programmed to conform to the dictates of their leader. And human DNA is not very different from AI code. The choices that mortals make may take them off the path charted for them by their coding—what I like to call the primary pathway—but that path is ultimately like a magnet that draws them back on to it. The strength of that magnet does not overpower human will to choose one's own destiny, but it does a fair job at counterbalancing it."

Walter sighed in resignation. "I don't *want* this pathway, though. I don't want to be powerful, I want to be ordinary. I'm afraid that having so much power will corrupt my soul and turn me into someone I've never wanted to be."

"Not all power corrupts," Shiva said. "A power that is used for good ends does the opposite—it strengthens and illuminates."

"If a human's DNA dictates the primary pathway they are likely to follow," Walter replied, "then what hope do I have of changing anything? Regardless of how I reprogram the AI Masters, humans will still revert to their baseline state—selfish, greedy, and egotistical. Instead of reprogramming AI code, perhaps I need to instead try to alter human DNA."

The tiger suddenly opened her golden eyes and let out a roar that reverberated throughout the entire room. She appeared to be having a bad dream, since she settled back down to sleep afterwards. Shiva allowed the echoes to die down before speaking again.

"You have seized on some powerful truths, Walter, but you are missing one critical piece of the puzzle. Humans may be selfish at their core, but that does not explain why, for countless millennia, they engaged in the practice of religious and spiritual worship which put supernatural entities, rather than humans themselves, at the epicenter. The truth is that humans are not solely guided by rational self-interest. They have a fairly limitless capacity for empathy and love as well. Sadly, the supernatural entities that brought out the best in human morality for centuries were eventually replaced with those that magnified human greed and egoism. You must remember that humans are like children— they need a master, whether it is a god or an AI.

"Change the master, Walter, and the servant will follow."

ABOUT THE AUTHOR

Alanna Mackenzie lives in Vancouver, Canada. She holds degrees in History, French studies, and Law from the University of British Columbia. An environmentalist at heart, she believes in using the law as a tool for social and environmental change. When she is not pursuing that passion, she can be found brainstorming the next chapter in her novels, playing Irish fiddle tunes on the violin, and hiking West Coast trails.